BGM & BADLAND PUBLISHING PRESENT

SERVED AGAIN: TRAP OR DIE!

Audentes Fortuna Juvat

A Classic Novel
By PLEX

BADLAND PUBLISHING, LLC

SERVED AGAIN: Trap or Die!
Copyright 2016 by: PLEX
Written by: PLEX
Cover design by: PLEX
Graphics by: Cedric 'Ckills' Killings
Book design by: Pam Quigley
Published by: BadLand Publishing, LLC
P.O. Box 11623
Riviera Beach, FL 33419
www.badlandpub.com

A BADLAND PUBLISHING BOOK
P.O. Box 11623
Riviera Beach, FL 33419
(561) 892-4746

www.badlandpub.com

ISBN: 978-0-9839123-9-2
First Edition

First edition

DEDICATIONS

I dedicate this book to Diamond Deon Pless. I love you, son...

ACKNOWLEDGEMENTS

To all of my friends, I really love and appreciate y'all. I've been through so much this year. And without y'all I know I wouldn't have made it. Thanks for being there and seeing me through it: Kimberly Adams, Pam Quigley, Daphne Johnson, Shanika Brown, Ms. Toni, Tikeisha Reid, Marquiesha Pless, Artoria Pless, Kawannah Rouland, Pam Little, Allison Carter, Elsa J. Joseph, Viviana Ruiz, Cybrian Jones, Sekeithia Jackson, Tacha McNeil, Tammy Chambers, Sharon Y. Pless, Erica Montgomery, Sherry Tyson, Shundra Hardy, Roshaundra Rolle, Kateva Ward-Jinks, Dawn (Pless) Westbrook, Antionette Lewis, Lakeisha Waters, Shannon Wilson Glover, Ali Moore, Cynthia Smith, Tanzy Banks, Sabrina Williams, Gail Nelson, Shuantavia L. Dixon, Sheronica Byrd, Candace Deas, Keisha HBIC Jones, Alchani Shabazz, Jennifer Logan, Arlena Pless, Buffy Uter, Black Girl, Natasha Lewis, Tracey Carter, Jai Pless, Ms. Jay, Marquita Harris Walton, MsNeet Truly Blessed, Shaquana Killings, and anybody that I might've forgot, I apologize.

Fellas, this is for y'all, because y'all fed me when I was hungry and hit me off when I was dead broke. Be it money or wise words, y'all came through: Mike Harper, Cedric Killings, Troy Cannon, Boobie Williams, Travis Pless, Troy 'Disco' Jones, Wayne E. Gladden, Dip Taylor, Jed, Solo, Benny Redd, D-Boi, Bino Jones, Roddrick Vann, Dwayne Linder, Boosie Pless, Arthur C. Pless III, Big Gemo, Travis Pless, Mike Pless, Cal, Vert Bradshaw, Fat Rat, Mal, Reggie, J-Roc Carter, L-Boogie, Dewey P. Newton, K-1, Big Bondy, Malik, Big Lue, Christopher Freemen, Seven Supreme, Skip Coleman, Bling, KP, E4, Trub Brown, King Pre, Turk, Mike Brown, Cracka Black, S. Terry, E, Pookie Boy, Ninja, Chuck, Shakim, Smiley, Jack, Zoe (Ali), City Boi, LA, Benjamin Hardy, Simon K. Machines, James Harrison, Al Poon

Witt, Carlos Poodle Dubois, Terrance Dowdell, Eric Hardy Sr., Harold McKinney, Odell Bacon Jr, Reginald Walton, Chaviss Brownlee Jr., Seth Ferranti, Bryan K. Sumlin Sr, Ismael J. Guzman, Bradshaw Palmer, Mitch, Lucky, Man, Homie Joe, Will, Jahhead, Blue, Big Dream & Lil Dream, that gambling-ass nigga Rich, Frye, Tayvis Dodson, JB, Ronald Tinsley, Black, Conrad, Turner-Bey, Pop, Poppa Stoppa, Poppa Charlie, G, Tra Owen, Young Money, Herman Stephens, Kevin Stone, P-Dog, King, Big Jack, Steve Ka$h, Juvy, Fats (Wayne), Snap, Pookey, Jimbo, Big Joe Hollywood, Lil Chris (Hayes), Young (Kiddo), Gino, EJ (Eric Jones), Credit (Cruddy), Gerald Adams, General, Teck Freeman, Chris (S.C.), Future (Chi-Town), Norman, my lil' BG (Markee Ruff), Joe Black, G, Derry Evans, Rozay, Man Man, Big Money (East Chicago), Chino, Ben Kramer, Tom Tom, Big Fridge, Cap (Ya Hear Me?!), Green Eyes, Spoon (T4L), Pac Man (Coco), Muff, Cracka Vert, Kwame Teague, Ca$h, Big Nation, and all of my dogs that's bidding hard and staying sucka free… One Love!

In the process of creating this book and getting it to you, my loyal readers, I lost my son to the streets. He was only twenty-two years old. I promise you, accepting the fact that he was gone, and realizing that I would never see him again, never get to talk to him, that was the hardest thing I've ever had to do in my life. I know this may sound cliché, but no parent should ever have to bury their child. They should be around to bury us!

I don't know the exact details concerning my son being murdered. I was no angel at twenty-two, so I can't imagine him being one either. However, twenty-two years is such a short time. I can remember being twenty-two, lost, trying to figure out which way was up. All I wanted at that time was to have fun. I remember running with Bush, Pookie Boy, Dwayne, doing us; making just enough money to eat, smoke some weed, drink some beer, feed Diamond, Marquis, and Marquiesha; and starting all over again the following day. We were just living, having fun.

I never could have imagined at the time that one day I would have to bury my son. I always knew in my heart that I'd grow old and he'd be there to take care of me, to drive me around and make sure that I ate my vegetables. He was supposed to have a son, name him after me, and get mad at me for spoiling him. But all that's dead. It died with him, when niggas killed him. Senseless. *My son died for nothing.*

The sad part is that it won't end with him, because we as a people, black males, we have too much heart and not enough brains... more guns than we have sense... everybody wants to lead, but nobody wants to follow. And the qualifications to lead are not there. They're too immature, too high, too unwilling to listen and learn; too much trap music and gangsta movies... and too quick to

6

tell when they get caught doing what they've done. *Senseless*. We didn't just lose my son, because the dude that did it is just as much a victim, *lost to the streets*. If somebody doesn't kill him, his homeboys will eventually tell on him, because ni#@as are pu#@y. Too quick to kill over nothing. Too stupid to see that THE GAME IS OVER. I see little dudes coming to prison every day with sentences ranging from twenty-to-life, looking sick, because their partners told on them and they're broke. Ni#@as doing thirty years and can't get a visit, can't get his phone calls accepted, can't go to the store, because he ain't got no money? Smart nigga, you can't tell him nothing, but he can't read and can't spell! Yet this ni#@a was on the streets leading a crew. And even worse, he's got a son that looks up to him. Sad, but so true.

I do my best to teach them. Help them through this sh#@. Because I wanna see them go home better men. I do it in hopes that somebody out there will take the time to teach mine something, help them through the bullsh#@. I sit these young ni#@as down and tell them what I'd want a ni#@a to tell mine: *be cool shorty, it ain't worth... don't give a ni#@a nothing you can't afford to lose... think about your children... let him live, dog, put the knife down, he's got a family just like you... save your money, bruh, don't be hustling for nothing... shorty, don't get that man's stuff if you can't pay him... boy, take your ass to school and apply yourself, because ain't nothing in the streets but death and more prison time.*

But y'all dudes on the streets are not doing y'all part! Y'all giving these lil' boys guns and drugs and are not giving them proper instructions. Y'all ain't giving them a chance to be children. Y'all pu@#y-ni@#as are misleading them! It's two sides to the game: SUCCESS. *That's the money, hoes, cars and clothes.* FAILURE. *That's long prison terms and early death.* It's leaving your mother, your wife, and your children to fend for themselves. It's a lot of lonely nights in a cell by yourself. It's a great possibility that your son's gonna lose himself out there, end up following a ni#@a that doesn't mean him any good; and he'll end up dead or rotting away in a funky-ass cell just like you. But y'all ni#@as don't tell the lil' ni#@as about that. You're taking away their ability to make an intelligent decision, because you can never choose wisely if you only have half the information... It's wrong. And y'all are some real f#@k-ni@#as for misusing them like that.

I'ma keep doing what I do and I pray that y'all ni#@as do better. Life is too precious to just keep throwing away. Time is too valuable to be wasting in prison. We're too intelligent, as a people, as black men, to keep doing the same sh#@ and expecting something different to happen. *Madness.* It's time to alter our course. Do away with the senseless altercations. Give our lil' ones an alternative to the streets. *Talk to them.* Show them a better example. They'll follow if you give them something worth adopting...

[Moment of silence for my son]. *I love you Diamond Deon Pless.* I miss you so much! But I'm gonna push on, I'ma do every day just like you're right here with me. And I won't let the world forget. *Like father, like son...*

One Love,
PLEX

Prelude

The chirp of the birds and the gleam of the morning sun woke Tracey. She was drained, yet so fulfilled. Last night had been a helluva night. The mere thought of the love she'd made ignited a delightful tingle between her dark, shapely legs and brought a smile to her cute, wholesome face. Life had changed so very much for her over the past two years. She'd been blessed to love twice. Something that rarely, if ever, happened in life. Some people, as sad as it may seem, lived to *ripe-old-ages* and never experienced the joy of true love. Ma B, her wise and loving mother, had always advised her, *baby, when you feel it just go wit' it. You won't need nobody to tell you what it is because it'll make you feel like nothing before has made you feel... be responsive and responsible, child. And don't let nothing come between you and true love. Because it's like lightning. It never stikes in the same place twice.*

Tracey lay there considering her mother's words. She thought about her parents and how merry they seemed after so many years of marriage. Their love had produced five healthy children. Three of which were married and following their parents' excellent example. She might have been married herself had she not lost her daughter's father to the war on drugs. He'd been a very decent man, not perfect, but so handsome and loving. He was a provider and they had been a team. And with the birth of Jai, her greatest source of happiness and motivation, they'd become a family. But then came the Feds and the destruction of what they'd worked so hard to build. For two years she'd waited and hoped. Appeals came and passed. Each ended in denial and heartbreak. Sometimes, most times, life had seemed unbearable. It had been cold and unloving. *Lonely.* Unbelievably sad and frustrating. Yet she'd made it.

Somehow, some way, she'd struggled through the despair that had become her life.

A tear frolicked at the corner of her eyes. Tracey briskly wiped it away. Realizing that those days, those feelings were no more. Life was anew for her. With Hitman in her life she had reason again to be merry. For lightning had struck twice in the same spot – her heart.

Tracey rose from her cozy queen-size bed and walked naked to the bathroom. At age 25 her B-cups and her firm, round ass had not began to yield to the pull of gravity. Everything stood perky, something that she was proud of. Especially after having birthed a child.

After doing what women did in the bathroom every morning, Tracey headed to the kitchen. Jai was away with her grandmother and Hitman was out in his streets. A place that he loved and she hated. Yet she understood. The streets were a part of him. Just as they'd been a part of Jai's father. *Lord I miss him*, she thought, setting the ingredients out for an egg omelet. She also knew that she would be missing Hitman if he didn't *right-his-ship* and rid himself of the urge to command the streets. Because even though she understood, she was conscious of the fact that the system had *no understanding for the streets and the people that ran them*. Jai's father had been a supreme general. Yet, the system had eaten him alive. As it would anyone *with no regard* for life or law. Hitman was, or had become the same way, *lawless*. He was so much like her child's father that it frightened her at times. Whenever she discussed the many lucrative avenues of legitimacy he'd always laugh and say, *"trap or die, shawdy."* To which she had frowned and told him, "Hitman, this is serious. This is not a rap song." Again he'd laughed, *"Nah, this my life... and if the street was a battlefield, I'd earn stripes."*

Tracey finished her breakfast, cleaned the kitchen and prepared herself for a day of shopping. She deserved it. The business that she and Sharon had started was doing drug numbers. And though it took up a great deal of her time, it was well worth it. There was nothing in the world like being your own boss and controlling your own destiny. It was a feeling that drove her. It was probably the same feeling that drove so many young blacks to the streets. It provided them with a lucrative means to an end. The only problem was, most of them never got to see that end. Because the majority of them got caught up in the *lifestyle* and lost focus of their goal, causing them to prolong their stay in the streets. That extended time, nine times out of ten, either led to the penitentiary or the cemetery. Either way, nothing was gained, another black talent lost.

Dressing neatly in a green Nadia Terrell denim dress that hugged her every curve, she slid on her black leather Prada riding boots. Satisfied with the head turning 32-26-36 that stood before her in the mirror, she snatched up her black leather Prada bag and hit the door.

...touch what I never touched befo'/ seen what I never seen befo'/ woke up and seent the sun/ sky high (sky high) sky high (sky high)... Friends, Romans, countrymen/ lend me yo' eardrums/ It was a beautiful day off in the neighborhood/ yellows and greens and blues and browns/ and grays and hues that ooze beneath dilapidated woods... Ain't a thang could explain what pertains/ to cocaine it's a stain that rain/ see summer roll 'round niggas holla 'bout change...

Tracey smiled brightly hearing the tune of Goodie Mob's *BLACK ICE* beating up her block. It was one of Hitman's favorite songs. With added pep in her step, Tracey made her way to the porch just in time to see Dee hopping out of her fresh black F-150

Kingcab on *all-days*. She looked a bit sad. Yet Dee was so *wish-washy* it was impossible to judge her mood.

"What's up, Dee?" Tracey asked, smiling her pretty smile.

"Ain't shit," Dee replied dryly. "Here, this for you."

"What is it?"

"Look and see," Dee said rudely as she jumped back in her truck and sped off.

Tracey could've sworn she'd seen dried up tear streaks on Dee's face. Which was indeed strange. Dee wasn't just Hitman's older sister, she was a hardened street soldier. Dee was harder than most dudes that ran the streets.

Tracey looked up into the heavens at the many thick clouds and the bright sun. It truly was a *beautiful day off in the neighborhood*, so while her gaze was settled on God's dwellings, she smiled as bright as the sun that shined down on her chocolate complexion and thanked Him, her God, for all that He'd afforded her.

Now her attention was drawn to the neatly folded piece of paper that Dee had handed her. She slowly opened it and read:

Dearest Tracey,

This is the hardest letter I've ever had to write in my young/old life, and I'm in tears as I scribe it. Reason being, it feels as if I'm going against everything that I've been raised to uphold. Love, loyalty, and liberty have always been the driving dynamics of my decision making. Nevertheless, I find myself betraying those principles in an attempt to spare you, my friends, and my family the dangers and harassment that associating with me was sure to bring.

These last two and one-half years have been the best of my life. And I can honestly and wholeheartedly say that it is because of you that I know true love. What I have experienced with you I will forever carry in my heart. The times we've shared will always flood my memories. I love you, Ms. Tracey Carter, and nothing on Earth will ever change that.

I smile now, tears streaking my face, thinking back to the very first night I met you. You looked so good in that brown dress. Now I'm picturing you, naked, the first time we made love. I was nervous. Lady, you was the best I've ever had.

I gotta go now, Tracey. You just stirred in your sleep and I don't want you to wake up and see me like this. By the time Dawn hands you this letter I'll have been long gone. Where? I'm not sure. But when I'm settled and things are safe, I'll contact you. Meanwhile, if you need to get a message to me just contact Riff-Raff.

Meanwhile, Tracey, I sincerely apologize for any pain I've caused you. My intent was not to hurt or mislead you. My aim was, and will forever be, to love and protect you. And to do so, I first had to let you go, in hopes that you'd understand and know that my eventual return will be forever. My mother once told me, "if you love something son, let it go. If it was meant, it'll return even stronger." Will you be strong for me? Because I'm definitely going to fight and do whatever it takes to make it back to you... I love you!

One Love,

Hitman

Tracey's breath caught in her throat. Tears ran from her eyes. Her hand trembled terribly as she held the letter that Hitman had written while she slept last night. Her legs became weak. Her whole world had imploded in less than a second and she was on the verge of breaking down.

"Ooooh, God, wwwhhhyyy?" she heard herself cry out.

What could've been so bad or adverse that he'd simply up and left her? How could he ever believe that he was protecting her by distressing her so? Had it been real? Was it all merely a cruel game that had been played at her expense? Where was he and how could he do this? Tracey wanted to know as she cried her way back inside the house. After reading the letter twice more she picked up the phone and dialed Rfif-Raff's number.

* * *

"So what you gon' do, boy?" Riff-Raff asked Hitman. He'd never seen his partner looking so sad and broken.

"It's too early to tell, lil' buddy," Hitman answered sadly. He'd pulled off the *lick* of a lifetime. Yet he felt so sick and lonely inside. Because the *lick* and the life he'd chosen to live had cost him everything he loved.

Riff-Raff shook his head sadly. "You just up and left the woman, my nigga?"

Hitman nodded his head yes. He'd left without saying good-bye. Because he knew that if he looked her in the eyes, he'd have still been in Americus, wrapped in her loving embrace, and possibly bringing harm and ruin to her and all of the people he held dearest.

Riff-Raff knew that the big kind-hearted country boy was hurting. Because he'd also had to leave his wife and children once, while he went away to serve a state prison sentence.

"Why you ain't just take her with you? 'Cause, my nigga, she woulda went! Lil' momma loves you, bruh-bruh. I know she woulda went."

Hitman shook his head no. "Nah, man. I couldn't ask shawdy to just up and clear it like that. I mean, she gotta business and a daughter to tend to. And, man, I don't even know exactly where

I'm goin' or what I'ma do. Riff-Raff, I don't even know if I'ma be on the street or above ground tomorrow. That was a serious *lick* we hit! And somebody gon' want they shit, you feel me?"

"Yeah, bruh-bruh, I feel you. Plus them crackas gon' be hot! Yeah, you couldn't drag lil' momma in no shit like that," Riff-Raff agreed, realizing that Hitman had done the right thing, because it's exactly what he would've done. There was no way he'd knowingly bring harm to his family.

"So dig, lil' buddy, I'ma hit you in two days with my info'. You're the only nigga I'm givin' my shit to, so don't give it to *nann* muthafucka. Tracey is gon' call. Do anything that she needs done. And forward any messages from her to me."

"You got that, kinfolk," Riff-Raff said and hugged his big partner. "You be careful, my nigga. And holla if you need me."

"No question, lil' buddy."

"Riff-Raff! Riff-Raff, telephone!" Riff-Raff heard his wife yell. Both he and Hitman already knew who it was.

"I'm gone."

"I already know," Riff-Raff said, watching his friend jump in his Vert and ride off, southbound. Riff-Raff then walked inside to talk to Tracey...

"We must agree on common sense. That we were brought here by our enemies (the white race) and made to SERVE them. We are a PRODUCT of our enemies own making... Whatever we are today... It is the WORK of our enemies (the white race)..."

- Elijah Muhammad

Shit Don't Stop

CHAPTER 1
Let's Get It!

Hitman woke up to the smell of country breakfast. Riff-Raff's wife, Cassandra, had outdone herself with the big spread of foods that covered the table. Hitman ate until he nearly popped the button on his pants.

After eating he called Tracey. It would take her at least three hours to travel from Americus to Riff-Raff's farm. So he and Riff-Raff had three short hours to make *dope-boy-magic*.

In the trailer that sat on the rear of Riff-Raff's land, where Hitman had the 100 kilos stashed, the two men went to work. One breaking the *bricks* and measuring, the other dropping and whipping. In two and a half hours, using three microwaves and six sets of Vision Ware, they'd turned twenty kilos into thirty. Hitman put the thirty kilos of *hard-white* in two suitcases, said his good-byes to Riff-Raff and his family, and left with Tracey.

Hitman smiled at her hungrily as they rode along the highway. It had been nearly two weeks since she'd left him in Miami and she was looking good enough to eat in her tight Baby Phat T-shirt, Baby Phat Capris and crispy white K-Swiss. She had her hair in a short wrap, lightly streaked. Babyface's *Sunshine* was playing as they entered Americus City Limits.

They didn't talk much. But it was very clear that they were both happy to be in one another's company. Thoughts of the last time they'd made love played in Hitman's mind as the car came to a stop at his house on Roland Street. The first thing he saw was his Ninja GXR-750.

He smiled like a kid on Christmas. "Shawdy, you wanna ride?"

"Yeah. Why not?"

Hitman grabbed the two suitcases, ran in the front door of his house and straight out of the back door. Clarence, his father, had an old bread van sitting just outside of the back fence. Sliding the door open, Hitman jumped in and hid the two suitcases, after removing four kilos. The streets were dry and the only safe side was the Southside.

"Here, put this on." Hitman handed Tracey a helmet and a backpack.

They both climbed on the *crotch-rocket* and Hitman fired up the high performance engine. It roared and vibrated beneath them.

Holding on to the man she loved, with this powerful machine vibrating between her legs, had Tracey *feeling some type of way*. She realized that those two weeks apart had been a long time.

"Look, shawdy," Hitman said over the noise of the engine. "Hold my waist tight. Lean with me when I lean and don't let go for nothin'. Aiiight?"

Tracey nodded her head yes and Hitman gunned it.

The wind felt good as they breezed through traffic. Shifting through the gears, they leaned in and out of traffic. He stopped the bike at the red light, next to the Post Office. Putting his feet down to balance the motorcycle, Hitman lifted his helmet visor and stretched. It had been years since he'd rode. He looked to his left and looked right into the evil blue eyes of Detective Rodgers.

"Hey!" Rodgers yelled, his face registering surprise, and began opening his car door.

Hitman shot Rodgers the middle finger and gunned the motorcycle's throttle.

Tracey yelped and squeezed Hitman around his waist as the bike's front tire lifted up in the air and they flew out in traffic.

Hitman was in third gear by the time he got the front tire back on the ground. Down shifting, he bent a corner and accelerated up the next street. Nel and Rodgers were just leaving the red light that he'd left them at.

The fast bike skidded to a halt in front of Sneakers. Hitman turned to address Tracey. "Say, baby, take this phone and go in Sneakers. Hit this button, it'll speed dial BamBam. Give him the bookbag and get the money from him. He'll take you home."

Taking the phone, Tracey nodded and got off of the motorcycle. It was her first and last ride, she promised herself.

Hitman gunned it. He was up the block before she made it in the shoe store.

When Hitman leaned right and hit the one-way, Nel and Rodgers were on him. He shifted and hit fourth gear as he approached the Greyhound bus station. Leaning hard to his left, he began down shifting and locked the rear tire. The rear of the bike went into a slide. Going with the momentum, he gunned the throttle, the GXR swung 180 degrees; now facing the way he'd just came, Hitman flew right past Nel and Rodgers going in the opposite direction, the bike's front tire high in the air. Hitman stood up on the pegs and pressed his chest to the tank. When the tire kissed the street, Hitman popped the clutch going into fourth gear. He was glued to the tank, scared that if he lifted up the wind would snatch him out of the saddle. He shifted into fifth and just held on. Only God knew how fast he was travelling. The choppy yellow line that marked the lanes had become one solid line. The three lane highway seemed to have narrowed to the size of a sidewalk. Objects no longer seemed permanent, because they all flew by in a blur.

Nel and Rodgers were out of the race. However, they radio'd for help. Giving the patrol car Hitman's description and the direction he was headed. The patrolman watched from a side street as Hitman blew by the last patrol car at the Theatre on the edge of town.

"He's gone," the patrolman radio'd back to Rodgers.

* * *

When Hitman cut the slick Ninja GXR-750 off, he could hear the fan humming on the performance bike's cooling system. He'd rode the bike hard, making it to Riff-Raff's farm in two hours. He got thirty more kilos and headed back to Americus in Cassandra's car. He thought hard on the situations as he rode. Action really had the law pissed off, so he knew that he had to move smart and creep silent.

His first stop was B-Easy's mother's house. The Regal was parked beneath the carport. B-Easy was in the front yard with his daughter and his baby's mother. Hitman parked and got out.

"Boy, what's up?" B-Easy greeted his big homie, looking as if he was a little uneasy himself.

"I can't really call it, lil' dog."

"Them crackas have been trippin'! They come through Eastview tearin' it up everyday. And they say it ain't gonna stop 'til they catch you and Action."

"Me?!" Hitman questioned.

"Yeah. Them crackas want you, boy." B-Easy eyed Hitman. "That's why I ain't been goin' through there lately. I just been chillin', 'cause I don't need the heat. You feel me, big homie?"

Hitman felt him. B-Easy didn't want to go back to jail. And Hitman couldn't blame him. Yet he needed him, so he had to ask, "Dig, Easy, you gotta lay low and be smart, you're doin' the right thang, dog... But, yo, I need you. I got thirty *bricks* in the car and I can't take them home. Besides Black, you're the only nigga I trust. And Black can't keep them, because if them folks are on me they're on him, too."

B-Easy did not want to do it, but he was a soldier. Hitman was his Old G. And most importantly, he knew that Hitman would never ask him to do something that he wouldn't do himself. "Where they at, homie?"

"Right here." The kilos were in three overnight bags. They grabbed them and took them to the washroom on the side of the house. "Each bag got ten *bricks* in it."

"Okay."

Hitman gave B-Easy a bundle of bills. It was $5,000.

"What's this for?"

"For you, dog."

"Nah, man, keep your bread. I'm good. You always lookin' out."

"And I always will. Keep the money," Hitman said and left for the Southside.

BamBam was standing in front of Lil Bit's house with one of his little homeboys. The little dude, not recognizing the car that Hitman was driving, pulled out a little handgun.

"What's up, BamBam?" Hitman said, exiting the car.

"Shiiid, you tell me, kinfolk." BamBam walked over to where Hitman stood.

"Ain't much to tell... you see ole-girl up at Sneakers?"

"Hell yeah. Everythang was everything, kinfolk. And all of it's gone! Ain't nobody got nothin'!" BamBam shook his head. If he hadn't been the one that sold the dope, he never would've believed that four kilos could sell, in straight ounces and eight-balls, in two hours. "I gave ole-girl $100,000 and I got another $100,000 for you right now."

"Cool, I 'preciate your loyalty, dog. And I want you to know that I don't respect what Action did to your man. It was fucked up and I don't support shit like that... I'ma send you eight more bricks, and dog, I know it won't replace your man, but keep four of them for yourself. Just make sure that Lefty's people are always straight. You feel me?"

That was love, BamBam thought. Hitman always tried to make things right. "Thanks, big dog, that's real good lookin' out."

Hitman collected the money and got in the wind. He needed his cell phone, but Tracey had it. He turned the car north and headed to her house. Tracey had a neat little house that sat midway the block. Baby Jai was out front playing and her Honda was parked.

"Boy!" Tracey exited the screen door and stood on the porch as Hitman got out of the car. "You a fool! I don't know who taught you how to ride a motorbike, but you made them police look too stupid! When your friend picked me up from Sneakers, I made him take me to DQ and to your house to get my car. All of the folks in the DQ was talkin' 'bout was *how the boy on the racin' motorcycle ran the police.*"

Hitman laughed. "Well how 'bout that?! I'ma star now."

"*Hmph!*" Tracey snorted. "I don't know 'bout all that."

Laughing, the two walked inside and took a seat. The conversation immediately turned serious. Tracey drilled Hitman about his future. In her eyes, he had made it. He'd done everything that other dealers from in and around Americus had failed at.

"Why are you still willin' to risk it?!" She looked into his face. There was no way for him to mistake her expression as anything less than sincere. "Baby, you know I know what I'm doin'. In one year, with your friend's farm and all, every dime of yo' money can be clean and workin' for you."

Hitman shook his head. He wasn't ready for that. "We'll see. Where's my phone?"

"I'm glad you asked. Please get this thang! It has been ringin' like crazy."

And she wasn't lying. When Tracey came back out of her bedroom the phone was ringing in her hand. She hurriedly gave it to him.

The caller ID showed that it was his sister. "Yeah?"

"Boy, where the fuck are you at?! And why you ain't been answerin' your damn phone? I been callin' you for two days!"

"I'm answerin' now. What's up?"

"I got somebody 'round here that you really need to holla at. I'm talkin' 'bout *right now*!"

"Who?"

"Don't matter who! Just get your ass 'round here!" Dee said.

"Dee, I can't come through Eastview. Y'all meet me at that lil' gas station store on twenty-seven, headed to Cordele."

"Aiiight." Dee hung up.

Hitman gave Tracey the other $100,000 that he'd collected from BamBam and left to meet his sister. Based on the way Dee acted over the phone, he knew that the situation was serious. Pulling up to the gas station, he saw Dee's truck. He blew the horn to let them know that it was him driving the unfamiliar car. Dee got out. And Hitman was surprised to see the pretty brown-skin chick that had the altercation with Action getting out on the other side. *What the hell does she have to talk to me 'bout?!* he wondered as the two women got in the car with him.

"Nelva, right?" Hitman asked her.

She smiled, happy that he'd remembered her name. "Yeah, that's my name."

Dee just sat there.

"So, Nelva, what's up?" Hitman inquired.

Nelva took a deep breath and said, "Well, there's a lot goin' on… First of all, I'm Nelva Brown. My father's Nel Brown."

Hitman frowned and looked at Dee. It felt like someone had *sucker-punched* him in the stomach.

"Please don't look like that, because it's not what you're thinkin'. I came to help you," Nelva explained.

"And how is that?"

Nelva sighed and began telling Hitman everything that she'd heard at the meeting between her father and the two Federal agents. She left nothing out. And she felt a lot better when she was done.

The words *Feds, indictment,* and *life sentence* had Hitman sick to his stomach. He ran his hands over his face as he pondered the gravity of the situation. "Dee, sis, we gotta find this nigga." His voice was nervous.

Nelva wanted to ask, *What you gonna do when you find him?* But that would be being nosey. And truthfully, if they were going to do what she knew they had to do, she did not want to know.

"Okay, I'll get on it, bruh," Dee said. She'd never seen her brother scared before.

"Meanwhile, I got like twenty-six bricks in town. We gotta move them fast, before this whole shit with Action blows up."

Dee nodded. "TrapGirl and WattsDog are in town. They've got money for five."

"Aiiight, good. I'ma need you to take BamBam eight... you and Black can work the other thirteen. It's all in the bread van... if that runs out before I get back, it's another thirty by B-Easy."

"Where you goin'?" Dee asked.

"Away from here!" Hitman assured her.

Dee dapped him up and she and Nelva got out.

* * *

Hitman spent a sleepness night at Tracey's house. His mind was in a million different places. They got up early the next morning, dropped Baby Jai off to her grandmother's house, picked up the $100,000 that TrapGirl and WattsDog owed for the five kilos, and took a car service to Albany. They had a first class flight to Miami to catch and $300,000 that needed to be delivered to Santino.

After being at Santino's house for two days, Tracey had learned lots of new Spanish recipes and Hitman had visited damn near every strip club in Miami with Flaco. The two of them had become super-tight.

Hitman had plans to stay in Miami for three more days. He had yet to call Dee, but knew that he needed to. The situation with Action was not going to handle itself. And nobody was going to move until he said so. With a heavy heart, Hitman got his Blackberry and went in Santino's backyard to call his sister. Dee answered on the third ring.

"Yeah, nigga, what's up?"

"Dee, Act's in the *Dele*... ya heard me?"

"Yeah, I figured that," Dee said.

"You remember that bug I put in your ear a while back?"

25

"Yeah, I remember." Dee did not like the way the conversation was going.

"Okay, well, make sure you tell Action when you see him."

Dee nodded her head as if her brother could see her. "I'm on it, bruh... anything else?"

"Nah." Hitman hung up. When he turned to go back in the house, he saw that Santino had took a seat on one of the lounge chairs that sat by the big custom Jacuzzi.

"Come. Sit," Santino said, waving Hitman over.

Hitman sat down. Stared off in the direction of the back fence. A lot was on his mind. Mainly the situation with Action. He loved his friend.

"You like it here?" Santino asked, pointing at the big backyard.

"Oh, yeah, it's real cool." The question caught him off guard.

Santino nodded. Smiled. "My wife and me. We want to thank you... Me, my wife, my son, we think of you as family." Santino sat and thought for a minute. "I have many houses. Some bigger than this. Rent, me make money... Drugs, no good. Kill or go to jail... I, me do it for me family never poor. Me old, life over. But mucho money... you, what you do with you money?"

Hitman shook his head. He was not expecting this sort of conversation for Santino. It was almost like talking to Tracey or Black. He didn't have an answer for the old man, so he simply shrugged his shoulders.

"You, you have much money now... give me some, five-hundred-thousand. Me make money good for you. Houses, bank account, money investment bonds. All in you name," Santino explained.

Without one second's hesitation, Hitman agreed. There was no particular reason why he agreed, he just did. For some reason he trusted the old man.

Arm in arm, the two walked back in the house like father and son.

* * *

TrapGirl was back from Tennessee and hanging tough with Dee. With a fifth of Remy Martin V.S.O.P. and an ounce of 'dro, the two were feeling nice as they rode and looked. They had been in Cordele for about an hour, cruising 15th and vibing. It looked like Spring Break out there (back when it was still being held in Daytona).

Dudes were riding real slick: Donks, *big boy* trucks, Lexus Coupes, and Act Legends. Both Dee and TrapGirl were impressed with the Cordele dudes' car game.

Scanning the scene, TrapGirl spotted the dark-blue Galaxy parked in the projects at the top of the Avenue. They quickly parked the rental and hopped out, blunts and drink in hand.

"Damn, boy, you M-I-A like a *mug*, dog! What's up?" Dee stated.

"No bullshit!" TrapGirl added. She eyed Action close as they approached him. TrapGirl noticed that he still had that green soldier rag dangling from his right rear pocket. That made her feel good.

Action swaggered over and the three of them hugged and exchanged Face Mob handshakes. He was real happy to see them. He loved his hometown, but Face Mob was where his heart was and would always be. "Damn, it's good to see y'all!" he exclaimed.

"Nigga, you know what it is! What the fuck is you doin'?" Dee asked, passing him the blunt she had.

"Shiiid." Action hit the blunt. "I been layin' low... what they doin' in the Lil' A?"

"Come on, nigga, you know exactly what it is. We gettin' money and duckin' the police and the fake muthafuckas," TrapGirl answered.

"Yeah. And everybody lookin' for you," Dee added.

"Oh yeah? It's bad, huh?! Black and Hitman really fucked up with me this time, huh?" Action knew that he'd let his team down by doing the dumb shit he'd done. Killing Lefty was a bad move and Action now realized that. But he also knew that he'd do it again, because he hated Southsiders with a passion.

Dee sucked her teeth and frowned. "Maaaan, fuck Hitman and Black! You did what you had to do, homie. This Face Mob, you feel me?! Every now and then somebody gotta dangle that soldier rag and let their nuts hang to the floor... Black and Hitman gotta respect your mind just like you respect theirs."

"Yeah, we're family and that was mob business you handled... so it is what it is, kinfolk," TrapGirl stated, hugging Action as she spoke.

They stood out in the projects smoking, drinking, and shooting the bullshit for about two hours before they ran out of liquor. High as hell, they climbed in the rental car to go get some more drink. Dee drove, Action rode shotgun, TrapGirl sat in the back. Leaving the liquor store with three more fifths of Remy, they cruised the Avenue. Dee made a left turn and banged the curb. The car dipped and skidded before Dee straightened it out.

"Damn," Dee yelped. "Y'all two aiiight?"

Action nodded.

TrapGirl bussed out laughing. She was high as hell.

Taking her cue, Dee and Action bussed out laughing as well. The three sang along to Juvenile and BG's *Feeling Right* as Dee drove towards the northside of Cordele, past the slaughterhouse, up near the Farmers' Market.

Slowing the car, Dee frowned and looked at Action. "Cuz, you hear somethin' clickin' on your side? Sound like the front tire."

"Nigga, I don't hear shit!" Action said, laughing.

Dee shrugged and drove on. But minutes later her frown returned. Meek Mill's *'Bout That Life* was playing. Dee turned it down and said, "Now tell me y'all ain't hear that!" She stopped the car.

"Yeah, no bullshit, I heard it that time. It's a loud click, like the tire 'bout to come off," TrapGirl added, opening her door.

"Nigga, get out and check the shit!" Dee told Action.

Action shrugged and got out. He looked, saw nothing. He then kneeled down on one knee to get a closer look. *Tat! Tat! Tat!* the .38 kicked in TrapGirl's little hand. Action never saw it coming. His head splattered like a ripe watermelon dropped on concrete.

TrapGirl looked up and down the long two-lane highway before tossing the murder weapon in the grass that bordered the road. Seeing no one, she got in the car's passenger seat, tears in her pretty young eyes, and Dee pulled off. They rode back to Americus in complete silence... *Hollow-point seen, no more sleep lost. Just a new opportunity for the bettors....*

* * *

Two days had passed since Hitman received the text from Dee. It simply read, *I told the homie what you said... He's got nothing to say...* Hitman was relieved. But what he'd done tore him up inside. Action had been like a brother to him. One tear. Just one he'd shedded and his mourning was over. Yet Mommie sensed a change in him.

"You do something... something bad. But it be okay. You do it for good," she'd said before giving him another beaded chain. This one was blue and white.

Hitman thanked her and he and Tracey prepared to leave. "Flaco, you gonna run me and Tracey to the airport?"

They were standing beside Flaco's convertible Delta. He'd just finished cleaning the rims and tires. "I can do that, my niggie."

"This is a bad car you got here," Hitman exclaimed. He loved the Vert.

"You really like it, my niggie?!"

"Hell yeah."

Flaco shrugged and threw him the keys.

Hitman caught them. "You're lettin' me drive?"

Laughing, Flaco said, "You can do whatever you want, my niggie, it's yours."

"What?!"

"Fool, I talked to my dad. He told me everything... my niggie, I really respect what you did. You my brutha now, my niggie. What's mine is yours."

Hitman smiled. He was touched by the man's sincerity. "Thanks, dog... what's mine is yours as well."

They embraced. An hour later Tracey and Hitman were cruising up the Turnpike, top down, with the wind blowing through their hair. Teddy Pendergrass was singing about a *50/50 love... How it felt so good*. Hitman agreed because he'd never felt better.

* * *

They stopped and spent two days with Riff-Raff and his family before continuing on to Americus. At which time Hitman picked up forty-five kilos. The authorities in Cordele had found Action's body, so the blitz on the Northside by the police had subsequently been subsided. Eastview was back open and it seemed that things were back to normal.

There was $925,000 waiting on Hitman when he walked through the door. He gave Tracey $400,000 and the keys to the Vert. She kissed him and left. He then gave Keisha $515,000 and Santino's address. The $15,000 was for Keisha and the $500,000 was the investment money that Santino had asked him for.

Grabbing the forty-five kilos of crack, Hitman went over to Eastview. B-Easy, WattsDog, Dee, TrapGirl, and Black were all there. The only person missing was Action. And he'd never be there again. It felt strange to Hitman, discussing their future with such an important piece of their past no longer there to play his position.

"Dig, y'all, I heard 'bout what happened to Action and it's really fucked up. I'ma miss my dog, but bein' the soldier he was, I'm sure he'd want us to keep gettin' it. So that's what I'ma do... but y'all look here, stack your bread and start lookin' for a way out. I've got eight bricks for all five of y'all, fifteen a piece... That's $120,000 a piece, $600,000 altogether. I don't care how y'all work it, together, separately, it don't matter. Dee just needs to have $600,000 for me when y'all finished."

They agreed and he left with the last five kilos. They were BamBam's. With very little conversation he sold BamBam *the work* for $113,000, which Hitman took straight to Riff-Raff. The cool little dude deserved every penny of the money. He'd turned those last 100 kilos into 150. So Hitman still had forty-five *bricks* of *hard-white* left in the little trailer. He seriously thought about taking the *work* back with him, but something inside of him said *don't do it*. Following the force that guided him, Hitman left the *work*.

Young Jeezy's *Still On It* played as he drove along, fingering the beaded chains that Mommie had given him. For some reason he felt a strong sense of apprehension. Paranoia. He did his best to shake the uneasy feelings but they just would not go away.

As soon as he passed the hospital, en route to his house, police cars came from every direction. The thought of taking them on a high-speed chase crossed his mind, *but for what*?! His safe was safe and he was clean. He needed some rest anyway. Hitman pulled over and allowed the police to take him.

* * *

"Uncuff him," Nel ordered upon entering the small interrogation room.

Rodgers sighed loudly and walked over to do as he'd been told.

As soon as the cuffs were removed, Hitman rubbed his aching wrists in an attempt to stimulate his blood circulation. He knew that the racist *cracka*, Rodgers, had purposely placed the restraints on too tight.

Rodgers was truly the sadistic, extremist type. An Albert Pike worshipping, Hitler loving, Klan member. He'd simply traded his white sheet for a badge. "Cuffs wasn't too tight, was they, boy?" Rodgers joked, a sadistic smile on his face.

A wide smile stretched across Hitman's face. He replied, "Don't much bother me, buddy. I like them tight... like that *freak-nasty* sista of yours before she got strung out on crack."

The white officer's face turned fire-red at the thought of his little sister coupling with a nigger *street-punk.* Had it just been a loose accusation Rodgers would have simply brushed it off, but Rodgers was fully aware of his sister's drug problem and her association with black dealers. "Why, you little punk!" Rodgers said, stepping towards Hitman.

Hitman rose and the two men locked up. Rodgers aim was to overwhelm the smaller man. But Hitman slipped Rodgers' hold, went low and hoisted the big officer over his head.

"Hey, put him down!" Nel yelled.

Doing as Nel Brown had told him, Hitman brought Rodgers' down hard. Nel turned his head just as Rodgers back impacted with the table that Hitman had been handcuffed to. The old table collapsed, sending table legs and wood chips flying across the room.

"Uuuugh, shit!" Rodgers groaned when he hit the floor.

"That's enough!" Nel yelled, pushing Hitman up against the wall. His partner had forced the issue and suffered for it, but that was as far as things were going to go on his watch. "Get out of here, Rodgers, I'll handle it from here."

Embarrassed and angry, Rodgers got up and stared Hitman down before limping out of the room.

"Sit down," Nel ordered Hitman.

Hitman took a seat and rested his face in his hands. He was tired.

"You know why you're here?"

"Citizenship award."

"You really think life's a joke, huh?"

"Nah, but I think you and your partna are pretty funny."

Nel Brown looked at the young, strong, black man that sat before him. So smart and full of potential. Yet so shortsighted and unconscious. He hated the direction in which the system forced so many impressionable young blacks. *The insidious and pervasive nature of the drug problem amongst the black community is nothing short of genocide*, Nel thought. "Son, can't you see what these white folks are trying to do to you… to us? Just two years ago you were on the football field, a star. Now you're on the killing field."

Hitman, unfazed by the black cop's words or by his play at brotherhood, just stared at him.

"Well, I'm sure you know that your friend Action is dead... found him with a few plug-size holes in his head," Nel said, trying to get some kind of reaction from Hitman.

"Do you know what absolution is?" Hitman asked.

The officer nodded.

Hitman nodded in return. "Then you know what happened... You can't just be willin' to live for it and not be willin' to die for it." Staring Nel in the eyes, Hitman asked him, "Are you willin' to die for it?"

Nel studied Hitman's face. His expression was austere. The detective had seen many self-proclaimed street dons and crazed goons, but none like Hitman. For he was neither. The kid had the air of a gentleman, the viciousness of a caged rattlesnake, and an uncanny ability to calculate under pressure. So Nel wasn't sure if he'd simply been asked a question or had his very life been threatened. He decided to ignore Hitman's question and ask one of his own. "Son, did you kill your friend?"

Hitman shook his head. "Nah, officer, I loved Action like a brutha. Besides, I was in Miami."

"How about Dawn, did your sister kill him?"

"I don't reckon, but how 'bout you ask her, 'cause like I said, I was in Miami."

Nel Brown did not let up. For the next four hours he drilled Hitman with question after question, never once straying from the subjects of drug and murder. Hitman was not surprised by any of the allegations that were hurled at him, because truthfully, he'd done them all and they both knew it. The thing was, he wasn't going to admit it and Nel couldn't prove it. The Feds had packed up and left with Action's untimely demise. And Nel Brown had nothing.

After wasting four hours, Nel finally took Hitman to booking. From there he was taken to a cell block. As fate would have it, he ended up in the same cell block that B-Easy and Action had been housed in. He thought about his dead partner when he saw the words: *Action The Face Mob General*. It was scratched into the bunk that Hitman settled on. *Action? Damn, bruh*, Hitman mused, wondering if maybe something existed beyond this sphere of life. If it did, Hitman prayed that Action would be bequeathed the best of it...

* * *

Bail was denied and the game of chess began. Of course, there would be no sacrifices on Hitman's side of the board. And being as he was black, the *crackas* had the first move; which they made by charging him with first degree murder and conspiracy to murder. Hitman's counter move was hiring Marquis Wimberly — a spitfire lawyer out of Miami that ate murder and drug cases for breakfast. Then the waiting game began.

Tracey and Sherry visited once a week. Keisha, on the other hand, was there everytime they opened the visiting hall. She also wrote and sent him sexy *panty-shots*. Keisha was there for her homie-brother-provider in whatever capacity he needed her, whenever and however.

Time seemed to pass slowly in the beginning — as he accommodated himself to his new environment. Confinement. His only escape was between the lines of inverted narratives. Literary sequences. Exciting tales spun by talented black writers. Hitman read every black novel that he could get sent in to him. The more he read, the more he wanted to know — about himself and the plight of the so-called black man in the wilderness of North America. So at his request, Keisha started sending him books by the Honorable Elijah Muhammad, Arthur Cruz, Huey P. Newton, Malcomn X, and W.E.B. DuBois.

"Excuse me, main man, I'm not tryna get in your business or nothin', but is that your girl?" Eugene, the unit barber, asked Hitman one day as he cut his hair. Eugene had been in the county for a while.

"Who, the red chick I was at visit with yesterday?" Hitman questioned, figuring that he was asking about Keisha because she visited so often.

"Nah, nah, pimp, that lil' chocolate shawdy you be kickin' it with."

"Oh, Tracey, yeah... we jam real tight."

Damn! the barber thought, because he really dug Tracey. He'd seen her out at visit a few times and decided to ask, hoping that she was Hitman's cousin or something. Seeing that he was wrong, Eugene quickly changed the subject. "I heard 'bout ole Action. He was a cool dude. I was in this unit when him and B-Easy was here... yeah, I used to cut their hair every week."

Hitman didn't comment. The subject was still raw with him. Besides, his motto was *trust no one*, and he didn't know the barber well enough to be letting him into his space. Hitman kept his association with dudes in the county to a bare minimum. Because the truth was, outside of Face Mob he had no friends.

With damn near a year under his belt, Hitman had put together a real nice workout program that afforded him just enough leisure time to read, eat, shower and use the phone. He talked to Keisha and Tracey everyday. He never called Dee because he didn't want to bring any added heat her way.

The last forty-five kilos that were out at Riff-Raff's farm were long gone and he had no way of getting any more, so Dee and the mob were on their own, getting it the best way they knew how.

Week by antagonizing week, the months passed. Monotonous. Tedious. From the food he ate to the programs he watched on TV, there was no variety. Just more of the same. Overlapping redundancy. Yet while he sat his lawyer was busy building his defense. The crafty Marquis Wimberly had gathered video taped statements from Tracey, Santino, Mommie, the owner of the Rollexxx strip club in Miami, as well as copies of his plane tickets and phone records showing that Hitman had been far away from Cordele when Action met his untimely demise. Everything looked good for him. It was all just a matter of waiting.

"Soooo, sweatheart," Tracey sang cheerfully one day as they sat at visitation. "How are you doin'?"

Hitman rubbed his hand over his smooth crown of wavy hair, sighing as he spoke. "Tired. I'm sick and tired of this damn place. It's been two and a half years almost, damn. What the fuck are they waitin' on?"

"It's gonna be okay, baby." Tracey eyed him. She'd truly grown to love him. And she really missed his touch, his tender *thug love*. "God won't ever put more on you than you can handle."

Hitman sighed again, loudly. "Well, baby, I sure wish He didn't thank so much of me," he capped sarcastically.

"Boy!" Tracey laughed out loud. "You are so crazy... but you'll be out of here before you know it. And on that day, what are you gonna do?"

He thought for a minute, smiled seductively at her, and said with assurance, "I'ma show you just how much I been missin' you.

Then," he paused before saying, "it's gonna be straight work-call. I'ma bleed these streets for everything they're worth and punish everything that's movin' outside of my circle."

Tracey felt her heart flutter. It was like a brief snatch from a nightmare. Reoccurring. Her daughter's father had thought the very same way. She saw so much of him in the strong, handsome, loving black man that sat before her. He had been about the same age as Hitman when the Feds picked him up and gave him thirty long years to serve. He still wrote her and Baby Jai, called and expressed his regret for the decisions he'd made. Decisions that had destroyed their little family and the dreams of a future together. *One more shot at it*, was all that he yearned. Tracey shook her head slowly. Sadly. It saddened her, because she did not want to lose Hitman like she'd lost Jai's father. "Baby... don't you care if you lose your life to the street?" she asked him.

"Shawdy," he began evenly, "I think I lost my life already, a long while ago... right now, I'm tryna get it back, if that makes sense."

Tracey did not know. But she spent many nights, lonely nights, thinking about it. Thinking how much she really loved and missed him. Thinking how strong and loving he was. She thought about the things they could be doing, salacious and titillating, if only he was home with her...

Time continued to tick away as she thought. And Mr. Marquis Wimberly continued flooding the judge's chambers with letters, petitions, and legal authority. They had already violated Hitman's rights to a speedy trial and it was clear to everyone involved that the prosecution's case was extremely weak. The judge, to everyone's surprise, gave a standing order that the prosecution had to proceed or drop the case. And with much reluctance, and to the dismay of Rodgers and Nel Brown, the prosecutor chose the latter.

He dropped the charges. Hitman smiled brightly as he and Mr. Wimberly exited the courtroom.

"Hey," Rodgers called out, stopping Hitman. "I'ma be watching you, boy. And if you so much as crack bad corn, boy, I'll be there to smell it."

Nel Brown said nothing at all. He just watched. And his silence bothered Hitman more than anything that Rodgers could fix his big mouth to say.

Fuck it, Hitman contemplated. *We're all men... they've gotta job, to serve and protect. And I've gotta job, to serve with no regard for law or life... It's trap or die.*

Chapter 2
Welcome Home

After a very brief exchange with his handsome, dark-skin lawyer, Hitman exited the busy courthouse. He did not even bother to pick up his personal property from the property room, he just left. Stepping outside, he found the day bright and sunny, but extremely cold. He inhaled deeply. The fresh air was exactly what he needed. It had been nearly three years he'd sat fighting his case. *Damn, I'm free,* he mused. Then he heard a horn blow. He looked and saw his sister's truck.

"Where's my muthafuckin' money at?" Hitman said as he slid into the truck and slammed the door close.

Dee frowned and punched the gas. The dual Flow Master pipes growled as she pulled away from the small courthouse. "Well fuck you, too, lil' brutha," she stated, cutting her sexy slanted eyes at him.

"Why you ain't come see me?" he asked, looking her over. She was fresh in a blue leather jumpsuit, with different company sponsor patches sewn all over it. With it she wore a red leather jacket and all red leather Reebok Classic high-tops. Her long hair was pulled back into a neat ponytail.

Dee sucked her teeth at him. "Nigga, you know damn well I wasn't comin' to nobody's jail to see nobody... so, next question."

"Where's Black and them at?" Hitman hadn't heard anything from Black in almost a year.

"Black's either in Sam's ass or out on Southern Field."

"What's poppin' on Southern Field?"

Raising an inquisitive eyebrow at her twin brother, Dee asked, "You ain't heard?! Your boy got the DirTek business out there."

"DirTek?!"

"Yeah." She nodded her head knowingly as she drove along. "Your boy Black done gone legal. He's gettin' it, too. They're the only hose company around here, so him and the cracka Bill Hagan are makin' all the money." Dee cut her eyes at Hitman to peep his expression before saying, "He come through every now and then, but he ain't on it no more."

Hitman did not particularly like what he'd just heard. Action was gone, now he'd lost Black as well. It had always been himself and Black against them all, for as long as he could remember. He looked over at Dee. She seemed to be relishing his discomfort. Before Black it had been her at his right hand. And now that Black was gone on to other things it would be her again.

Dee stopped at their favorite chicken joint and they went inside to eat. While eating two large platters of wings, fries, onion rings, and shrimp, Dee ran down everything that had transpired during his thirty-three month absence. It was not really much to report, because their trap had been closed a helluva lot more than it had been open.

"Can't keep no dope, bruh," Dee explained, her pretty mouth full of fries. "Niggas don't wanna serve me. Sometimes I'll go over to Cordele or Albany and get a few plates, but that's mainly when TrapGirl and WattsDog come down from Chat-Town. Other than that I just been chillin', layin' back, waitin' on you, 'cause for real, bruh, they taxin' and the *plates* really *ain't* worth coppin'. You feel me?"

Hitman nodded. He'd spent a nice piece of change fighting his case for nearly three years. And now it was time to get it all back, with interest. "So ain't nobody doin' nothin'?"

Dee finished off a spicey wing and drunk from her Cherry Coke before saying, "Oh, yeah, ole Heavy's back, but like I told you, he ain't tryna serve me. They on that Southside shit again, bruh."

"Oh, yeah?"

"Yeah."

"Who he workin' with?"

Sucking her teeth, Dee answered her brother. "He givin' it all to Big Dream."

"Big Dream?!"

"Exactly. They're the only show in town. Ounces, quarters, eight-balls, and gram-slabs. The work's good, too. Ya heard me?"

Hitman thought silently as he finished off his food, allowing his mind to grind and properly digest the information. He had a million dollars in cash and nobody to spend it with.

"So what we gon' do, bruh?"

"I don't know..." He stood up. "But let's go."

Hitman had Dee to stop off uptown. They walked into *Da Coffee Shop: Tranch de Vie*. The shop was nice. There was a long counter, sort of like a bar in a club, that ran the length of the open room. The counter was fashioned from blonde-oak, leather, and brass; two attendants worked behind it. The place smelt like a fine blend of exotic coffees, teas, and chocolates.

Over along the far right wall was a row of eight computer desk stations. Thick beige carpet covered the floor. It matched the leather couches, love seats and bean bags perfectly. People, singles and couples alike, both black and white people, occupied the comfortable settings, some even sitting around on the thick carpet. All of them reading, drinking one beverage or another, or tapping away at a computer keyboard.

Hitman and Dee continued on towards the back, where Hitman approached a sexy yellow-bone. The chick was older. Beautiful green eyes. Thick honey-blonde dreadlocks that stopped just above her perfectly rotund posterior.

"Sister Furqana?" Hitman asked the woman.

"Yes," she replied, smiling brightly at him. "I'm Sister Furqana."

"I'm Clarence Man," Hitman introduced himself. "And this is my sister, Dee."

The beautiful shop owner recognized the name Clarence Man as the name of the guy that she'd sold so many books to and occasionally corresponded with through letters over the past few years. She immediately reached out and hugged them both. It warmed her heart to see him free.

"It is so good to finally see you in person," Sister Furqana announced gleefully.

"You know they can't keep the black man down forever," Hitman replied.

Hitman had promised her that he would visit the shop upon his release.

The three of them made their way over to the bar and ordered three green teas. Together they sat and talked for almost an hour. Sister Furqana was a very intelligent woman. She reminded Hitman of his mother.

"Well, baby, welcome home," Sister Furqana said as she walked them out.

"Thank you."

"You think about your life and value your freedom. Don't continue to let the powers that be dictate your actions through their trick-knowledge."

Hitman nodded and they parted ways.

As Dee pushed the slick truck, Raw Nitty and Choppa's *Break Up The Block* rumbled loudly through the speakers...

...if the pound go buck/ then the AK gon' chop/ gimme two like me/ we'll shutdown the whole block... whip up and break up the whole block/ flip up and cake up the whole block/ got enough whips to take up a whole block... Choppa like Jam Master Jay/ I'm the big gun blaster/ drum three-round burst/ make the rounds spit faster...

Hitman smiled as they hit Rouland Street. *Home sweet home.* The neighborhood looked the same as he'd left it, but his house looked different. There was a chain-link fence surrounding the yard now and broken toys were spewed all over the lawn. A rainbow of crayon marks ran the length of the walls on the porch.

"Who did this?"

Dee laughed. "Them lil' gangstas."

"What lil' gangstas?"

Without waiting for Dee's answer, Hitman opened the front door and walked inside. The inside of the house looked worse than the outside did. There were more toys and twice as many rainbow designs on the dirty interior walls. Little handprints and food stains accompanied the crayon marks on the floor and walls. Hitman could not believe what he was seeing. Trash laden. The place was sordid. Amongst the toys and candy wrappers lay Clarence. Passed out drunk.

Hitman turned to Dee, who stood laughing at his expression. He sighed and turned towards his room, but Dee called out to him.

"Aye, bruh, you probably don't wanna go in there," she said and continued laughing.

"Why?!"

She shrugged her shoulders. "Just 'cause," she said.

Ignoring her warning, Hitman proceeded towards his room. But before he could open the door it flew open, almost bussing him in the face. As he weaved left to avoid the door two little boys came flying past him, with Sherry chasing behind them.

"Quan! Cameron!" Sherry yelled. "Y'all better get back here!"

One of the little boys ran in the bathroom and the other one ran for the front door, but Dee had his passage blocked. He turned and ran off to Sherry's old room.

Hitman peeped around Sherry into what was supposed to be his bedroom. What he saw almost brought tears to his eyes. The bed frame that once held his mattress and box spring was piled in a tangled heap near the closet. Beside it sat his clothes and shoes, amongst more broken toys and empty fast food containers. His mattress set on the floor. His safe lay sideways, open, filled with Lego blocks and Frosted Flakes. The fronts of the dresser drawers had been pulled off and the large oval mirror was cracked.

"I paid four stacks for that bedroom set!" Hitman yelled.

At that instance Sherry looked and noticed her big brother standing there. "Oh, hey, Man! When did you get out?"

He stared at her. He was about to tell her *something good*, but she cut him off.

"Wait a minute, Man, I'm 'bout to go kill these two lil' *badass* boys!" And off she went to make good on her threat.

Hitman looked to Dee for some sort of explanation.

Dee laughed. "Welcome home, bruh... The two lil' gangstas are your nephews. You remember Quan, right? Well, he's gotten to be too bad! And lil' Cameron wanna be just like him. They are terrible."

"What happened to them?!"

"Shiiid, they're spoiled."

Hitman shook his head sadly. "How do you live here like this?" He waved his hand about the room.

"I don't," Dee stated. "Me and Kim gotta crib in Hosana Circle. Them lil' soldiers been ran us off."

"How many bedrooms you got?!" His voice was desperate.

"I already know." Dee was dying laughing at him. "Get your stuff, nigga."

Twenty minutes later they drove up to the new house. His Vert was parked in the driveway, beside a red 5.0 Convertible Mustang. The house was nice.

"Where's my bike?"

"It's in the back, in the shed."

As soon as they walked in Hitman spotted Lil Kim. Little panties, big pussy. She was cleaning up. "Hey, Hitman," she spoke and went in the bedroom.

Hitman returned her greeting and continued towards his new bedroom. Dee had furnished it nicely. King-sized bed. Oak dresser, nightstands, and cabinet. On the bed lay a large duffle bag. Opening it up, Hitman stared at stacks and stacks of big-faced hundreds and fifties. An instant smile creased his handsome face.

"That's one-million-twenty-five-thousand. A hun'ed-fifty thousand went to your lawyer and twenty-five went on your third of the cost of this house... the bedroom set was on me," Dee explained as she entered his room.

Hitman smiled. Dee had already known that he couldn't live under the extreme conditions that Quan and Cameron were putting down at the other house. "Thanks, sis."

"No problem, nigga... welcome home," she said and left his room.

Chapter 3
The Station

The station was buzzing as officers moved throughout it, dutifully performing one task or another. Enforcement. Binding obligation to the constituents of Americus, the largest city in Sumter County. Americus was a predominantly black city, where ethnic groups remained firmly within their racial boundaries. This unwritten segregation exited in every social institute in Sumter County except for the police station. The Captain and Nel Brown saw to it that racial harmony flourished in their work place. Black, white, and Mexican officers worked hand-in-hand to serve and protect the community at large.

Nel Brown came into the station a little earlier than he normally came in. He'd spent the night at his daughter's house. She was away, on vacation in Seattle, Washington, and he'd agreed to keep an eye on her place while she was away. Nelva had been gone for three weeks and was due back any day now.

Passing his desk, Detective Nel Brown went straight to the coffee pot and fixed himself a steaming mug of the black liquid.

"Rough night?" his partner, Detective Rodgers, asked when Nel returned to his cluttered desk.

Nel grunted and sipped at the hot coffee. The two men had been partners for a very long time. "Did Clarence Man pick up his personal effects?"

Rodgers shook his head in the negative. "No, sir, he sure didn't."

"Okay. Where's the phone?"

"Right here… we just got it back."

"Fine. Pack it all up and mail it to him. Be sure to get it out of here today, because I don't want that lawyer of his calling down here bothering the Captain… seeing as it'll be my ass that the Captain chews off."

"I'm on it," Rodgers stated. He snatched up the phone and blended in with the orderly pell-mell that was *the station….*

Chapter 4
The Embrace

It had been another long, tiring, uninspired day at work for Tracey. It seemed that she had to fight harder and harder every day to pull herself through the monotony of her life. Tonelessness. *I've got to do something... make a change... God, I wish that Hitman was out,* she thought to herself as she drove home. Her beautiful daughter, Jai, sat in the passenger seat. Baby Jai was the absolute light of Tracey's life.

"Ooow, Ma!" Jai yelled excitedly as Tracey whipped her car into her driveway. "Look, Ma, look!"

The entire porch was littered with roses. Big pretty bouquets of them. White, pink, yellow, purple, and red. They were beautiful. And sitting in the midst of them was Hitman, smiling brightly. His Vert was parked curbside. B-Easy and Dee were sitting inside of it.

Jai quickly jumped out of the car and bolted off. The pretty little girl with the long hair and almond-shaped eyes really liked Hitman. "Whose flowers are these?" she asked him.

"They're for your momma," he answered.

"All of them?"

"Yep, all of them." He saw the disappointment register in her facial expression. "But this is for you."

Jai saw the grey Toy Poodle and lit up like a Christmas tree. "Ooow, thank you, thank you! What's its name?"

"That's gonna be up to you and him."

Tracey had walked up by then and busied herself smelling the flowers. Hitman admired her. Dress slacks. Silk button-down blouse. Smart little four-inch heels. She wore her hair in a short wrap like Malinda Williams. Tracey was so sexy and cute.

"Ma, look, ma!" Jai exclaimed, showing Tracey her new Toy Poodle.

Tracey nodded at her daughter, smiling that smile of hers, and then looked at Hitman. She was so happy to see him. He stood and the two of them embraced. A slow, tight, comforting embrace. Three years of uninspired toil was completely eradicated in that single hug.

While Dee and B-Easy put all of the flowers in the house, Tracey and Hitman went in her bedroom to talk.

"It's so good to see you," she purred.

"I feel the same way, baby." Hitman gazed into her lovely eyes. "It's been a very long time comin'."

She nodded. "For me, too."

"Well, I'ma need you to do somethin' for me."

Again she nodded. Her eyes never straying from his.

"I've gotta few things that I gotta do right quick, but then I want you to fly down to Miami with me."

"Okay."

Their lips then met. He loved the taste of her tongue. The softness of her lips. He held her tight as their tongues danced—her tender body pressed lovingly against his own. *The embrace.* It was perfect. He wished that he could hold her forever. But he couldn't because he had to embrace the streets...

Chapter 5
Little Urchins

The weather had gotten considerably cooler since night began to fall. In the wake of approaching darkness, Hitman's Vert slowly cruised the streets of Americus. B-Easy drove. Dee rode shotgun. Hitman sat in the backseat, the convertible top down, sipping on a fifth of Night Train. Wale's song, *Bricks*, played loudly as they rode. They'd been riding for over an hour. Hitman was on a new campaign and he wanted the street populance to know that their ruler was back.

"Damn, bruh, it's cold as witch titties out here," Dee complained.

"Yeah, no bullshit," B-Easy concurred.

When the Vert came to a stop at the red light, next to the hospital, they noticed the gold Lincoln Navigator that sat beside them. Big Dream was behind the steering wheel of the slick SUV. Heavy was stunting on the passenger side.

Big Dream happened to look over and saw Dee eyeing him. He waved. A smug grin on his chubby black face. He knew that he had the better hand at the time and he made it his business to make sure that everybody else knew it as well. A lot had changed in the three years that Hitman had been gone. With Heavy, CurveBall's old connect, supplying him with heavy weight, Big Dream was serving everybody on every side of town. The streets were his and he decided who ate, and he'd decided that he didn't want to see the Face Mob with anything on their plate.

Dee pointed her finger at Big Dream like it was a gun, aiming, she pulled the trigger as the light changed and the Vert skated off.

Their next stop was in Eastview. Hitman couldn't wait to see Keisha. He jumped out of the Vert and took the stairs two at a time. Keisha's door was locked so he knocked on it hard. She opened the door, wearing boyshorts and a bra, and her eyes almost popped out of her head.

"Oh my God!?" Keisha screamed, jumping up into his arms and wrapping her legs around his waist. "I can't believe this," she whined, tears running down her face. She was so happy to see him.

Hitman carried her across the threshold like they were newlyweds on their honeymoon. Keisha kissed him right on the lips. Thoughts of Miami, the time they'd almost had sex, worked their way into his mind. Add that to the fact that her soft, hairy pussy was pressed against his stomach, and he felt an erection growing in his pants.

"When did you get out?" Keisha asked, her lips nearly touching his as she spoke.

"I believe it was 'bout noon," he answered, quickly putting her down.

She sucked her teeth and rolled her eyes at him. "Okay, so why you ain't been came 'round here?"

"I've been busy," he said, flat and to the point. "But what's up?"

"Ain't shit." Keisha eyed him. "You seen Tracey?"

"Yeah."

Keisha sucked her teeth again. *This niggas's a trip*, she thought before asking, "How 'bout your house, you seen your house?"

Hitman shook his head sadly. "Yeah, I saw it."

Seeing the look on his face, Keisha bussed out laughing. "Them lil' urchins that your sista had are some demons! They brung them lil' muthafuckas 'round here for me to baby-sit and, boy, let me tell you." Keisha paused and shook her head. "Hitman, God be my witness, I swear that was the first time I ever wanted to shoot children in the muthafuckin' head."

"Come on, now, they ain't that bad," Hitman replied.

"Shiiid," Keisha stated seriously. "You just don't know them, that's why you sayin' that dumb shit."

"I know Quan, girl," he corrected her.

Keisha shook her head. "Ut'un, no, that lil' boy ain't the same lil' Quan he used to be... no, he's changed, Hitman. I ain't never seen a lil' boy that bad. Dennis' momma won't even let him come over their house no more, 'cause he set their house on fire."

"What?!"

"Yeah. Sherry took him to a lil' child counselor and they said it's 'cause Dennis is gone. They say he rebellin' 'cause he missin' his daddy. Crackas wanna put him on medication and all, but your daddy said hell nah; Mr. Clarence wasn't goin' for that... and shiiid, Cameron just as bad. Sherry spoils them."

Hitman felt bad, because if it was true that Quan was rebelling because he missed his daddy, then it was all his fault because he was the one who had ran Dennis out of town. *Damn*, he thought, looking stupid in the face.

* * *

Hitman was good and twisted off the cheap wine and Remy X.O. that he'd been drinking all night with Keisha, Dee, and B-Easy. Slowly, carefully, he made his way up the walkway in Tracey's front yard as Dee and B-Easy pulled off in the Vert.

Before he could make it to the porch the automatic sensor lights came on, damn near lighting up the whole yard. The front door came open as he mounted the steps. Tracey stood there smiling at him. He could only imagine what was beneath her T-shirt.

"I thought you'd stood me up."

"Not in this lifetime, baby," Hitman assured her.

Smiling, she turned and led the way to her bedroom.

Hitman stared, his eyes locked in on the seductive sway of her sexy hips and ass.

As soon as her bedroom door was closed, without so much as a hello, the two were in each other's arms; their lips locked in a lustful cohesiveness. Zealous. There was no mistaking the love that fueled their passion. Unsophisticated. Constraint's conquest provoked their kiss.

Tracey fell to the bed, legs sequestered. Hitman peeled away his clothes while she discarded her T-shirt and panties. Her chocolate body was beautiful. Breasts firm and delectable. He volleyed from one erect nipple to the other, nibbling and sucking. He worked his way down her flat stomach and found himself between her dark, shapely thighs. Using his forefingers, he parted the silken lips of her vagina and lapped her pearl-tongue before sucking it into his hot mouth like a shucked oyster. A low growl caught in her throat and her entire body shook.

"Ooooooh, yeeeesss," she moaned, taking the back of his head into her small hands and arching her back. Tracey spread her legs as far apart as she could spread them and slowly oscillated her hips to the smooth rhythm of his talented tongue.

Abandoning her swollen clitoris, Hitman covered her lips again, sucking her long tongue into his mouth as he plunged the full girth and length of his shaft into her warm pool of silk. The pleasures of her love possessed him. Sweltering. Contracting around him. The milky nectar of her pussy saturated the sheets beneath them. Inundating as he plunged and withdrew. Each stroke a little deeper than the last.

"Daaaamn, I ...miss you," he moaned, lost to the world outside of her.

"Baby, I ...miss you, too," she sang, her voice sultry; emitting the sort of sensation that one might perceived audibly if sunshine ever voiced its warmth.

"...pussy good, baby," Hitman intoned. He was overcome with emotion and fighting the compulsion to declare his love for her.

"Then... cum in it, baby, because... it's yours," Tracey assured him.

He kissed her hard. Sucking her tongue and lips. Their embrace grew tighter as the rhythm of their love-making quickened. Faster. Deeper. They both moaned and froze. Their love consummated in the heat of passion...

* * *

When Tracey woke up the next morning Hitman was gone. There was so much that he had to do. He put away the buy money in the van that Keisha would be driving to Miami. He called Flaco down in Miami to make sure that everything was a go. And lastly, he and Dee took the long trip down to the farm to pick up Riff-Raff. The three of them were near the old Walmart when Dee's Blackberry started ringing.

"Yeah, run your mouth... Yeah, he right here... So why you ain't just call him last night? ...Whatever, girl, we on the way." Dee hung up the phone.

"Who that?" Hitman inquired.

"Your sista, Sherry," she stated as if Sherry was only Hitman's sibling and not her own. "She say a package came for you yesterday."

They were only a few blocks away, so Dee drove straight there.

Dee parked outside the fence and the three of them jumped out. The front door to the house flew open and out came the two little gangsters, running and yelling.

"Hey, Uncle Man!" Quan yelled.

He had on the religious beads that Mommie had given Hitman and he was wearing Hitman's platinum chain with the diamond cross and engagement ring on it. Cameron had his uncle's cell phone plastered to his young ear as if he was talking big business.

"Unc, hey, Unc! I'm talkin' to your girlfriend!" Cameron yelled.

"What the fuck?!" Hitman questioned, seeing the two of them with his personal property. "If y'all lil' devils don't give me my shit!"

"Ut'un!" Sherry said, stepping out onto the porch. "Man, you ain't gotta talk to my damn kids like that!"

"Hell you say... somebody need to talk to them, 'cause you sure ain't tellin' them shit, and that's for damn sure." Hitman grabbed his nephews and quickly relieved them of his possessions. Cameron tried to fight for the cell phone, but he gave it up after Hitman hit him upside his head.

They all went inside, Cameron and Quan both glued to Hitman's legs. It seemed to Hitman that the house was in a worse state than it had been just yesterday.

The boys left Hitman to attack an unconscious Clarence.

"Hey, Uncle Man, look!" Quan yelled as he came off of the couch's armrest like Jimmy Superfly Snooka, landing elbow first in Clarence's stomach.

Clarence quickly came out of his drunken slumber. He had fire in his eyes! But seeing that it was his worrisome grandson he just shook his head and laid back down.

"Boy!" Hitman grabbed Quan and slapped him hard across his butt. "Are you crazy?"

"Don't hit him, Man!" Sherry screamed.

"You're right, I need to be hittin' you, 'cause you're the one that's got them like this!" He really wanted to beat Sherry's ass. "Where's my shit at, so I can go."

Sherry rolled her sexy China-doll eyes at him and looked in her old room for the package that she'd signed for yesterday. It wasn't there. She then tried Hitman's old room, thinking maybe she'd sat it in there. No luck. Returning to the living room, she looked around and came across an empty shipping box. "Cameron, boy, did you open this box?" she asked.

Cameron shook his head. "Ut'un!"

"Stop lyin', boy! 'Cause you had my damn phone!" Hitman checked him.

"Ut'un!" Cameron stuck to his story.

"Where's my money? It was fifteen hun'ed dollars in my property."

"Now, I ain't seen no money," Sherry said. "But we do need some."

"Cameron, you seen your uncle's money?" Dee asked.

"Ut'un!"

"You talkin' 'bout this?" Quan yelled, holding up twenty, fifty, and hundred dollar bills that he and Cameron had colored with crayons.

Hitman wanted to kill Sherry and both of her badass children. "There goes the money you needed right there," he said to Sherry and left before she could reply...

"All science is merely a means to an end. The means is knowledge. The end is control. [So] the end always justifies the mean. Beyond this remains only one issue: Who will be the beneficiary?"

- William Cooper

The Beneficiary

Chapter 6
Speed and Deception

After landing at Miami's International Airport and renting a nice custom van, Hitman, Tracey, Dee, and Riff-Raff were now en route to West Palm Beach. Dee rode in the passenger seat as Riff-Raff drove. Junior Mafia's *I Need You Tonight* played softly. The song caused Tracey to replay last night's events in her mind. The thoughts provoked a slight shiver to wash over her, a smile playing at the corners of her small mouth. She was so happy with her life.

"Do you know who this is?" Hitman asked, interrupting her thoughts.

Tracey, sitting beside him on the van's first row of seats, looked at the cover of the book he was holding. The book was black and red in color. There was a picture of a handsome, light-skin man on it. *Message To The Blackman* was written above the man's head. Pointing to the name, Tracey said, "Says right there, Elijah Muhammad." She shrugged. "Who's he?"

"He's from Sandersville, Georgia... never passed the fourth grade, but since 1968 to now he's got over ten books in print... he was a millionaire when he passed," Hitman explained.

"How'd he do that?"

Hitman shrugged. "Simple, by thinkin' and teachin' others to also think." Hitman turned the book over to its rear cover and read it. "Look... *Elijah Muhammad is the most powerful Black man in America... he has done what generations of welfare workers, committees, resolutions, reports, housing projects and playgrounds have failed to do. He has done all these things, which our church and government has spectacularly failed to do...* Now, that ain't him writin' 'bout his damn self, that's James Baldwin and the folks from Reader's Digest talkin' 'bout him."

Tracey had never heard of him before. She'd graduated from college and studied some Black History along the way; however, Mr. Elijah Muhammad had never come up.

Probing the book's cover a little further, she saw the word *Muslim*. "He's a Muslim... you gonna be a Muslim also?"

"Nah, I'ma be smart and I'ma be rich. That's my aim. I wanna be able to *do for self.* I don't wanna have to ask a cracka for shit." Hitman thought for a minute, then said to Tracey, "I was trippin' when Riff-Raff said he wanted to leave Miami and get a damn farm. But for real, that was a smart move he made! Because a nigga with no land and no means to produce really ain't no real nigga. You feel me? A nigga gotta get that land and build his finances."

"So that's what you're doin'? You think some land and money's worth your life? Pastor says hell's gonna be filled with people that think that way."

"Hell?" Hitman questioned. "Tracey, we livin' in hell already. And God ain't made no heaven for no nigga. That's why white folks are so busy makin' their heaven here. They know that it ain't no life after death... When your time comes you're done... shiiid, bad as I wanna see my momma again, I've often wished it was, but I know it ain't. So I'ma do like white folks and make my own heaven on earth."

Tracey didn't respond. *Hell*, she couldn't respond. All she knew was what Pastor had told her. And it was clear to her that Hitman didn't have any faith in that. But it was okay, because Pastor had also told her that God forgave and protected fools.

In the distance they heard a loud rumbling sound, like thunder. But as they got closer to their destination they began smelling smoke, burned rubber, and the scent of gas hung heavy in the air. There were dozens and dozens of cars everywhere. Groups of dudes stood beside the cars drinking beer and talking trash. There were also plenty women out on Gardens Road and they were not the shy type.

"Yo, Riff-Raff, pull right over there." Hitman pointed to a Spanish dude with a big Lazarus chain on. He stood next to a two-tone gold and black 1970 Foose Challenger with racing stripes.

Seeing them approaching, Flaco cut his conversation with the blonde beauty and greeted them. "Damn, my niggie, what's up?" He hugged everybody. "I'm glad that y'all could make it."

"This the slow-ass car you've been talkin' 'bout?" Hitman pointed at the Challenger.

"Slow?! You got me bent. This'll cook that fuckin' Delta, trust me." Flaco fired up the engine. It growled deeply, causing the body of the car to rock slowly in rhythm with the engine's stall-delay timing.

"Boy, what you got under there, a four-hun'ed?" asked Riff-Raff.

"Hell nah. That's Mopar performance, dog." Flaco popped the hood. "That's a Hemi 426 with Indy heads. Edelbrock dual carborators. And I'm sprayin' a two-hun'ed-fifty shot. Dog, that's over fifteen-hun'ed hours in labor, at a hun'ed dollars an hour! Plus over seventy thousand in parts."

"Quarter time?" Riff-Raff asked.

"Depends on who's drivn'. High eleven's with me. But my driver, Midget, ten or better. Just depends."

"Where's the dude at that we rapped 'bout?" Hitman wanted to know.

"With the *work*?"

"Yeah."

Flaco looked around for a minute. Then, seeing the triple-green two door 1974 Caprice at the line, he said, "There he go."

Everybody looked to the line. A thick, black Amazon stood there in cutoff jean shorts, a tight-T, and high heels. She held a red flag high above her head, smiling and showcasing her huge breasts. The anticipation built as the two cars revved their engines. Then, without warning, she dropped the red flag and the race began.

The red 1974 Nova came off of the line clean. The green Caprice spun and came out sideways. The driver didn't let up though. He caught his next gear and jammed the accelerator.

The Nova was out front by a few car lengths. The Caprice shifted once more and blue vapors blew from its dual exhaust. It was now running straight. The Nova was in its rearview. Ten seconds had passed... *Speed.*

"That nigga there's drivin', boy!" Hitman said excitedly.

"Yeah, Brim, he's the dude with the *work*."

As they talked, the Caprice pulled up and Brim jumped out, a frown on his brown face. He walked over to the Nova and got an envelope from the driver. He flipped through the bills to be sure that it was $10,000 and walked back over to his car. His engine was smoking a bit.

Flaco and Hitman walked over. They caught the tail end of Brim cursing out his mechanic, for what he deemed a poor performance, seeing as the car probably needed new heads.

"Yo, Brim, check this out," Flaco said as they approached.

Seeing Flaco, Brim said, "You seen that? Gave him a link and still went and got that shit! And that's with a fucked up head."

"Niggie, you fucked that head up when you sprayed all that shit!" Flaco shot back.

"I tell you what, you line that ugly-ass Challenger up and I'll make you tear the transmission outta that bitch, just like last time... Ten's, my nigga."

"Man, Brim, fuck that shit you're talkin'." Flaco pointed to Hitman. "This is my man from G-A. He want them thirty."

Brim looked Hitman over. *Nigga sure don't look like he coppin' no thirty*, he thought before saying, "Say, you got the money, my nigga?"

"You got the units?" Hitman questioned him in response.

Nodding his head, Brim replied, "Yeah, I got the units, but they ain't out here now."

"Well where you wanna meet?"

"I got tickets to the Dolphins' game tonight. Game starts at nine, so y'all meet me in Miami Lakes 'bout seven-thirty. You know where my spot's at, right?"

Flaco nodded.

"Aiight, I'ma holla at y'all boys," Brim said and walked over to a *badass* Spanish chick.

* * *

After leaving Flaco, Hitman and his crew checked into their usual hotel on 80th Street and 7th Avenue. It had been a tiring day. Tracey and Hitman were in their hotel room watching *Love & Basketball*. Their stomachs growled simultaneously.

Laughing, Tracey said, "I guess you're 'bout ready to eat."

"Yeah, we probably should eat, huh?"

"Room service?"

"Nah, I like real food. I'ma hood type of dude." He snatched up the phone and called Riff-Raff's and Dee's room. They agreed to meet downstairs in ten minutes.

"Baby, I'll meet you down there, I have to use the bathroom before we leave," Tracey told him.

Hitman kissed her, grabbed his Blackberry and exited the room. As he walked up the long hallway towards the elevator he saw what appeared to be a group of prostitutes. Four of them: A white girl, a red chick, and two dark skin babies. Their little shorts and miniskirts left nothing to the imagination. As he got on the elevator with them he noticed the little red chick whispering something to the white girl, they then giggled like little girls. Seeing them reminded him of Sherry. He silently thanked God that his little sister had better sense. It always saddened him to see a female catching a bad break in life.

"You see something you like, lil' daddy?" the red chick asked. She was fast and deceptive.

Hitman didn't realize that he'd been staring until she made the slick remark. "You talkin' to me?" was the only thing he could think to say.

The four females all giggled. "Yeah, I'm talkin' to you." Red eyed him. She had a husky voice and a sexy little body. She bravely leaned into him, resting her body against his. "You lookin' a lil' lonely over here, baby. You want some of my company?"

Hitman found her little act cute. She was a *bad little chick*, pretty and well developed, but he wasn't interested in her on that level. "Sure, I'd love some of your company."

"Well, if you got the cash, I most definitely got the time," she sassed.

He nodded, enjoying the game. "How much cash do I need?"

"Seventy-five for the *brains* and one-fifty for *other thangs*."

Reaching into his pocket, Hitman pulled out about $8,000. "When's the last time you seen your daddy?"

"My daddy?" she asked. That was the very last thing she'd expected a stranger to ask her. "I don't know, maybe 'bout eight years ago, when I was eight-years old. That's before he went to prison."

He'd figured as much, because no man would allow a daughter as beautiful as her to run the streets doing what she was doing. He knew her father had to be either dead or locked up. "Come on," he said, hugging her tight in his strong arms. She melted in his embrace. They stepped apart when the elevator's doors opened.

"You straight?" she asked him.

"Here, shawdy." He gave her $1,000. "That's a lot more than what you asked for, but it ain't no where near what you're worth... Stop sellin' yourself short, lil' momma. You could really make some nigga happy."

She pocketed the money. "You're a real dude."

"I try... but, umm, I know another real dude that would be too happy to see you."

"Who?!"

"Your daddy. You should go see him."

She agreed and Hitman headed for the parking lot. Riff-Raff was already down there, leaning against the van smoking a lace-blunt.

"You wanna hit this?" Riff-Raff asked.

"Hell nah!" Hitman had not smoked a blunt since he'd been released from jail. After going three years without it he realized that he really didn't need it.

As they stood there waiting on Tracey and Dee, Hitman saw the red chick and her crew exit the hotel. The crew headed out towards 79th Street. Red walked his way. She looked sad or upset.

"Damn, shawdy, you lookin' kinda lonely. You want some of my company?" he teased, using the line that she'd used on him earlier.

She couldn't help but smile. "I am lonely."

"What about your friends?"

"Them hoes ain't my friends." She frowned up her pretty face. "Them jealous bitches caught beef 'cause you broke me off some money and not them."

Hitman nodded. "What's your name?"

"Jasmine." She was sixteen. She and her mother had major issues. They hadn't spoken to one another in nearly a year. As for her daddy, she missed him, but hadn't been able to go see him.

Hitman talked to her about school and self-worth. He told her how special and beautiful he thought she was. He really liked her vibe and enjoyed talking with her.

They had just traded information when Tracey and Dee walked up.

"You make sure that you holla, aiiight," he said sincerely.

She smiled. Jasmine loved him already. "Okay, I'ma do that. But, umm, can I get another hug?"

They hugged. She really did not want to let him go. But she had to. He had a girlfriend who was standing right there and Jasmine didn't want to be disrespectful towards the chick — though she'd already decided that she didn't like her. Breaking the embrace, she said her good-byes and walked off.

"Who was that?" Tracey asked.

"My lil' buddy. Jasmine."

Dee licked her lips. *If bruh don't know what to do with it, I bet I do! Damn, Miami got some bad chicks*, she thought as she climbed into the van and Riff-Raff pulled off.

Chapter 7
Cop and Go

The van's clock read five-twenty as Riff-Raff drove back to the hotel. When they entered the lobby Hitman saw Keisha and Flaco sitting at the hotel's bar eating wings and drinking.

"What's up, niggie?" Flaco greeted them. "Yo, Brim's ready for us."

"Good."

Flaco and Dee jumped in the van with Riff-Raff. Hitman, Tracey, and Keisha followed in the other van. By the time they reached Brim's two-story home in Miami Lakes, Hitman had *removed* the buy money from its stash spot. He placed the $360, 000 in two bags. With the bags in hand, he got out and sent Keisha and Tracey back to the hotel to wait for him.

Brim stepped out in true Dolphin valence. Green and orange leather fitted. He donned a pair of baggy orange leather pants, matching orange leather jacket. Beneath the jacket he had on a fresh green Ricky Williams jersey. Green, orange, and white Bathing Ape sneakers.

He hit his remote, lifting the bay door of his six-car garage. Riff-Raff pulled the van inside. Once the bay door was closed, Hitman peeped the garage's contents. 1000 Ninja. 1200 Suzuki. 600 Benz hard-top. Chevy 3500 Dually. Two jet skis. 600 Benz convertible. *This nigga's cuttin' it!* Hitman thought to himself. Flaco had told him that Brim was a *jack-boy*. All he did was rob banks, check cashers, and big time drug dealers.

Without speaking, Brim opened the rear of the big Dually and tossed a big green duffle bag to Hitman. "Thirty units, my nigga... Check it however you check it, snort it, cook it, whatever, just give me my money... cop and go! I gotta game to catch."

Riff-Raff opened the bag and started checking the cocaine. Hitman went ahead and paid Brim. Just as he did, the door leading from the house to the garage opened. It was the Spanish chick from the race. Leather Dolphins jersey-dress and six-inch heels. Long black hair. Full lips and sexy eyes. Olive complexion. She had the prettiest, shapely legs.

"Brim," she whined. "How long?"

Brim didn't answer her. He just handed her the money. "Put this up."

She took it and disappeared.

With her gone, Dee and Riff-Raff started stashing the cocaine in the van's stash spot. It took them twenty minutes to get everything put up properly.

Hitman thanked Brim and they got on their way. They stopped at the hotel. After checking out and praying, Keisha took the wheel of the van with the thirty kilos stashed in it and hit I-95 North. Riff-Raff drove the other van with Dee, Flaco, Hitman, and Tracey. Destination, Americus.

* * *

Dee was driving. They passed the Farmers' Market in Cordele, then made a left onto a small dirt road. The road led out to Drayton, where Hitman had leased a five bedroom brick house on Franklin Road. He was paying Tracey and her partner Sharon $1,850 a month for the property.

The clock in the van read five-twenty in the a.m. Tracey picked up Hitman's Blackberry and dialed. "Hello... I didn't mean to wake you... yeah, okay, I'm maybe thirty minutes away... yeah, okay, y'all be ready... okay, bye."

Darkness surrounded them as they rolled past fields of barren land. Every so often an old shotgun home or barn would dot out on the landscape. Someone cracked a window. The clean country air swept through the van.

Tracey spotted a single light pole shining in the distance. "Right there, Dawn, *that's it*, turn right there."

"Dee, shawdy, my name's Dee!" she corrected Tracey. Dee literally hated the name Dawn.

The house sat on an acre of land. There were no houses around, just trees and empty fields. It was perfect for what Hitman needed. Mainly because it was in Dooly County and not Sumter.

Keisha's van pulled in behind them. They all got out. After removing the thirty kilos they went inside. The house was sparsely furnished. But for the next two or three months, for Flaco and Riff-Raff, it was going to be home.

"Y'all gon' be straight?" Hitman asked.

Riff-Raff and Flaco nodded.

They exchanged hugs and dap, leaving them to whip and weigh the work.

Keisha, Dee, Hitman, and Tracey headed on to Americus. Dee drove. Plies' *100 Years* played as they rode along, everybody brooding individual thoughts. As Dee brought the van past the theatre that sat at the edge of town, it was like déjà vu for Hitman. Out of nowhere police cruisers and unmarked police cars swooped down on them. At the head of the pack, waving his badge and gun, was Detective Rodgers.

"Okay, goddamn it, everybody out of the van!" Rodgers yelled, slapping his hand against the van's window. "Come on, goddamn it, let's move!"

Everybody got out of the van. The police officers and their drug-sniffing K-9's got in.

Tracey and Keisha were placed in one police unit, Dee and Hitman were placed in another one.

Dee shook her head sadly. "Bruh, this shit don't look right."

Hitman said nothing. He continued to watch the police tear up the van.

"Bruh, how they know we was comin'?" Dee asked. "Tracey, that's how! She the only one that used the phone. Bruh, I —"

"Dee!" Hitman finally cut her off. "Dummy up, sis... we're in the back of a police car, you feel me?!"

Dee nodded, realizing that she'd slipped. The police could've easily been listening in on them or recording everything that was being said in the police car.

An hour passed. Nothing had been found. The dogs had been walked through and around the van several times. Teams of Task Force Officers had come and gone. Rodgers had even searched the van twice himself. Hitman smiled as he saw Rodgers and one of the Task Force Officers begin to argue openly. The argument ended with the officer going back to the van and searching it again.

Rodgers walked over to the car that held Tracey and Keisha. The three of them talked for a while, then Tracey and Keisha were allowed to get back in the van.

With rocks in his jaws and fire in his eyes, Rodgers walked over and snatched the door open on the squad car that Dee and Hitman sat in. "Get out!" he screamed.

Hitman looked at him. "Are you sure?" he asked, smirking at the red-faced officer.

"I'ma personally wipe that goddamn grin off of your goddamn face before it's over with. That I'll assure you, boy."

"You mean, like you did that day in the interrogation room?"

A flash of pure hatred registered in Rodgers' eyes. His lower lip twitched as he began to speak, but he caught himself and stormed off. He could hear Hitman laughing loudly as he climbed into his car and sped off...

Chapter 8
Heaven on Earth

Tracey sat across from Hitman in the huge luxurious hotel suite. The room, which was actually like an apartment, was absolutely beautiful. It boasted a lovely dining area, a small kitchen, a living room with vaulted ceiling, and a large bathroom. The hotel sat in the middle of downtown Americus. It was the perfect getaway for those that could afford the $375 rooms.

After the exasperating brush with Rodgers earlier that day, Hitman decided to pick up Jai, Tracey's daughter, and get the exclusive suite for the three of them to just chill. They'd been ripping and running and really needed a little downtime to unwind.

Hitman gazed at Tracey through tired eyes. She was exactly what every real man needed in his corner. "It feels like heaven, don't it?"

She nodded. A cute little smile on her face. "It sure does."

"It feels like heaven because *that's what it is...* baby, when things are goin' good and you're thinkin' good thoughts, heaven ain't hard to find."

Tracey nodded again, because she was in agreement. He'd given her heaven on earth, because before they'd gotten together she'd truly been catching hell.

"Bein' able to make you smile, havin' the means to make my people comfortable, that's my paradise. And I thank God for givin' me the strength to make it." Hitman thought to himself. He'd done so much. He was very proud of what he'd accomplished. "I can't see myself livin' average. And I see a lot of myself in you, so it's hard for me to understand how you can work so much harder for them crackas than you will for yourself."

"Ut'un, see, it takes money —"

Hitman cut her off. "You got four-hundred-thousand. It takes more than that?!"

Tracey's thin eyebrows rose in surprise. "When did I get four-hundred-thousand dollars?!"

"When I put it in your hands." He eyed her. "That's what the money's for, to be used to better our situation. You feel me?"

"No," Tracey said, shaking her head slowly. "That's your money, Man."

"And that's them crackas' job that you go to everyday. They can fire your ass anytime they want to, because it's theirs. They created it and they control it! That's why we gotta have somethin' for ourselves, that we own and control."

Tracey sucked her even white teeth. "Oh, and what you're doin' is gonna get it?"

"Respice Finem."

"And what's that s'posed to mean?"

"Look to the end, because it always justifies the mean, baby... like that nigga 50 Cent, I'ma get it for us or die tryin'."

"But, Man, baby... this, this stuff... the way you're livin', baby, this can't last forever. I need..."

Hitman kissed her. "You're right, baby, nothin' in this life lasts forever. So we gotta get it for as long as it does..." He smiled that smile of his. "...you feel me? Ride this thang till the wheels fall off.

And at that point, no matter how bad it is, we'll have lived a helluva life."

Somehow she found herself nodding yes. He always seemed to make her understand. *Soul mates? Are we temperamentally suited to each other?* Tracey wondered. Yes, it was plain to see that they truly had something special. *Love.* It was the closest thing to heaven on earth...

Chapter 9
Like Deja Vu

Hitman sat on a milk crate in Eastview Apartments playing checkers with the old man, Mr. Chunk. This was how Hitman spent his days as of lately, getting his ass kicked in checkers and soaking up lessons on life from Mr. Chunk.

"Boy, you know why I beats you so?" the old man asked, laughing at Hitman. "I beats you 'cause you don't never set up your next move."

Besides the game of checkers going on between Hitman and Mr. Chunk, there wasn't much else going on in Eastview — the apartments were dead.

Dee sat on the second floor, on a crate, smoking 'dro and texting.

B-Easy was in the trap, laying sleep in front of a small color TV.

Shop had been open for two days and things were moving very slow. They had gram slabs and half-gram slabs for forty and twenty dollars. So far they'd only managed to serve a little over four and a half ounces.

Riff-Raff had easily turned the thirty kilos into forty-six. The cocaine was good. The problem was serving it. Hitman and his crew had been out of the loop for so long that Big Dream and Heavy had effectively locked down the city's clientele.

With these thoughts heavy on his mind, Hitman excused himself from the game of checkers and called BamBam on his Blackberry. He hadn't talked to the Southside hustler since he'd been out of jail and figured that it was probably about time he did. Hitman heard BamBam pick up and began speaking, "What it do big timer...? Yeah, nigga, it's me... yeah, I been out for two, three days... Yeah, hell yeah....! In the View... Homie, you already know what it is... aiiiight, in a minute."

Just as Hitman hung up Tracey pulled up in her white Honda Accord. A black Sierra Denali was trailing her. Hitman paused at the foot of the stairway and watched Tracey, Black, and his girlfriend Sam exit their respective vehicles. Black had put on a little weight since Hitman had last seen him.

"Man, what's up?!" Black greeted his friend with lots of love and excitement. He'd really missed seeing Hitman in the three years he'd been in jail. "How've you been?"

"You already know," Hitman answered, smiling. Seeing Black was love, because he truly loved him. They'd shared so much over the years. "It's just good to be free, bruh."

"I heard that."

Hitman turned and greeted Tracey with a hug and kiss.

They all walked up to Keisha's apartment. Keisha was laying there on the couch in her sexy little panties and bra. Hitman shook his head. *This damn girl must hate clothes, 'cause she ain't never got none on*, he thought.

"Girl, go put some damn clothes on," Black said.

Keisha rolled her pretty eyes at Black and sauntered off, her hefty red ass cheeks jiggling the whole way. Her bedroom door slammed loudly as she closed it.

They all laughed as they sat down.

"That damn Keisha's still crazy as a bag of flies," Black commented.

"You ain't never lied, baby," Sam agreed with her man.

"Say, Hitman, I gotta surprise for you, playboy."

"Oh, yeah?" Hitman looked at Black. "And what's that?"

"Bruh, I got the DirTek out on Southern Field and business is boomin'. Dog, everyday I see new game, new ways to advance in this corporate shit. You should come out and help a nigga, 'cause together we'd kill the corporate world."

Hitman nodded. "Aiiight, Black, what, you tryna run some of this trap money through there and clean it up?"

"Hell nah, bruh." Black stood up. "This shit is legit, my nigga. I'm doin' big numbers! And at the same time, I'm bleedin' the cracka Bill Hagan for information that you can't get out of no book or classroom. I'm buildin' some nice political ties with city and county officials.... Bruh, this cracka Bill know a lotta people."

"Okay, and?" Hitman inquired. He did not see how any of this had anything to do with him.

"And, my nigga, I want you to come work with the company! I can salary you forty thousand a year. And this time next year, after you've picked up the game, we'll have another DirTek up and runnin', only it'll be yours and mine. What's up?"

Hitman saw the excitement in his friend's expression. He'd found something that he loved. Hitman smiled broadly. He was proud of his homeboy. "Dig, Black, I got five people on a thiry-five-thousand dollar salary right now. But that ain't per year, bruh, that's per week. So if you need some bread or somthin' to open up your company, cool, I'll give you that shit. But, bruh, I don't need no job."

"Nah, bruh, it ain't 'bout the money. I'm straight. It's 'bout us, me and you, dog. I want it to still be 'us,' dog, workin' together."

"Black, my nigga, we still are workin' together... Maaan, I remember ever since we was lil' niggas, I've been strugglin' like hell to *get in the game*; while you've been savin' your cash and doin' everything you could to *get outta the game*. Together, dog, we did it!" Hitman paused to check his homeboy out before continuing. "And for real, homie, a nigga real proud of you."

The two men hugged.

Sam and Tracey had to fight back the tears. The situation was just that real. Hitman and Black were friends. *Pals.* And even though they were different in so many ways, the contrast made them that much more the same.

"Thanks, dog," Black said. "And you know if you need me..."

"Yeah, yeah, I know." Hitman playfully cut him off. "You're still Face Mob, homie. But dig, I got these streets. You just handle that corporate shit. Ya heard me?!"

"I hear ya, bruh."

Sam stood and they all said their good-byes. Hitman was going to miss Black...

* * *

About twenty minutes had passed since Hitman had called BamBam. Hitman smiled when he saw his little partner pull up in a fresh black Chevy 1500 Kingcab. The truck had 24" chrome Hurricane rims and chrome running boards and crash bar. BamBam hopped out with one of his little soldiers.

"What's up, boy?!" BamBam greeted him excitedly. He was happy to see his partner out of jail.

"It ain't shit, Bam, my nigga."

They dapped and hugged. BamBam's soldier stood off to the side.

"So what's good, boy?! I need somethin'," BamBam stated.

"Twenty-six-five."

"What?!" BamBam questioned. "Hitman, this me, dog."

"Yeah, I feel you, but that's what it is. The work's one hun'ed, though... my price get better, your price'll get better." Hitman shrugged.

BamBam sighed loudly and scratched his nappy beard before saying, "I got nineteen-five on me right now."

"That's cool. You just bring me them seven later." Hitman took the money, tossed it in Tracey's backseat and walked over to the trap apartment. B-Easy jumped up out of his sleep. "You're lucky I'm not the police... where that shit at?"

Slow as this shit is you ain't gotta worry 'bout no police comin' 'round here, B-Easy wanted to tell his big homie, but instead he just got up and got the dope. Handing Hitman the backpack, he said, "Here, that's everything, twenty-nine ounces."

Hitman took the backpack and left.

Dee was now standing by BamBam's truck smoking a blunt with BamBam and his soldier.

Hitman was about to walk over to where they stood, but out of nowhere a bunch of vans and SUV's came speeding through the parking lot. Without one moment's hesitation Hitman spun and took off running. He cleared the corner of the building before the first officer was out of his car.

Running along the six-foot chain-link fence, Hitman's eyes frantically searched for the hole that someone had cut in the old fence so long ago. When he spotted it, he got low and cut through the opening like Adrian Peterson breaking through the line of scrimmage.

Behind Eastview was a steep hill that led to a thick patch of high brush. Beyond the brush was a big cemetery. Hitman came down the hill wide open, cradling the backpack in his arms as he ran. He could hear walkie-talkies and footfall behind him as he approached the bushes, but once he ran through them, scratching his arms and tearing his clothes, it seemed his pursuers stopped.

Hitman continued running, jumping tombstones and cutting across grave plots. He was past the church and up the street before he heard a siren...

* * *

"Lil' sorry muthafuckas," Big Dream said aloud as he poured the last of the cheap dog food into the dog's bowl.

He was in his huge backyard feeding and watering the dogs. His sons were supposed to be doing this, but they never seemed to get around to it. *But, damn it, they don't never forget to come get my, goddamn you me, money!* he fussed in his mind.

Big Dream found himself a nice shaded spot beneath one of the many trees that took up space in his backyard, tossed the empty dog food bag on the ground with a growing culmination of empty cans and beer bottles, and lit himself a Newport. *Sure could use me a cold beer*, he thought.

As he stood there he heard the thundering bassline of Trick Daddy's *Shut Up*. A big Lincoln Navigator pulled up. Heavy got out wearing Polo from head to toe and about $100,000 in jewelry.

"What it do, Big Dream?"

"Slow motion, boss... what's up with you?"

"I seen that lil' red piece that you be kickin' it with. She was up in Atlanta with some more *badass* hoes last night," Heavy informed his partner. He left out the fact that he'd fucked her.

Big Dream knew exactly who he was talking about. "Maaan, fuck that bitch," Big Dream said and lit another Newport.

That's just what I did, Heavy thought and shrugged. "True that, but, umm, what you got for me?"

"Shiiid, boy, it's been slower than Polar bears fuckin' in the winter. Goddamn you me, it ain't never been like this," Big Dream complained as he walked over to a dog kennel and came back with a bag. "This thirty right here. And goddamn you me, I had to tie my Reebok's tight to get that damn money."

Heavy shook his head and thought. Big Dream had been doing damn near two kilos a day up until Hitman had come back. "How long before you finish?"

Big Dream sighed. "Boss, it could be two hours or two weeks. I'm really duffed... Hitman's back, man, so we got our work cut out for us, goddamn you me."

Heavy took the bag of money from Big Deam and left.

* * *

Tracey stood on the second floor with Keisha, watching as the chaos unfolded below them. A score of officers ran into the trap apartment and had yet to emerge. The officers that ran off after Hitman came back limping and out of breath. Tracey could not believe that the lawmen were actually allowed to harass and manhandle people the way they were doing it. It was uncivil and racist.

Just outside of the apartment another group of policemen had Dee, B-Easy, BamBam and his little homeboy, all stretched out on the sidewalk.

Police officers and their K-9's were combing the entire area.

"What was in the bag?" Detective Rodgers asked B-Easy.

"What bag?"

"The bag that your friend, Hitman, ran off with!"

"Maaan, I ain't seen no damn bag," B-Easy answered.

Being spiteful, Rodgers stepped on B-Easy's outstretched hand. B-Easy tried to pull his fingers from beneath Rodgers' shoe, but the spiteful cop just applied more pressure, causing B-Easy to scream out in pain.

"What's the matter, fucking punk! Not so tough after all, huh?" Rodgers removed his foot and turned his attention to Dee, who lay on the sidewalk beside B-Easy. "You're going to get your wish, you little dyke bitch... When they catch your brother with that bag of drugs, I'm going to see to it that they send your ass off to a rough federal prison full of bitches just like you... yes, sir, for a long, long time."

Dee didn't respond. She just laid there. BamBam to her left, B-Easy and BamBam's partner to her right. They were all pissed off. Police had turned over everything in the apartment complex and hadn't found anything. Dee was about to complain when she heard something come across one of the officers' radios. It sent Rodgers into a rage.

"Goddamn it, fuck!" Rodgers screamed.

Dee laughed. "Looks like I won't be gettin' my wish after all, huh?!"

Rodgers gave her a mean look before yelling, "Come on, let's get out of here!"

The officer on the radio had said there was *absolutely no sign of the runner*. That was music to Dee's ears.

As Dee and the others were getting up off of the ground, Tracey and Keisha came running over. They told Dee that Hitman had just called with instructions to come pick him up. Piling into the van, they headed for the Southside.

* * *

After giving the sweet old lady $250 for picking him up and dropping him off at Lil Bit's house, Hitman gave the dope to one of BamBam's little soldiers and took off walking. As he walked he called Tracey on his Blackberry, telling her exactly what street he would be walking up so that she could pick him up.

He looked a mess. Welts covered his arms and neck. His clothes were torn. *Helluva day*, he mused. *I sure hope Tracey hurry up and get here!*

Making his way across the parking lot of Monroe's Hotdogs, Hitman peeped a police cruiser slowly patrolling the area. It continued up the block, then made a U-turn. His mind told him to run, but when he turned around there were three more police units speeding in his direction. The lead car skidded to a halt and Detective Rodgers jumped out.

"Go ahead, track star, try your luck... see if you can outrun a fucking bullet...go ahead, run!" He ordered Hitman, praying that he'd make any sudden move. Rodgers wanted any reason, no matter how minute, to shoot Hitman.

Hitman saw the strain in Rodgers' face. The racist cop was agitated, like a coiled viper, and ready to strike. *Not today cracka*, Hitman reasoned and simply raised his hands up above his head.

Rodgers holstered his weapon and rushed Hitman, elbowing the defenseless man in the back before slamming him down on the Plymouth's hood. He then punched him in the ribs.

"Damn, cracka, what —"

"Shut the fuck up!" Rodgers cut Hitman's protest short. "You know it's an official ordinance concerning runaway niggers in the South."

"Cracka, fuck —"

Rodgers cut him off again with another short-hook to the ribs. Only this time, Hitman reacted by swinging his left elbow. It landed sharply in Rodgers' solar plexus, knocking the wind out of him. Hitman quickly spun around and snatched the helpless officer up around the collar. But before he could do anything, Nel Brown and two other policemen stepped in.

"Okay, okay, that's enough!" Nel Brown stated.

Fuming, Rodgers yelled, "That sonofabitch assaulted me! I want him —"

"Hey! Rodgers," Nel Brown exploded. "Can it, okay, I *said that's enough!*"

Rodgers didn't like the fact that Nel was talking down to him, especially in public. But all he could do at present was nod his head.

"Now go, I'll handle it from here."

Rodgers ambled off.

Detective Nel Brown carefully searched Hitman. He found nothing but Hitman's Blackberry and $1,100. Nel turned Hitman around to face him. He noticed the dried blood and welt marks on his arms, neck, and face.

"What happened to you?"

"Nothin'."

"Why'd you run?"

"I was scared."

Nel nodded. There was something about the young man that made Nel like him. He couldn't explain it, but Nel Brown knew that if he would've been blessed with a son instead of a daughter, his son would've probably been just like Hitman. "Son, you know I can arrest you, right?"

"If that's what the law requires of you, lawman, do your job."

Smirking, Nel said, "No, that would be petty, and you'd be out before I finished doing the paperwork. So I'm going to let you walk. You know why?"

Hitman shook his head no.

"Because you really look like you've had enough for the day." Nel began walking off. "Besides, when I do decide to check you, it's going to be mate."

"Fuck you," Hitman said. However, he'd only said it loud enough for himself to hear the rude remark.

Dead tired, he began his walk. He hadn't made it off the block before the van pulled up. He jumped in and Dee pulled off. His mind raced as they rode. He needed to know how in the hell had the police been able to keep such close tabs on him? The trap hadn't been back open for no more than three days and the traffic had been minimal. No, something or somebody was not right. He'd been through the bullshit before and these recent run-ins with the law were like déjà vu....

Chapter 10
Mister Seventeen-Five

After a day of rehabilitation under Tracey's supervision, Hitman had time to heal and rethink his ordeal. He'd had three run-ins with the police in two days. That was something he did not want to get use to. So he had to figure out *what or who* the problem was. Dee thought Tracey was the source of their misfortune. "Bruh, I'm tryin' to tell you some good shit. Either that bitch is the police or she's one unlucky muthafucka. In either case, we don't need the hoe 'round us, bruh," Dee had said just last night. However, he didn't believe it. True, she'd been on the scene all three times, but that didn't mean she'd caused it.

Restless, Hitman got up and did 1,000 push ups and sit ups. He then jogged to the Food Lion across from the National Guard Armory. He bought a V-8, two protein sports dinks, and a pack of Gatorade gum. After consuming his drinks he jogged off at a fast pace. Past the Brick City Projects, down across the railroad tracks, he didn't stop running until he got to Eastview apartments.

Mr. Chunk, his checkers partner, was sitting in their usual spot. "Hey, there, boy! Where you been?" the old man called out.

"I've been settin' up my next move," Hitman answered.

The old man doubled over laughing at that. He loved to sit around and play checkers with Hitman. He'd tell the younger man all sorts of stories, which Hitman enjoyed just as much.

Business was still super-slow. But Hitman had learned a few things from playing checkers with Mr. Chunk, and one of those things was patience.

Hitman had also succeeded in getting Tracey to use the $400,000 that she was holding for him to expand her business. His talks with her had finally hit home. She quit her job and rented a nice building in downtown Americus. Her and her partner Sharon were buying up foreclosures and *fix up* properties. Everything that they couldn't *flip* for a quick profit, they rented out. Money was coming in and she was now doing something that she loved... and more importantly, she was doing it for herself.

* * *

After paying Dee, Riff-Raff, Keisha, B-Easy and Flaco, Hitman was $300,000 to the good and headed to Atlanta to celebrate with Flaco. It had taken them a little over two weeks to dump the forty-five kilos, but the $360,000 investment had been a good one and things were rolling along smoothly as planned.

Hitman still needed a plug. And with $1,300,000 at his disposal, he was looking for a *godfather*.

Atlanta was right up the road from Americus, a mere two to three hours drive. Yet the two cities were a lifetime apart. Atlanta was a lot bigger and offered a larger variety of consumer products and services — as well as opportunities to go to prison and/or get killed. None of that appealed to Hitman. He didn't even want to go to Atlanta. He hated big cities, because everybody in such places always wanted to be three-quarter's slick.

Pulling up to the club, Hitman scanned the parking lot for a place to park. There was nothing in the parking lot under $50,000. The Atlanta dudes were representing with their car game.

"You ready, my niggie?" Flaco asked. "I ain't never had no Georgia pussy before, my niggie."

"Whatever, fool," Hitman replied dryly and got out of the car. He simply did not want to be in Atlanta at no damn club. He would have rather been at home with Quan and Cameron, who he'd been spending more and more time with as of lately. After all, it was his fault that they didn't have their fathers in their young lives.

As Hitman and Flaco approached the club they came across a large gathering of people, mainly females, near two parked cars. One car was a Bentley sports coupe, the other was a Porsche 911. They were both all black in color, BMF on the front plates, and beside them stood a pint-sized Steve Erkle looking dude. He was grandstanding, too, wearing enough clear ice to cool the sun.

Hitman stopped, stared at the dude, then yelled, "Seven-Fizzy! Boy, that's you?!"

The dude turned his attention to Hitman. He smiled. "Hey, what's up, *big country*?! What're you doin' in this neck of the woods?" Seven-Fizzy relied.

"Just hangin' out. Ya heard me?" Hitman capped. "This my cousin, Flaco. I'm tryna show him a good time while he's down my way."

"Okay, good to meet you, *home*... But yo, Hitman, what they do? You still servin' them pies, 'cause I'm the man now!" Seven-Fizzy pointed to his attire and then gestered towards the two expensive vehicles.

"That's you?" Hitman questioned.

"Is that me?! You better look up, *home*. It's all about *blowing money fast* and I'm plugged, *home*. I got it for cheap!"

"Yeah?" Hitman was loving what he was hearing. "Give me some numbers."

"What's my name?"

"Seven-Fizzy."

"Okay, put a one in front of it and I got it like that all day," Seven-Fizzy bragged.

Just as he'd spoken, one of Seven-Fizzy's partners called out to him. "Mr. Seventeen-Five, what we gon' do?"

"Y'all go 'head on, V.I.P. it up! Tell them to put it all on Seventeen-Five!" Seven-Fizzy told his partner.

Hitman had to give Seven-Fizzy his due *props*. The man had *come up* big in a dangerous game and hadn't crossed anybody to do it. That was rare, so when you saw it you had to respect it.

"So what you need, playboy, one or two units?" Seven-Fizzy asked.

Hitman laughed. "Nah, dog, unless you just throwin' them in with my order, 'cause I don't cop less than twenty. You feel me?"

"Okay, I feel you."

"Good. Can you get me thirty-five?"

"All day, *home*... Mr. Seventeen-Five got them yams for you... Your place or mine?"

"My place."

"Well, I'll see you in the Lil A, playboy... but right now, it's party time! I'ma show you and your cousin a damn good time. Y'all see anythang, I mean *anythang*, that you want tonight, you got it. And it's all on Mr. Seventeen-Five!"

Chapter 11
Switch Sides?

Heavy spotted Big Dream sitting at a rear table in the dimly lit club. He was sitting with a cute red-bone, eating chicken wings and drinking liquor. It was happy hour at the Astro and lots of people came in to take advantage of the twenty-five cent wings and half-priced drinks.

Heavy walked over and sat down. Without saying hello, Heavy asked, "Dream, my nigga, you got that?"

"Yeah, hell yeah... just got off the last two onions this morning, goddamn you me. I been jungle hustlin' for you, boy." Big Dream sucked the sauce off of his fat fingers and downed his drink before turning to the chick. "Baby, give him that bag."

The chick went in her big designer purse and pulled out a brown paper bag. She gave it to Heavy.

"This all of it?" Heavy stuffed the paper bag in his Polo boxer briefs and picked up one of Big Dream's wings.

"Yeah. Twenty-seven thousand."

Heavy grabbed another wing and ate it as he thought. The money was coming slow. Ever since Hitman had come home. If Hitman was that strong and Big Dream was too weak to compete for his fair share of Americus' drug market, then maybe he was working with the wrong dude. *I might need to be workin' with Hitman*, Heavy seriously thought about switching sides.

"Say, Dream, what's up with the nigga, Hitman? Is his prices that good or is niggas just scared of him? 'Cause this shit's movin' too slow, dog."

Big Dream polished off another wing and sucked his fingers. "It ain't Hitman." Big Dream shook his big head. "It's a Spanish dude in town. He got onions for six-hun'ed. But if you buy six or more, they're five-hun'ed a piece."

"What?!" Heavy frowned. "Dream, you a muthafuckin' lie! Ain't no nigga in Georgia can afford to serve ounces for five or six-hun'ed." Heavy knew that Big Dream was ultra-slick. He figured that Big Dream was probably slow-rolling the dope and lying about this Spanish dude's prices to get him to low his prices.

"Boy," Big Dream said with certainty. "If I'm lyin', the Lone Ranger rode a Harley and Tonto was a hoe! Now jump out there..."

"Where's the dude from? Where he be at?" Heavy asked, now convinced that Big Dream was telling the truth.

"He Spanish, hell, I reckon he from Spain," Big dream answered. "All I know is that he got *fi' hard* for five-hun'ed and he comes to the trailer park, down from Wal-Mart, twice a day. Niggas be lined up to get served, too!"

What Big Dream didn't tell Heavy was that he'd been one of those niggas lined up to get served. At five-hundred a piece, Big Dream couldn't pass that up. That's the real reason why Heavy's money was so slow as of lately. Big Dream was taking Heavy's money and flipping it before he paid Heavy. He'd bought thirty-six ounces, twice. And the work moved fast because the product was good. Big Dream had built his money up and was now in prime position. Either Heavy had to beat the Spanish dude's prices or Big

Dream and everybody else would simply switch sides. It wasn't complicated, it was business...

Chapter 12
It's That Girl

Hitman lay in the bed, sleeping like a big baby. Flaco had dropped him off at four-thirty a.m. So there he was, on his back, calling the dogs. Partying with Mr. Seventeen-Five had left him drained.

As Hitman slept, he felt something thick and warm filling his mouth. Then it ran down his cheek and onto Tracey's sheets. Hitman was still in dreamland, so he just swallowed hard and continued snoring. That's when his senses exploded. His weary mind rang the alarm and he jumped up out of his sleep. A small shadow flashed by the door, but he paid that little attention, because his mouth was on fire.

"Got-damn!" he yelled and hopped out of bed. Rushing to the bathroom, he nearly tripped on an empty Tabasco bottle that laid on the floor.

Hitman drank cup after cup of water from the bathroom sink. Yet his mouth seemed to burn more. He decided to brush his teeth and tongue.

Somewhat relieved, Hitman got dressed and went in the kitchen. Tracey was at the sink. Her daughter, Jai, was standing by the fridge. Cameron and Quan were both sitting at the table eating.

Seeing Hitman, Tracey asked, "You ready to eat?"

"Yeah."

"Okay. Did you leave the hot sauce in the room, baby?" Tracey asked Hitman.

"Yeah, I sure did. Who sent it back there?"

"I did," Tracey answered, not knowing what had happened. "The kids said that you –"

Cameron and Quan jumped up and ran. But they didn't get far. Hitman caught them and spanked their little asses.

After breakfast, Tracey and Jai took off to Coleman, Florida. That's where Jai's father was serving his prison time. That left Hitman alone with *badass* Quan and Cameron.

Laid back on the couch, hand in his pants like Al Bondy, Hitman surfed the cable network. Cameron sat beside his uncle, hand in his pants also, watching TV and doing whatever he saw his uncle doing. Hitman had no idea where Quan was and he didn't care to know, as long as he didn't bother him or burn the house down.

Still surfing channels, Hitman heard his Blackberry, which was on his left, Cameron on his right, start ringing loudly.

"Aye, Unc!" Cameron yelled. "Unc!"

"What?"

"Your Blueberries rangin'!"

"Shut up!" Hitman barked at him before answering the phone. "Yo...? What's up, boy...? Seven-Fizzy came through, huh...? So y'all cool, huh...? Oh yeah, it ain't clean, huh...? It is what it is, bruh... Yeah, do what you do and we'll holla later, 'cause I'm a lil' busy right now... One."

It seemed that Mr. Seventeen-Five had *some shit with him.* Hitman had spent $612,500 with him, but instead of delivering grade-A fishscale, he'd dropped off some recompressed shit. So instead of whipping thirty-five kilos into fifty-two and a half,

Riff-Raff was only able to bring back forty-five kilos. That cut $141,750 into his profits, which was not good at all.

Still thinking to himself, Hitman peeped Cameron out of his peripheral, peeping him. But when he turned to face Cameron, the little urchin turned his head. So, Hitman, drifting back to his thoughts, peeped Cameron watching him again. Yet, when he faced him, he turned his head again. *Fuck is up with this lil' nigga*, he wondered. Faking like he was about to face forward, Hitman looked back real quick and caught him.

"What you lookin' at?!" he asked Cameron.

"Umm, nothin', Unc... Nothin'."

"Then look at the TV."

Hitman knew that Cameron was up to something. The little *thug-in-training* was always up to something. He turned back to the TV. And from somewhere in the house he thought he heard someone talking. Then he remembered Quan. Of course, he knew that Quan was crazy, so him talking to himself wasn't out of the ordinary. But then he heard a low bleeping sound and the *tap-tap* of keys being pressed.

"I know this lil' muthafucka ain't fuckin' with that woman's computer," he said.

"Uncle Man!" Cameron called out loudly.

Before Hitman could answer him, he heard his Blackberry ring. He looked to his left and saw that his cell phone was gone.

"Uncle Man! Hey, Uncle Man!" Cameron yelled again.

"What?!"

"I thank Quan got you Blueberries."

"Shut up! 'Cause you helped him get it!" Hitman got up. "Quan!"

Hitman went around towards the den. While he searched in there Quan eased out of the hall closet and dashed for the front door.

"Fuck!" Hitman yelled and ran off behind him. The little urchin was pretty fast; he made it to the end of the block before Hitman caught him and scooped him up. "Come here, lil' nigga! Where you goin'?"

As Hitman swung his nephew around, he saw two unmarked police cars posted up.

Carrying Quan back to the house, he noticed another detective car at the far end of the street. *How these bitches knew I was here?!* he wondered. He could hear Dee answering, *It's that girl, bruh! She's the police!*

Chapter 13
Got Us Again

The white late-model van slowly eased through the trailer park, followed closely by an old station wagon, which no one particularly noticed. While the van made a quick U-turn and parked with its engine running, the old station wagon continued on for about twenty yards and parked facing the van. The driver of the station wagon sat behind the car's tinted windows and watched as a long line of hustlers waited, all hoping to get served. Everyday, twice a day, for the past three weeks, the van had showed up and served six kilos of hard, in all ounces. The dude inside of the van never got out. He served everybody through the van's side window, which was tinted, so nobody knew exactly how many people were inside the van.

It normally took about an hour to shake the whole six kilos, but for the past three days they'd been doing it in only half the time. The reason being, Big Dream and Heavy had become enthusiastic consumers of the van's product. They bought three and a half *bricks* everytime. Which in all actuality was contrary to what Big Dream had had in mind. His initial plan was to force Heavy's hand — make him lower his price. Instead, Heavy had fell in line — started copping his work from the van — because it was cheaper and safer than driving to Jacksonville and trying to outmaneuver the authorities. Heavy had copped fifteen bricks in three days, showcasing his hustle and purchasing power. Now it was time to step the plan and his game up.

Approaching the van's window, Heavy popped, "You know my order, dog, I'm sure... but check this out, I've spent big change with you, my nigga. I'ma boss, just like you. And, my nigga, bosses don't stand in no line and deal out in the open like this. You feel me?"

"So what's up, my niggie, what you sayin'?"

"Niggie?! Hold up, my nigga, where you from?"

"Fuck where I'm from, what's up?"

"This is what's up, I'm from Florida, my nigga. And it sounds like you are too! So that mean we homeboys, my nigga, and you need to put a nigga down!" Heavy capped hard, hoping to seal the deal. "Look out for the *home team*, and at the same time, take the heat off of yourself. 'Cause, dog, this ain't the crib, and these niggas sour easy. Look where you're at and peep how you're doin' it, my nigga."

The dude in the van was silent for a minute, thinking. "Okay, slide me your number."

Heavy passed the dude his digits. "What's your name?"

"Flaco."

"Okay, Flaco, I'm Heavy," Heavy introduced himself and the two made their three and a half kilo, $63,000 deal and parted ways.

* * *

In the three deals that they'd conducted with Seven-Fizzy, not once had the *work* been copacetic. And being a man of business, Hitman understood losses; nevertheless, what Seven-Fizzy was doing equated to robbery.

Hitman peeped out of the window to see if his newfound admirers were still interested in his affairs. Sure enough, the unmarked police vehicle was still there. Hitman smiled, he was about to set up his next move. He was glad that Sherry had come and picked up the boys, because they would've definitely gotten in his way.

Dialing B-Easy's number, he hit send and waited. "Aye, boy, I need you... aiiight, where you at...? Cotton Avenue, boy, what the hell you doin' on the avenue...? Oh, aiiight, look here, I'm on Lafayette... Yeah, come snatch me... Aiiight, One."

Hitman hung up and went in Baby Jai's room. He grabbed her backpack and dumped her school supplies on the bed. Next he went in the bathroom, grabbed a few things and then went in the hallway closet to gather up the last of what he needed. Slinging the backpack over his shoulder, Hitman jogged for the front door, having heard a car horn outside.

B-Easy was driving a pearl-white TransAm. He eyed Hitman as he jumped in with the backpack, but didn't question him. B-Easy knew where his money was coming from, plus he knew that Hitman would never purposely put him in harm's way.

They were out in traffic. B-Easy hadn't noticed the police following them. He was high off 'dro and caught up in the lyrics of T.I.'s *Praying for Help*.

"Yo, turn up here, dog," Hitman instructed. He saw that the three police cars were still behind them.

B-Easy looked over at him. "What's up with you, playboy, why you lookin' like that?"

"Don't look, but it's three police cars behind us."

"Po-lice?!" B-Easy echo'd and turned around to see.

Didn't I tell him not to look?! Hitman thought, shaking his head.

They'd just passed the package store on Lee Street, right down from Staley Middle School.

"Turn left right here, dog," Hitman told him.

B-Easy was now perspiring as he made the turn. The road ran at an angle alongside the school yard. The railroad tracks ran along the right-hand side of the road.

As soon as the TransAm passed a large thicket of brush that sat next to the railroad tracks, just beyond the school, Hitman tossed the backpack out of the window.

The lead police car was driven by Detective Rodgers, Nel Brown rode on the passenger side. "Pull over! Right there! He threw the bag!" Nel Brown yelled.

Rodgers pulled over. The other two units stopped alongside him. Rodgers jumped out and raced for the bag that Hitman had discarded. He snatched up the bag and opened it.

"Fuck!" he yelled. "He got us again!"

"What is it?" Nel asked.

Rodgers emptied the bag. A bunch of tampons, pads, pantyliners and douches fell onto the hood of the car. Nel Brown shook his head sadly. Rodgers burned inside. He was tired of Hitman. And he vowed to show him just who the *pussy* really was...

Chapter 14
Love & War

"Come get them! I mean right now, Man!" Sherry yelled into the phone as soon as Hitman picked it up. "And don't bring them back! 'Cause I swear to God, I'ma kill them…"

"Who, who you talkin' 'bout?"

"Quan and Cam!"

"Girl, what is…"

"No, ut'un! I'm serious, Man, I'm finish with them! You better be here in ten minutes or their muthafuckin' asses are dead," Sherry assured him. "They're on the porch with their stuff!"

The line disconnected before Hitman could say anything further.

From that point on his life was a tale of complete chaos. Selling drugs and raising two little badass boys were a sure recipe for a nervous breakdown. He had to outlast the law, outslick his adversaries, keep his nephews in check, and make Tracey know that she was loved and appreciated.

He had not been staying with her as of lately, because Quan and Cameron were a little too much for her. So the three of them, against Dee's protest, were living at the house on Hosanna. And after only two weeks they had the entire house to themselves, because Dee and Lil Kim moved back to the old house on Rouland.

Business in Eastview had picked up just a little bit. They were now moving a half-kilo a week; which was slow as hell, but better than the six ounces a week it was moving when they'd first opened up.

"Dee, this shit is slow as fuck!" B-Easy said. "How is Hitman payin' us so much money? 'Cause this spot ain't makin' no money."

"He got the trap out on Southern Field," Dee answered.

"Nigga, that spot makin' less than us!" B-Easy stated. "Dee, bruh losin'... Heavy and Big Dream and them got the city now. Even BamBam and them coppin' from them."

"Shit pickin' up."

"Nah, Dee, we loss... Southside got the best hand."

"So what you sayin', B-Easy?"

"That we losin'! And I know that Hitman ain't no loser... I'm sayin', why he ain't doin' nothin'? Why we ain't goin' at them niggas?"

Dee knew that B-Easy was one of the loyalist soldiers on the Northside; so for him to be questioning the situation, shit had to be really bad. "Look, Easy, we ain't goin' at them 'cause my brutha ain't gave us the green light... until he does, long as you're gettin' paid and bruh holdin' it down, don't question it, just roll with it."

B-Easy nodded.

Dee got up and walked out of the trap apartment. She saw Hitman sitting on a crate playing checkers with Mr. Chunk, like that was the answer to their problems. Dee was disgusted with her brother, because she'd been thinking the same thoughts as B-Easy, only she'd never expressed herself to anyone. She simply trusted things to pick up. She simply hoped that Hitman would tune in to the whispers of the streets. People were saying that Face Mob was over and that Heavy and Big Dream's team had took the city. Fuming, Dee jumped in her truck and left.

* * *

Whenever Hitman wasn't faced off with Mr. Chunk on the checkers board or romancing Tracey, he spent his time at *Da Coffee Shop: Tranche de Vie,* building with Ms. Furqana. She was a very interesting woman. She'd read a lot of books and experienced a lot in life. Talking to her was like actually living her experiences yourself. Hitman spent a lot of money on books for himself and his nephews. He made sure that the three of them spent at least an hour a day reading.

Today Hitman bought six books, two for himself, four for his nephews; and three green teas. Ms. Furqana was tallying up his purchases when his Blackberry rang.

"Yeah...? Again, huh...? Dude just ain't gonna play fair, huh...? Yeah, I know exactly what I said, and believe me, I got dude. I got both of them, I'm just biddin' my time. You feel me? Fattenin' the hogs for the slaughter... Yeah, aiight... One."

Hitman paid for his things and exited the coffee shop. He seemed cool on the surface, however his insides were boiling. He wanted to seriously hurt somebody, because he didn't take too kindly to people playing with him. *Calm down*, he willed himself. He had to keep it emotionless in order to keep it in motion. There was a lot at stake.

Driving towards the house on Roland Street, Hitman phoned Dee and told her that he had *two of them thangs* for her and hung up his Blackberry. His mind was still on the conversation that he'd just had with Flaco back at the coffee shop. He pounded his fist against the steering wheel. The last thrity-five kilos that they'd just bought from Seven-Fizzy weren't just recompressed, they were each short two ounces. Seven-Fizzy wasn't just greedy he was disrespectful.

But that wasn't the worst of the situation. Heavy was fastly adding his own name to Hitman's list of *niggas to be dealt with*. Heavy's mouth, along with his shady business practices, were becoming a problem. Hitman had heard the bullshit: *Face Mob is over rated, just like Hitman... Jail made that nigga soft... The nigga went broke fighting his case... The Lil A belongs to Heavy...* And Hitman knew that Heavy was the source of the gossip. He also knew that most people believed the nonsense. What Heavy and the others did not know was that the Face Mob General was controlling it all. Heavy had no idea that the money he'd been short with every week when paying Flaco was actually Face Mob money. But he would surely find out in time.

Passing the hospital, headed down Mayo Street, Hitman noticed an undercover police car following him. It was Rodgers. Hitman hit his left turn signal and turned onto Roland. There were four police units already parked in front of the house. He parked and they all approached the car. Rodger had his big gun in hand.

"Get out! Come on, punk, you know the drill... hands up, up against the vehicle!" Rodgers ordered Hitman.

After patting him down, Hitman was cuffed and placed in a cage car.

The officers tore through the car. The slobbering K-9 came in and sniffed the scene. Nothing was found. Their forty-five minute search was fruitless.

Sherry, and surprisedly Clarence, came outside to see what was going on.

"Let's go!" Rodgers ordered. He was pissed off.

"What about him, sir?" a uniformed officer asked.

Rodgers looked at Hitman's crooked smile and barked, "Lock him up!"

"On what charge?"

"I'll make one up..." Rodgers answered.

"You can't do that!" Sherry yelled, running towards the car that Rodgers was getting in.

"You just watch me!" he replied and pulled off.

Hitman sat in the cold confines of the station's holding cell, thinking. His present predicament presented a serious problem. Up until now, it had been a game to him. Laughing at Nel and Rodgers as they kept major tabs on him, playing checkers with Mr. Chunk, while all of his dope was being served at the trailer park.

What the hell am I doin' here?! he wondered. All he'd done was call Dee. Next thing he knew the cops were everywhere. As he sat stewing over the matter, he heard arguing in a near office.

"Cut him loose, now!"

"But Nel, I can have —"

"All of us on charges of harassment!" Nel Brown barked at Rodgers. "Now you cut him loose and steer clear of him! You're off of this investigation as of right now."

Rodgers stormed out of the office. As he passed Hitman's cell, he eyed the young tough with murderous eyes. *I'll get you*, he thought and continued on.

* * *

Within the hour Hitman was back in traffic. Rodgers' satanic look was burned in his mind. The officer really had it out for him. Picking up his Blackberry, he thought over the past few weeks and realized that time was not on his side. His plans had to be expedited or he ran the risk of having them go sour before his eyes.

"Yeah…! What's up…? Wild shit, huh…?!" Hitman spoke into the cell phone. "Yeah, they'll be aiiight… I don't really know, cuz… But be ready anyway, though… Yeah, we goin' to the club tonight… Yeah…! Aiiight… Face Mob, nigga!" Hitman then called Flaco and Tracey to let them know that they were going out tonight.

After a quick stop at the barber shop, Hitman went by Keisha's to shit, shower, and switch his Dickie outfit. Quan and Cameron had been over her house all day. And she was too happy to see them leaving.

"Glad y'all gone, sorry ya stayed so long!" she said, laughing.

"You just be your crazy-ass at the club, girl. And remember what I said," Hitman told her.

"What-ev-er!" Keisha said, giving him the hand.

His next stop was around the corner to the house on Roland. He had to drag Quan and Cameron out of the car. They did not want to stay with Sherry, who had threatened to kill them if they came back. They were funny to Hitman, because he couldn't figure out how they could be so damn bad and be so damn scary at the same time!?

"What's up, shawdy?"

"Hey, Man," Sherry greeted her big brother with a hug. Then she saw her sons. She quickly darted on them with hugs and big kisses. Sherry loved her boys. But she was still so young and still trying to figure out her own life. Raising two boys was too overwhelming.

Hitman found Dee in her room. He quickly ran down a few things to her. She didn't quite understand it, but she decided not to question it, because she knew her brother. And to know the Hitman meant to believe in the Hitman.

"So I'ma see you tonight," Dee said and went to hit the shower.

Hitman headed for the front door, his blood pumping with anticipation. As he opened the door he heard a strange but familiar voice.

"Clarence Junior."

He turned and saw his father. He was sitting up on the couch staring at him.

"What's up, Clarence?" Hitman took a seat.

"You aiight, boy?"

"Yeah." Hitman nodded. "I'm cool."

"You don't look too cool to me. You look like you're in over your head... now, I know I don't say much, but that don't mean I don't know nothin'. It just means I know in my heart that I did my best with you, so I know you got the wit and the mustard to smooth your own affairs... And son, I know that you love your family and your friends..." Clarence paused and lit a cigarette. He blew the smoke towards the ceiling. "...but, son, these crackas and this racist system don't care much 'bout no love or friendship. They only care 'bout solvin' problems. And you, boy, you're a problem to them... and before too long, they gonna solve you."

Hitman listened. He knew exactly what his father meant. And he knew that Clarence was absolutely right. He just never expected Clarence to say what he was saying. Listening to his father was like talking to Mr. Chunk, only better, because it was his father.

"Now, boy... you can go on lovin'... and lose everything. Maybe even your life. Or you can get hip and do what your mind's been tellin' you to do. 'Cause I know your mind's sayin' somethin'... listen to it, son. 'Cause even though love is good, it becomes an impediment in times of war." Clarence stubbed out his cigarette and pulled the covers back over his head...

* * *

Hitman smiled, because the point was seen and it was not his loss. The club's parking lot was packed. Tracey parked the new teal-blue Infinity FX. She and Hitman got out. As they walked towards the club's entrance they heard Luke's *Facedown Ass Up* rumbling across the parking lot. It was Dee pulling up in her truck. Hitman and Tracey waited, they all walked in together.

The club was super-packed. Crossing the floor, Hitman saw that Heavy, Big Dream, Flaco, BamBam, and some other dudes were sitting in the section where Face Mob normally sat. Vickie was sitting in Heavy's lap.

"What's up, boy?" BamBam said when his eyes met Hitman's.

Hitman chunked him the deuces and walked on.

Dee mugged everybody at the table before she stepped off. She was truly pissed. Heavy and Big Dream were getting very disrespectful. "Bruh, what's Flaco doin' with them bitch-ass niggas over there?" she asked as they walked through the crowded club.

"I'll tell you later," Hitman said, spotting Keisha, B-Easy, and two of the other little homies over in the cut. "Just know that it's all good."

Just as they went over and sat down, the DJ dropped Usher's *Love in The Club* remix with Beyonce. Hitman nodded for Keisha to go and do her thing.

Keisha downed her double-shot of Scotch whiskey and stood. She wore an organic-green v-neck tube dress with the three-quarter sleeves. The tight, formfitting dress stopped just below her gold French bikinis, which could clearly be seen riding up into her opulent sex-canal and perfect red ass.

Tracey looked and frowned. As did most chickens in the coop.

Keisha just smiled connivingly and worked her body. Heads from every section in the club turned in her direction as she rode the rhythm of the song. The gold T-strap Marciano six-inch heels only added to her sex appeal. There was not a single set of eyes, male or female, that weren't fixated on the lasciviously winding nymph.

"Got-damn-it! You see that bitch?" Big Dream yelled.

"Hell, yeah... Lil' momma is off the damn chain!" Heavy drooled from the mouth.

Vickie shot Heavy an evil look.

"Fuck that shit, goddamn you me, I'm 'bout to go buy me some of that pussy... and I don't care what it cost!"

Big Dream pushed his way through the crowd. There was a dude standing in front of Keisha, dancing with her. Big Dream pushed him aside.

"Hey, man!" the dude said.

"Beat it, punk!" Big Dream ordered him and took up his position in front of Keisha.

The song changed, but not the mood. Prince's *Do Me Baby* was now playing. And Keisha was still performing her sexually explicit moves. Big Dream touched and moved with her.

"Damn, Keisha, baby." Big Dream eyed her hungrily as they moved together. "What you gon' charge me for some of this pussy?"

Keisha smiled seductively and backed up while patting her hairy pussy. "You wanna eat it?"

Big Dream looked at the imprint of her meaty pussy-lips in the gold panties and got dizzy. He swallowed the saliva that had formed in his mouth and said, "Hell yeah I'ma eat it. But I wanna beat it, too. And I don't care what it cost."

Keisha quickly lost her smile and frowned at Big Dream. "Nigga, don't fuckin' play with me! You know it's Face Mob over here, all day everyday."

"Fuck's that s'posed to mean?"

Keisha nodded towards Heavy and the rest of the people over in the section where Face Mob used to chill.

"Oh, shit, I'm just eatin' with them. I don't care nothin' 'bout that other shit."

"Whatever, Dream."

"Nah, baby, I'm serious. I'm my own man... and right now I'm tryna make you my ole-lady. Or at least buy me a mess of it, goddamn you me."

Keisha put her arms around Big Dream's neck and stuck her long tongue in his mouth. As they kissed Big Dream grabbed a handful of her big, soft ass and grinded his erection against her. She knew that she had him. Removing her tongue from his mouth, she stuck it in his ear before she began whispering. When she'd completed her spiel the song had ended. Keisha rubbed his hard dick with her soft hand and stepped back.

"Now can you handle that?"

"Shit, I can do that easy," Big Dream answered.

"When?"

"Hell, tonight!"

"You got thirty?"

"Thirty? Hell nah, but I can get them."

Keisha reached into her tight gold panties and pulled out a sweat-soaked piece of paper. The ink was smeared some, but the writing was visible. She handed it to Big Dream. "Call me when you're ready."

Big Dream smelt the paper and smiled.

* * *

"Damn, you look so good," he said, kissing her with a passion that he didn't know existed inside of him.

They were already naked, laying in her queen-sized bed. The only light was the glow from the flat-screen TV. From her soft lips, he worked his way down her smooth body. Attentive to each chocolate, cherry-sized nipple, down to her navel, and...

"No, stop..." she whined. "Let me." She rolled him over and took his erection into her delicate mouth.

With slow deliberate strokes, her beautiful head rose and fell, bringing him that much closer to climax. Unable to hold himself any longer, he pulled her up to straddle him. With one hand on his chest and the other on her stomach, she rode him slow and passionately.

"Oh, baby, you feel that?" she moaned. "I'm... just... cummin'!"

Their breathing got heavier and sweat covered their bodies. Expertly, she turned around and rode him backwards. He was amazed at the sight of his cum-covered sex organ disappearing in her grassy brown strath. It caused his lust to boil.

"Ooooh, Hitman!" Tracey crooned. "Baby, cum with me this... time, ba-be!"

"I'm 'bout to!" he groaned.

And the two of them exploded together. Satisfied. They slept in each other's arms.

* * *

Hitman knew that Rodgers had made their little rivalry a personal issue. And once things got personal with police things could only end one way — with one of them dead. He knew that Rodgers would not give up. So he had to kill the racist cop or leave everything and everyone that he'd grown to love.

After Tracey had fallen to sleep, Hitman got dressed and slipped into Baby Jai's room, where he found paper and pen. In tears, he sat in the dark and bared his soul throughout the paper's borders. He then took one last look at the woman he loved... but would probably never see again.

The clock on the Delta Vert's radio read 3:45 a.m. as he drove home. His Blackberry rang. It was Keisha.

"What's up?"

"You nigga. Why you sound all sad and down?"

Hitman lied. "I'm just tired."

"Okay, let me find out, nigga... anyway, tomorrow, 'bout six or seven. He say twenty a piece."

"Twenty? These niggas really think I'm sweet, huh?"

Keisha laughed. "That's 'cause you are."

"Whatever. I'm gone. I'll be on Hosana if you need me."

"You sure you okay?"

"Yeah, I'm good."

"Aiiight, I'll holla."

Hitman ended the call and listened to the growl of the car's powerful engine as he rode along. The sound was soothing. The clock now read 3:58 a.m. as he turned into Hosana Circle. Just beyond the mouth of the circle's entrance sat an old Buick with its hood up. Its owner was bent over toying with the motor. *Strange*, Hitman thought, but pushed it out of his mind and continued to his house.

He carefully backed the Vert in and went inside. All of the Henny and cranberry juice had his bladder on fire. He went straight to the bathroom. Holding his cum-covered penis, piss splashing into the toilet, he heard the neighbor's dog barking. He left the bathroom light on and slipped into the living room to peep out the window. He saw nothing except the old Buick. Its hood was down and the owner was gone. Hitman dropped the corner of the curtain that he'd been peeping out of and started for the bedroom; but the people's dog on the other side of his house started barking.

Fuck is up with these mutts? he questioned as he stepped into Cameron and Quan's room. He peeped out just in time to see a man in a ski mask and gloves creeping along the side of the house. *Oh, fuck!* he thought, slipping away from the window.

His heart was in his throat. There were no guns in the house. They'd caught him slipping and the mistake could cost him his life.

Staying low and close to the wall, Hitman killed the light in the bathroom, then tipped to his bedroom, at the rear of the house, and turned the lamp on. Now, crawling, he went into the kitchen. The idea was to make them think that he was in the bedroom. He was gunless, but he'd taken the element of surprise from them, and now had it on his side. He only prayed that it would be enough.

The clock on the microwave read 5:10 a.m. So whatever his assailants had in mind they only had about thirty minutes before first light. He sat and waited. Then, *Boom*! the front door was kicked open. Two mean wearing black ran past him, heading for the bedroom.

That was his cue. Hitman struck out for the back door, which was only a few feet away from where he stood. Just as he neared it, it too flew open. *Boom!* He was too close to reverse field, so he lowered his shoulder and dove. A loud thud sounded as the two men collided in the dark. "Uuurrrh!" the intruder groaned loudly.

Hitman wrestled the huge gun from the semiconscious man and clubbed him with it twice.

"Hey!" one of the other black-clad men yelled.

Boom! Boom! Boom! Boom! Boom! Hitman got off with the large gun. He heard a loud scream as he cleared the back door and jumped in the Vert.

Return fire erupted from the backyard just as the Delta's engine growled to life. Hitman slammed the gas pedal down and the Delta fishtailed out of the driveway and down the street....

Chapter 15
A Lesson from Mr. Chunk

The cock had barely crowed as Big Dream floated across town in his large SUV. A smile as bright as the coming sun spread from one ear to the other. He had vivid thoughts of what lay ahead for him, playing in his mind. Today was going to be his day. It had taken him $500, a half-ounce of cocaine, two ounces of sticky-greens, and an hour of arguing, but he had finally convinced Heavy to serve Hitman. The three of them, Heavy, Flaco, and himself, had left the *animal hoes* that Big Dream had paid to party with them, in the other hotel room while they argued over the issue in another room.

"Fuck Hitman! This is my town now, my nigga. Let's touch the nigga!" Heavy had said.

"Hell nah! Dude's not a fucked up dude. He can be an asset to us," Big Dream shot back.

"I think we gotta lotta assets of our own already. Why we need him?"

"You can't never have enough assets when you gettin' real money!" Big Dream stated with force. What he didn't say was that Keisha's pussy and the promise of her being his had really been the deciding factor for him. "Plus we gonna make a lotta money on the deal, and for me it's always 'bout the money."

"Dream, my nigga, ain't nothin' slick 'bout sellin' no country-ass nigga thirty petty-ass bricks," Heavy spat like a true big-boy. However, the truth was, Heavy was doing better than he'd ever done in life and it was all because of country-ass niggas like Hitman and Big Dream.

"Aye, look," Flaco spoke for the first time. "Shit could be serious though. And we'd really make some nice money, my niggie."

"How?" Heavy asked.

"How much you gonna charge the dude?"

"Shiiid, if I serve him I'ma charge him twenty a piece."

"Aiiight, look, that's six hun'ed thousand. I got five-hun'ed myself. If y'all got four-hun'ed thousand, I can get us a hun'ed bricks. That's fifteen thousand a piece, dog! And I'ma show y'all how to make a hun'ed bricks look like one-fifty, my niggie. This could really be big," Flaco explained.

Heavy thought for a minute. "You can really do that?"

"Hell yeah! This is our chance, niggie," Flaco emphasized.

This a million dollar score, he thought. "Okay, I got three-hun'ed. How 'bout you, Dream?"

"I got the other hun'ed."

"Good," Flaco said, rubbing his hands together. "I'll call my man, Mr. Seventeen-Five, and it's a wrap... we 'bout to really take this country shit over!"

While Flaco was calling his people Big Dream had called Keisha and told her to clean and season the pussy because the deal had been made.

All of that had taken place by 4:50 a.m....

* * *

Hitman felt something hit him on the chest. He ignored it. But whatever it was came down on his chest again.

"Unc! Hey, Unc!" he heard a little voice calling.

Opening his tired eyes, he saw that he was on the couch next to his father. Cameron was standing over him holding out his cell phone.

"You Blueberries, Unc! It rangin'," Cameron said.

Hitman took the phone from Cameron and saw that it was Keisha. "What up?"

"I thought you was on Hosana."

"I was. What's up?"

"I've been by there, nigga. They're ready."

"Now?"

"Nah, tomorrow!" she sassed him.

"What time is it?"

"Time to meet these people," Keisha said. "Get it together, nigga, they're at Dream's house."

"Nah, hell nah. Tell them B-Easy's house. It's on a main street, so nobody ain't got to worry 'bout no funny shit."

"What if they say no?"

"They can't say no. The work's already here and they need my money to pay for it. Nah, they can't say no."

"Aiiight."

"Bye." Hitman hung up.

Thoughts of last night flashed through his mind. The attempt on his life. He reached under the couch's cushion and felt the huge gun that he'd taken from one of the intruders.

The clock said that it was ten o'clock. He showered and readied himself for the day. As he opened the door, gun on his waistline, he saw an undercover sitting curbside. It was three houses up. *What the fuck?!* he thought.

"Unk! You Blueberries! It's you Blueberries!" Cameron yelled.

My Blueberries? Hitman thought, looking at the police car. *Muthafucka!* he mused, taking the bugged cell phone from his nephew. It was his *Blueberries*. That's how they'd been tracking him so easy. It all made perfect sense. He'd underestimated Americus' finest. Or had they underestimated him?

Hitman jumped in the Vert and went to Keisha's apartment. She was dressed and ready. Hitman called Dee and B-Easy, said a few things and hung up. He then turned to Keisha.

"Change of plans, baby. Call Flaco and tell him..."

* * *

The undercover vehicle followed Hitman to the cleaners, the gas station and was now following him to the Coffee Shop. Hitman went inside, ordered the green teas, and spoke briefly with Ms. Furqana before exiting the Coffee Shop's rear exit. The exit led to an alley on the next block. Dee was waiting for him.

"Where are we headed?" Dee asked.

"Just drop me off by Staley Middle. Then get B-Easy and go post up where I told y'all... Did you grab that money?"

"Yeah, it's in the trunk."

As they neared the school, Hitman saw Heavy's SUV parked curbside, in front of B-Easy's house. Hitman jumped out, got the duffle bag out of the trunk, and began walking in the opposite direction. Using his Blackberry, he called Big Dream.

"Yeah?"

"Aye, I'm outside, in the field at Staley. Y'all come pick me up. I'll be walkin' by the tracks." Before Big Dream could say anything he hung up.

"You hear that?!" Nel Brown asked Rodgers. They were parked in front of the Coffee Shop.

Rodgers sat on the passenger side of the unmarked police car wearing dark shades and a big hat. He'd just popped the last of his pain killers. "Yeah, I heard him," he answered dryly.

"How can he be at Staley if he's in there?"

"Beats me... God, my head is killing me," Rodgers moaned.

Nel Brown declined to comment. But judging Rodgers' appearance, more than his head was killing him. Both eyes were black and swollen, there were large knots on his forehead, and he had a terrible limp. He'd told Nel that he and one of this brothers were horsing around and things had sort of gotten out of hand. Nel felt it was a very unlikely story. But then again, Rodgers was an unlikely sort of guy.

"Come on, let's check it out," Nel finally said and opened his door.

When they entered the Coffee Shop they noticed Ms. Furqana staring at them.

"Mr. Nel! Are you two Mr. Nel and Rodgers?"

Nel looked at Rodgers with questioning eyes before turning back to the woman. "Yes, that's us, why?"

"I'm Ms. Furqana. I own this shop." She handed each of them a large green tea. Hitman had paid for them before he'd exited through the rear door. "Man said that the two of you were coming."

"He did, huh?" Nel sipped the tea. "Where is he?"

"He left about fifteen minutes ago."

The two officers left the shop in haste, knowing they'd been duped yet again. They jumped into the car and raced off to Staley.

When they came up Lee Street, Rodgers saw a huddle of men standing by an SUV. Nel quickly turned the car down the street. The men were at the rear of the SUV looking at something. Upon seeing the police car approaching them, the men all ran and jumped into the SUV as it sped off. Nel was right behind them. But before they could clear the block, the rear window was raised and Hitman threw out four duffle bags. Nel swerved to avoid them.

"Stop! Stop the car!" Rodgers yelled. "They're throwing out the drugs!"

"No, not this time!" Nel responded. "He got me with that one last time... no, sir... call a patrol to go check them."

Rodgers got on the radio and called it in...

* * *

"Shit, did you just see that?!" B-Easy asked from the bushes beside the railroad tracks.

"Hell yeah, I saw it!" Dee exclaimed. "Come on!"

They raced out of the bushes and grabbed the four duffle bags full of drugs and money. After loading the bags into their car, the two cleared the scene. *That boy's a damn fool,* Dee thought as they rode.

* * *

"Pull this muthafucka over! Pull over, dog! Let me out!" Seven-Fizzy screamed.

"Hell nah, fool! It's life-sentences back there in them duffle bags!" Heavy replied, driving wildly.

Big Dream had tears in his eyes. He'd just lost his life savings. He also knew that Keisha would never be his now. He just sat there crying as the SUV flew through red lights and swerved through traffic.

Flaco and Hitman were also quiet as Heavy turned sharp onto Mayo Street, sideswiping a pickup truck. More flashing lights were joining the chase.

"Aye, man," Seven-Fizzy yelled. "Pull over! Let me out!"

Heavy ignored the nerdy looking drug dealer from Atlanta. He had to evade the cops. The big SUV was doing about seventy-five miles per hour, southbound on Mayo, when Heavy tried to turn into Belinda Circle. Unfortunately, he missed the turn and ran slap into the porch of the corner house. The airbags deployed and so did the passengers. Hitman and Flaco ran across Mayo, to Eastview. Seven-Fizzy, Big Dream, and Heavy took off through Belinda Circle. They bent the corner wide open. Three police cruisers were right behind them. Seven-Fizzy jumped and cleared the tall fence that separated the projects from Belinda Circle. He landed and was gone... Heavy and Big Dream didn't make it...

* * *

Just as Seven-Fizzy was clearning the fence in Belinda Circle and Heavy and Big Dream were being taken into police custory, Hitman and Flaco were clearing the hole in the rear fence in Eastview. Down the hill, through the brush, off through the graveyard and they were gone.

"Let me see your phone," Hitman asked Flaco.

"What's wrong with your phone?"

Hitman didn't respond, he just snatched Flaco's phone and called Dee.

"Yo, where you?"

"Barbershop at the bottom of the hill."

In less than five minutes Dee was there.

"Boy, you a fool!" Dee laughed. "How did you know they wouldn't stop for the bags?"

"A lesson from Mr. Chunk."

"What?!" Dee questioned.

"Just somethin' that I learned playin' checkers..."

They placed three of the four duffle bags in Flaco's van.

"Look, Dee, this is five-hun'ed thousand. Give Riff-Raff one-fifty and make sure that Keisha and the family eat from here on."

"And where you goin'?" Dee asked.

"I don't know... but I gotta go. Give this letter to Tracey for me."

Flaco jumped in the van with the one hundred kilos, the million that they'd licked for, and Hitman's one million four hundred thousand dollars, and drove off.

Hitman hugged Dee and whipped off in the Vert as Dee's tears fell freely. It was the first time she cried in her adult life.

* * *

The Delta Vert sailed past the trailer park. Its powerful engine growling as the wind blew over Hitman's face. He'd won. Everything had played out perfectly. He knew that Heavy would eventually step to Flaco with an offer to work together. He just didn't know that things would be so sweet. But then again, slick *niggas always turned out to be sweet licks*. And Hitman would always put himself in a position to *serve them with no regard...*

"You gotta always be settin' up your next move," Mr. Chunk had told him. Hitman smiled, because Mr. Chunk had been one hundred kilos correct.

The Vert sailed on, Hitman's brain searched for clarity. *Why am I doin' this?* he wondered. He felt the large .45 on his waistband. It was Rodgers' gun. And he knew that the racist cop had come to kill him that night. A violent surge of emotions began to play at his mind. He had never ran from a fight. Every fight that he'd ever been involved in, no matter the odds, had always been one that he believed he could win. *All battles were fought, won or lost, in the mind.* Hitman shook his head and threw the gun in the ditch as he drove. He wasn't sure he could beat Rodgers, not in Sumter County. *Not like this...*

With the top down and his music up, Hitman breezed through Cordele and caught I-75, southbound. The Vert picked up speed. The wind blew hard. His eyes glossed over and tears began to fall... Tracey. Keisha. Quan and Cameron. Sherry. His father... They all needed him... All the good times together... he remembered. He continued south....

"When I look round, and see how few of the numbers who talk so largely of DEATH and HONOR are around me, and that those who are here are those from whom it was least expected... I am lost in wonder and surprise... An engagement, or even the expectation of one, gives a wonderful insight into CHARACTER."

- Joseph Reed [Sept. 1776]

TRAP OR DIE?

Chapter 16
Trap or Die?

"My niggie, you're crazy as a muthafucka, dog!" Flaco yelled as he came out of his parent's home. Mommie and Santino had moved back to Puerto Rico, leaving their son the two-story house to himself.

Hitman just smiled at his partner. They'd done it.

"We served them, bruh… we served them," he said, following Flaco into the side entrance of the big three-car garage.

"You fuckin' right! We served their ass!" Flaco snatched open the rear hatch of the minivan. One hundred kilos of cocaine sat neatly stacked in the van.

A big grin creased both men's faces as Hitman picked up one of the 1,000 gram squares and looked at it, loving the feel of the weight in his hand, knowing the amount of *filthy lucre* the *white girl* would bring. The letters BMF were stamped on every brick. Hitman did not know what those initials meant to other niggas, but for him it was *bring money fast.*

Placing the kilo back amongst the other 99, Hitman slammed the van shut.

He'd done it.

Still he questioned himself, *was it all worth it?*

He knew that he'd hurt Tracey bad.

Thoughts of Black crossed his mind. However, they'd grown so far apart. Black was a legitimate, law abiding, tax paying citizen now. *Was that so bad?* he wondered.

What would Dee do?

How would Keisha make it without him?

Who would make sure that Quan and Cameron read for at least an hour everyday?

Better yet, who would keep Sherry from killing the two *badass* urchins?

Damn, Hitman thought, missing his folks already.

"Niggie," Flaco said, looking at the muddled expression on his friend's face. "What the fuck is wrong with you?"

"Nothin', bruh," Hitman replied, trying to shake the mixed emotions. After all, he'd done what was best for everybody, hadn't he? Or had he done what was expedient for him alone?

"Well, you need to cheer your ass up, because we're rich, niggie!"

Hitman faked a smile and followed Flaco into the house.

Flaco blended two large *batido de triqo* drinks and passed one to Hitman.

They both downed almost half of the rich flavored breakfast shakes before any words were exchanged. Flaco was first to speak.

"So what we gon' do, my niggie?" he asked Hitman.

"Shiiid," Hitman said with certainty. "We gon' trap or die, bruh."

Flaco nodded his agreement and the two finished drinking their breakfast.

Chapter 17
Shit Don't Stop

EIGHTEEN WEEKS LATER

Dee stepped out of the bathroom naked, her full C-size breasts were damp from her morning shower. Dee had perfect breasts and a very nice ass — though she hated them both. She would have preferred to see them on some other chick — and hers more flat and nondescript.

Dee sat down on the edge of the large king-size bed and began lotioning her smooth light-brown skin. This disturbed Lil Kim, who sat up and looked at her lover. Lil Kim was a dime by anyone's [male or female] standards: five-foot tall, red-bone, almond-shaped eyes and delicate lips. She only weighed 118 pounds, but had an onion on her that brought dudes [and some females] to tears. Lil Kim and Dee had been together for forever it seemed.

"Where are you goin'?" Lil Kim asked as she watched Dee get Polo down and put on all of her jewelry.

Snapping the latch on her big rose-gold bracelet that said DEE in clear diamonds, Dee looked at Kim's little fine-ass and said, "To pay the bills, shawdy... you know how I do."

Lil Kim sucked her teeth and scowled at Dee, because they'd been together too long for her not to know when her lover was lying to her. *This bitch must really think I'm slow*, Kim thought to herself. *Who in their right mind gon' go trappin' with all that jewelry on?*

"So when you comin' back?"

Dee picked up a half smoked blunt of purple and flamed it before answering.

"Hard... to... say," Dee whispered between pulls. "I... gotta... collect some ends... and then... go holla... at... my... folks."

"Whatever, Dee!" Lil Kim hopped up out of the bed, naked except for her little boy-shorts. Her perky red titties bounced just a little as she stormed off into the bathroom and slammed the door shut.

"So you mad?" Dee asked over a loud trinkle of urine.

Lil Kim did not answer.

The toilet flushed loudly.

"Well, do you still love a nigga?" Dee questioned, silently laughing to herself. Lil Kim always tripped out when she got fresh and hit the streets. Which was crazy to Dee, because Lil Kim knew that the streets kept the bills paid and kept her little fine-ass shopping and riding good. *Besides*, Dee thought, *I was like this when we met... bitch, shit don't stop!*

"Leave me alone, Dee!"

Dee was about to respond when her cell phone rang.

She looked at the number, smiled, and decided not to answer it.

"Well, a nigga love you!" Dee yelled to Lil Kim and was gone.

She'd been expecting this call for two days now.

'Bout goddamn time! she thought as she walked past Lil Kim's new forest-green convertible BMW 328i and jumped into her triple-black Cadillac Escalade on chrome 24" custom rims.

Still *chiefing* on her splif, Dee pumped Plies' *36 OUNCES* through the SUV's four 15" subwoofers as she sped off the block.

Her phone began ringing again, but Dee simply ignored it. *I'll be there in a minute, bitch*! Dee thought to herself. *I waited, now your ass gon' wait.*

Dee was truly on top of her game — the town was hers. She'd proven everybody wrong that thought she'd fall off without her brother, Hitman, at her side leading the way. Eveything was all good without him and she'd done it all alone. Sure, he'd left her with $500,000, but he'd also left her with the responsibility of taking care of Keisha, the family and the entire Mob. However, Dee quickly realized that everybody screaming Face Mob was not really Face Mob and everybody with the same blood as hers was not really family. With that realization Dee began cutting ties and going for self, leaving those that were not strong enough to tread water in a position to drown — and she did not give a fuck about who didn't like it. The ball was in her court now. Players had to play by her rules or not play at all.

Her first stop was out on Southern Field. Dee blew the horn twice before B-Easy came out. She'd fronted him a nine-piece hard over a week ago.

"Goddamn, Dee, what's up, girl?!" B-Easy greeted her, smiling. "What that Mob like?"

"It's like 225 grams of *hard-white*, nigga," Dee said, eyeing B-Easy seriously. "You got my muthafuckin' money?" she asked, praying that he'd fucked it up.

"Damn, Dee, let me find out we beefin' 'bout something."

"Oh, you would know if we was beefin', cousin," Dee stated before pulling the big chrome .357 from beneath her seat and sitting it on her lap for B-Easy to see.

His eyes buldged as he quickly stepped back from the SUV.

Eyeing Dee, he yelled for his girlfriend to bring him the money.

The girl quickly came out and handed B-Easy the roll of bills. Dee discreetly blew the fine red-bone a kiss. She wanted Keisha so bad and couldn't understand why she'd settled down with a little nigga like B-Easy. Keisha rolled her eyes at Dee and scurried back inside, her big red ass jiggling as she walked. Dee finally tore her eyes away from Keisha's departing ass and focused on the money B-Easy had handed her.

"Nigga, what is this?" she asked with a scowl on her pretty light-brown face.

"Oh, that's just —"

The impact of the loose bills hitting him square in the face silenced B-Easy.

"I don't take short money, nigga!" Dee spazzed out. "So whatever it is, you bought yo'self with it, busta!"

Before B-Easy could explain Dee pulled off.

She was glad that he'd fucked up. Now she was completely done with him and didn't have to be bothered with him anymore. Dee couldn't understand what her brother had seen in B-Easy.

It ain't my job to take care of no grown-ass nigga, she thought to herself.

Dee had a serious *what have you done for me lately* attitude. Fuck who you were in the past or what you might be in the future — all that was gray. Dee saw things in black and white. Whereas Hitman analyzed character and invested in friendship, Dee judged people for exactly what they were at the moment and made no excuses for their shortcomings or weaknesses.

Hitting the Southside, Dee picked up money from BamBam and two other dudes that she dealt with on that side before heading out to Drayton.

Dee pulled her Cadillac Escalade around to the back of the house and parked next to a white Dodge minivan. This was not only her safe house, but it was her home away from home and she did not dare to bring anyone out there.

Hopping out of the SUV with all of the money she'd collected, Dee used her key to enter the back door. A big smile covered her face as she saw the shapely sepia body laying on the couch. In panties and bra, the woman rested on her stomach, reading a book. Her French cut bikinis were provocatively sunk deep into the crease of her smooth round ass. With her fine brown bowlegs slightly gapped, Dee could see the meaty ripples of her labia pressing against the silk fabric of her tight panties.

"Damn!" Dee gasped involuntarily, grasping her *own womanly folds* as if she had a penis.

Hearing the comment, the woman looked back over her shoulder at Dee, sucked her pretty white teeth in exasperation, and turned to continue reading her book.

Dee eased over and traced her middle finger along the line of the woman's panties. When Dee's finger reached the spot where the woman's panty line disappeared between her thighs, she quickly slapped Dee's hand away.

"Don't touch me!"

Dee laughed. "What's wrong? Why you trippin'?"

The sexy brown bombshell closed her book and sat up. Her succulent 32-C's jiggled a bit, arresting Dee's attention for a spell. Seeing where Dee's focus was, the woman shifted her positon and sucked her teeth again.

"I know your butt seen me callin' you this morning. I've been callin' you for the past two hours," she spat. "I can't believe how selfish and inconsiderate you are."

"I'm sorry, baby. I was out tryna get this money for us," Dee stated before lifting the duffle bag of money she'd collected that morning and poured it all in the woman's lap. It was so many stacks of rubber-banded money that it spilled onto the couch and floor.

This act of *stunting* did not have its intended affect on the woman, for she'd seen *plenty money* in her life. She was thirty-something and had experienced a lot in her life.

Without comment she stood up on her lovely bowlegs and started towards her bedroom.

"Nelva!" Dee yelled and stood to follow her.

"What?" Nelva yelled back over her shoulder, but never broke her stride.

Dee caught up to Nelva as she entered the bedroom and grabbed her arm.

Nelva grunted and snatched away.

Frustrated, Dee shoved Nelva hard onto the soft queen-size bed.

"Dee, don't grab me like —"

"Shut up!" Dee snapped, landing on top of Nelva and covering her sweet lips with her own.

Nelva's breath caught in her throat as Dee pulled her tongue into her mouth. She could taste the chronic that her lover had been smoking. Their tongues darted back and forth from one mouth to the other.

"This what you wanted, huh?" Dee asked, pulling Nelva's bra off before taking one of her dark-chocolate nipples into her hungry mouth.

"Ooooooooooooooooh," was Nelva's sole reponse.

Her center was wet as rain.

Dee snatched her panties off and roughly shoved three fingers in her pussy.

Nelva groaned loudly and grabbed Dee's ponytail, pulling her head up to where their lips could meet again. She was so hot for Dee. And to engage in the passionate acts of lovemaking that they threw themselves into was to live life over and over again for Nelva. Because Dee was not just her fervent lover, she was a definitive essential in her life.

"Oh, Dee, I love you," Nelva sang, pulling Dee's Polo shirt over her head.

Once the shirt had been discarded, Nelva snatched away Dee's sport bra, freeing her voluptuous brown titties. Nelva took one in each of her soft hands and squeezed them. She loved the feel of Dee's fleshly mounds in her small hands. Nelva sucked one brownish-red nipple, then opened her hot mouth for the other, but Dee pulled away. She quickly shed her Reeboks, Polo pants, and Polo boxer briefs before sliding back between Nelva's open legs — facefirst.

"Oh yes, oh yes, oh yes, oooh yeeessss!" Nelva moaned as she felt spasms beginning to erupt in her tumid clitoris.

Dee fingered her own *lady dick* as she slapped at Nelva's fervent opening. She could feel her own juices turning and running down her thighs. Her breathing quickened until it matched the rhythm of the finger spanking her clit. She was now on the verge of climax.

"I'm right there, baby!" Nelva whined. "But... I want... to... taste you!"

The two positioned themselves in a 69, each lover's lips and tongue affixed to the other's clitoris, both racing to satisfy their thirst for cum.

"Ooooh, shit!" Dee grunted and lost her nut, bathing Nelva's face with her lady-milk.

Nelva sucked and swallowed until her own legs began to shake and her liquid-love flowed for Dee to consume.

The two lay there unmoving for a while, lost in the aftermath of their passion. It was always this way with them. Ever since the first time Dee'd seen Nelva she knew that she had to have her. It took a while, but she'd finally gotten her chance. Nelva was down-and-out [drugs had gotten the best of her] and Dee had helped her to get herself back together — no strings attached. With her life seemingly back in order, Nelva had thanked Dee and took off to Seattle, Washington to tryst with her boyfriend Smelvin 'CurveBall' Sims, who was on the run from the Feds. However, her rendezvous didn't turn out to be the hot love revival that she'd thought it would be. True enough, she loved Smelvin, but their reunion had simply been *more of the same*; and she'd found herself missing home [Americus] and thinking about an alternative love [Dee].

When she'd returned to Americus she and Dee began spending a lot of time together, talking and going to a lot of different places — and also experiencing a lot of new things as a couple. Nelva told Dee all about her trip to Seattle and how things just didn't seem the same between her and Smelvin. She also told Dee about the trips to California that she and Smelvin had made to score large amounts of cocaine. Dee had immediately ran her spiel, convincing Nelva to plug her in with Smelvin, whom she'd known and dealt with before [through her brother Hitman].

"Your brutha still owe me for a brick," Smelvin had told Dee in their initial conversation. Which was true, he'd fronted the Face Mob a brick before he went on the run.

"That's it? One brick?" Dee had fronted. "I'll pay that with interest if you can get me thirty kilos a month."

"Thirty?"

"That's too much?"

"Nah."

"How much?"

Smelvin thought. "585,000. And you gotta come to Nebraska to get them."

"Nebraska? Shiiid, if I come to Nebraska they're gon' be free!"

Smelvin laughed. "Aiight, how 'bout 550,000? That's a lil' under 18,500 a piece."

Dee'd thought about it. She was paying $21,500 at present, however, the price on the retail bricks was actually $29,000. *Shiiid, I'll be killin' them!* Dee had thought before saying, "Aiight, you gotta deal, playboy."

That had been four shipments ago. The first three trips had been made by Keisha, but Dee had decided to punish Keisha by not letting her make this last trip and letting Nelva go instead. Dee had niggas from Macon, Cordele, Tifton, and Albany coming to the Lil A to get served.

Chapter 18
Why?

"Uuurrrrrrrrgh!" Tracey heaved, vomiting for the forth time. On her hands and knees, she stared at the eggs and toast that she'd just eaten, floating in the toilet. She'd been experiencing morning sickness for the past two months, and knew exactly what was causing it. As terrible as she felt mentally and as much as she fought not to believe it, Tracey knew that she was pregnant. Tears streamed down her sad face as the realization sunk in. *I'm pregnant again with no one to help me raise the child*, she thought to herself. The pain of her reality caused her to heave and vomit again, "Uuuurrrrrrrgh!" her insides erupted.

After catching her breath, Tracey lifted herself from the bathroom floor and cleaned herself up. Before leaving the small bathroom she sprayed a fragrant spray and stepped into the hallway of her spacious art deco styled office. Her partner and close friend, Sharon, was standing there eyeing her.

"Girl, what is wrong with you?" Sharon asked, working her neck as she spoke. She was also working the hell out of her baby-blue Nadia Terrell pantsuit and Ferragamo heels. Sharon was a beautiful pecan-brown with perky B-cups and a nice ass. Her china-doll eyes and sexy smile separated her from most chicks and she knew how to use them to her advantage.

"Umm," Tracey hesitated, thinking before she spoke. She had no idea that Sharon was in the office. And even though she and Sharon were business partners and quite close [Tracey's only child, Jai, was fathered by Sharon's brother], Tracey knew that Sharon could not hold water. So she simply said, "I think I ate somethin' bad."

Sharon looked at her friend and laughed. "Girl, it look like you've done more than ate it! 'Cause, baby, you're pregnant."

"What?!"

"Girl, you heard me," Sharon stated, waving a freshly manicured and bejeweled hand at Tracey. Sharon wasn't just business smart, she was street-wise and frank. "You think I'm crazy? You thInk I can't see the change in your appearance and mood? I'm not just an *investment god* and fashion icon, I'ma mother of one and a conscious observer, honey."

Yeah, that must mean nosey as hell, Tracey thought to herself.

She and Sharon had been friends for forever it seemed; and though they'd always dabbled with quick flips on cheap *fix up* properties, it wasn't until Hitman had given Tracey $400,000 to use as she saw fit, that she and Sharon both quit their jobs and really began to maximize their efforts. They'd opened the office doors less than two years ago and now managed more than $750,000 in cash and property. People from as far as Atlanta and Waycross contacted them about investments and/or managing property for them.

"Well, you can stop *jankin'* me, 'cause I sure ain't pregnant!" Tracey shot back. "Hell, I ain't did nothing to get pregnant," she lied, mustering a serious expression.

"Yeah, whatever, girl." Sharon walked over to her desk. "Where's that fine-ass man of yours been hidin', he in jail again?"

Sometimes I just wanna choke her, Tracey mused and rolled her eyes.

Sharon caught the look and realized that she shouldn't have said that. *I gotta stop being so insensitive,* she told herself. Her frankness often rubbed people the wrong way, however, Sharon only meant to be herself and enjoy what life had to offer her.

The two women worked in silence. Besides the pecking of keyboards, the closing of drawers or file cabinets, and the answering of the office phone, the soft melodies of jazz music was all the sound that the closed air-conditioned environment had to offer.

Tracey thought as she worked, fighting back tears. She felt as if she'd break down at any minute. It had been almost three months, two missed periods, and 122 sleepless and tearful nights since Hitman had left. She'd written him several letters through Riff-Raff, which he'd sworn to deliver for her, yet she'd heard nothing from him in return.

How could this be? she asked herself. *Why would he just up and leave me?*

People, everyone, had problems. But nothing, no problem, aside from an incurable disease, was so bad that it couldn't be worked out. So why had he left? And why hadn't he taken her and Baby Jai along – if it was so bad that he couldn't stay?

She loved him. And she knew in her heart that he also loved her.

So why? Why had he came into her life and left her so confused and heartbroken? She wanted to know. But more so, she needed to know what she was going to do with the new life that was growing inside of her.

Abortion? *No.*

Adoption? *There was no way she could give away a life she'd produced after holding it.*

Rear it alone? *She didn't have the strength to do it again.*

Tracey caught a tear before it could fall.

Realizing that her mind was too troubled to get any work done, she told Sharon that she was leaving and went home to write Hitman a *final letter...*

Chapter 19
Money & Power

Dee and her little partner laughed and joked as they entered Atlanta's MAGIC CITY strip club. Naked and half-dressed hotties were everywhere; some giving lap, tabletop, or wall dances; while others worked the stage or chatted with customers.

As Dee and her friend made their way through the throng of *big-money-ballers* and the women who were out to get their money, both ballers and strippers acknowledged Dee with head nods, dap, and what's ups. This only inflated her already swollen ego. Dee loved the spotlight to no end. Not only was she from a small town being recognized by *big-money-niggas* in a big city like Atlanta, but she was a female in a cutthroat game of dope and she was ruling it alone.

Finding a spot near the rear of the club, along the wall, Dee and her partner seated themselves and waved over a waitress. Dee ordered three bottles of *Rosé Black* for her and her partner and sent eight bottles of Cristal to the different dudes that she'd met and associated with over the past few months.

"And here," Dee added as an afterthought, passing the sexy young lady one-hundred one-hundred dollar bills. "Brang a nigga 10,000 in one's."

When the waitress returned with the order Dee tipped her $200 and popped her bottles.

The club was live with excitement.

This was Dee's arena. Her greatest reward to herself for the hard work that she put in every day. Sure, she loved the jewelry, the three houses she maintained, and the four cars and two trucks that she'd purchased, but none of that elated her like the strip club. The naked bitches, the music, and the power she held over it all. If she wanted to hear a certain song, she sent a bitch to tell the DJ that Dee had a request. If she wanted more bottles to pop, she sent a bitch to go get them. If there was a new *tender* in the club that she wanted for herself, she sent for the bitch. Because all bitches had a price. And Dee didn't mind paying it. After all, that's what money was for — to acquire the things she wanted in life. That's why she went so hard to get it. So when she approached a female about sex or a male about *big-money-business,* they respected her mind and more often than not obliged her request — because in seeing her they didn't see a *mere* female asking for a favor, they saw big money wielding its power.

"So, I'm sayin', Dee," Dee's partner said, sipping from her glass of *Rosé Black.* "When are you gonna be ready, 'cause I need to get back to Chat-Town like yesterday, shawdy."

Dee sipped from the bottle. "You still want three?"

Her partner nodded.

"Aiight, I'ma see what my people say befo' we leave. Hopefully, I'll have them for you by morning," Dee capped back and pointed towards the stage.

"Aye, yo!" the DJ announced. "This ya boy, Shakim Biochemical, the turn-table god! And comin' to the stage is the lovely, the super-thick, Ms. Amber! So niggas get yo' racks up! Throw some money, show some love, Ammmberrrrr!"

"What the fuck?!" Dee's partner yelled, watching as the sexy 5'11", 170 pound red-bone sashayed out to Tupac's HOW DO YOU WANT IT.

Her 36-Double-D's bounced in tune with her 44" ass.

Every step she took brought one more baller to the stage's edge.

Singing along to the song's lyrics, Amber eyed the men surrounding the stage. Her lipstick matched her fire-red leather skirt, bikini top and leather six-inch heels. Her blonde hair was wavy and cut low like a man's — hence the stage name Amber — but it worked beautifully with her doe-eyes, regal nose, and pouty lips.

As bills of different denominations rained onto the stage, the sultry nymph lost articles of clothing, revealing more and more of her perfect anatomy.

...so tell me/ is it cool to fuck/ whatchu think I came to talk/ am I a fool or what... positions on the floor/ I'm hynoptic/ erotic/ and I'm somewhat psychotic/ hittin' switches on bitches like I've been fixed wit' hydraulics... my up and down like a roller coaster...

Tupac spat as Amber dropped and popped her big round ass, before slowly winding her thick body like the tootsie roll — still crouched low with her legs spread wide open.

Amber was now ass-naked and putting on a helluva show.

Sucking one of her own voluptuous breasts, she spread her legs as wide as they could go, her six-inch heels firmly planted beneath her — *a la* Lil Kim's HARDCORE album cover — and used her free hand to play in her pussy; which had orange, yellow and red flames tattoo'd around it.

The crowd of ballers lost their minds and really began hooting and tossing money on the stage.

Dee squirmed in her seat, feeling her own center moistening with excitement. For this was the only bitch in the club that she hadn't been able to seduce with her money and sagacious mack tactics.

The song ended and Dee's partner hopped up, heading towards the stage. By the time Amber, sweating and tired, had collected her money and clothes from the floor of the stage, Dee's partner was standing there to greet her.

"Amber, huh?"

The sexy red-bone looked and gasped loudly. Dropping her money and clothes, she reached and hugged the person.

"TrapGirl! Damn, what're you doin' in here?"

TrapGirl pulled away. She was happy to see her friend, but a little uncomfortable with being hugged by a naked woman. "Nah, Keisha, I mean, Amber, I should be askin' your ass that," TrapGirl said. "Fuck are you doin' strippin'?"

By now Dee had walked up.

Keisha sucked her teeth and collected her stuff from the floor again.

"What that Mob like?" Dee asked Keisha, smiling wickedly.

Bitch, you really gotta nerve, Keisha thought to herself, but replied, "You really wanna answer to that?" She knew that Dee'd brought TrapGirl to the club to expose her and try to shit on her character.

"Damn, you bleedin', what's up with the attitude?" Dee fired back, laughing now. She loved to fuck with Keisha.

"Dee, whatever!" Keisha snapped, rolling her pretty doe-eyes. She then turned to face TrapGirl. "When you come in?"

"Earlier today."

"Okay, well, let me freshen up and put my clothes on. Then we can rap."

TrapGirl nodded and Keisha hurried off.

* * *

When Keisha emerged from the dressing room Dee was getting a wall dance. Money was scattered all around the stripper's feet like carpet as Dee leaned against the wall and the naked stripper bent and grinded her ass against Dee's pelvic area.

Dee smiled at Keisha and tossed a handful of ones in the air.

Keisha rolled her eyes and shot Dee the middle finger. *I can't stand that dyke bitch!* Keisha thought before waving TrapGirl over to follow her outside.

The two women walked over to Keishas's new white-on-white Lincoln Navigator. The SUV sat nicely on chrome 24" rims and the custom snow-white interior had KEISHA stitched in the headrests.

They climbed inside and Keisha started the engine, adjusting the air conditioning and the radio before sparking a half-blunt of 'dro that was sitting in the ashtray.

"So... what's... up?" Keisha asked, pulling the blunt and passing it.

TrapGirl hit the weed and replied, "Shiiid, you tell me... I mean, what the fuck is goin' on? Why you strippin'?"

Keisha took the weed back and hit it again. "I'm doin' what I gotta do, that's it, point-blank, per-re-iod. A bitch got bills and they gotta be paid."

"What about the trips?"

"TrapGirl, I ain't about to kiss no bitch's ass. That's dead!" Keisha stated with much venom. *"Know-what-I'm-sayin'?!* Bitches pop that Mob shit, but they don't really be 'bout it, 'bout it."

"So you sayin' Dee ain't keepin' it real?"

Keisha looked at TrapGiirl like she'd lost her mind. *"Ppsstt!* That hoe can't spell *real.*"

"So she ain't been hittin' you off?"

"Look, that bitch is the devil!" Keisha stated and re-lit the roach she was holding. "When Hitman left, all of the love and loyalty left with him... that bitch gave me fifty-grand and then asked me to go to Nebraska to get ten *keys* from Smelvin. I did it, the bitch gave me *ten-fuck-ass-stacks*... I made two more runs for her, call myself tryna keep it real, 'cause she Mob-tight, but guess what?! The hoe wasn't gettin' ten, the slimy bitch was gettin' thirty the whole while."

"Nah, Keisha, I ain't goin' for that. Dee wouldn't do it like that," TrapGirl shot back, not believing that Dee would do anything of the sort.

"Yeah, okay, you gon' see, just keep fuckin' with her. That bitch is power struck. She wanna be Hitman *soooo* fuckin' bad. Then she on that ole bull-dyking-ass shit! Wanna eat a bitch pussy and shit, but I ain't with that nasty shit!" Keisha exclaimed and began to tear up a bit. She wiped her eyes and continued. "I ain't never crossed Dee or disrespected her, ever! She can come all in the club and drop twenty and thirty stacks like it ain't nothin', but she know I'm hurtin' and won't do nothin' for me."

"Well, what you did with the $80,000 that she gave you?"

"I bought the house on Southern Field. Plus you know y'all had done fucked up all my furniture that was in the Eastview apartment, so I had to buy new furniture... plus I bought this truck and tricked it out, thinkin' shit was gon' be real like it used to be... But, TrapGirl, Dee on somethin' else. She just *spazzed* on B-Easy the other day and cut him off. It's like she ain't fuckin' with nobody that was real cool with Hitman, like she hatin' for real."

TrapGirl listened to Keisha vent, yet she still didn't believe the shit that she was hearing. How could she? Because as far as she knew, Dee had always played fair with her. Maybe Keisha had done something to deserve the treatment she was getting. Because she'd witnessed it herself over a hundred times. Someone would pull some foul shit then blame their misfortune on the person that they themselves had tried to deceive. *And B-Easy?!* TrapGirl thought to herself, *girl pleeaassee!* She couldn't figure out why Keisha had brought his name up. B-Easy was cool people to laugh and party with, but everybody knew he'd lost his desire for the trap when Hitman left. The nigga just wanted to chill and take care of his daughter. The streets were no longer in him. Keisha was the only person that couldn't seem to see that. And nobody could figure out how Keisha had fell for him. He was handsome and cool as hell, but he wasn't *about that life* anymore. Of all the niggas with money that were chasing Keisha and offering her everything, how had she settled for B-Easy?

"Look, shawdy, I don't like this strippin' shit for you," TrapGirl finally said.

"Well, me either, but it is what it is 'til something better comes along. Shit don't stop, TrapGirl. So I gotta get it, get it."

"Shiiid, are you lookin' for somethin' better? 'Cause strippin' and fuckin' with B-Easy ain't gon' never amount to nothin'," TrapGirl schooled. "I'm sayin' like, you wasn't watchin' Hitman? All those years dog *put-on* and held it down for everybody. He whatn't doin' that shit just to be doin' it! Not for us to fall off on no weak-ass stripper shit."

Ut'un! No this lil' bitch just didn't try me! Keisha thought before saying, "No! See, TrapGirl, I'd expect that shit from somebody else, but not you... But since you wanna go there, you really got me fucked up. I did everything that was asked of me everytime my name was called, no matter what! I've trafficked for free, fucked and sucked niggas, and kept all kinda shit in my 'partment. I followed! You know why? 'Cause everybody ain't no fuckin' leader! Some of us need help. Everybody ain't good at managin' money and runnin' a operation. Everybody can't hustle crack... So you think what you wanna think 'bout me, just know I'm doin' me and I ain't kissin' nobody's ass to get by!" Keisha finished and exited her truck.

Chapter 20
Truth Is?

The next morning Dee woke up beside a beautiful Caucasian stripper that she'd brought back to her hotel room from Magic City. Her head was pounding from the champagne and wild *all night* sex.

Dee jumped up and showered, not bothering to wake the chick, then headed over to TrapGirl's room. TrapGirl was up and ready to go.

The two jumped in Dee's triple-black Cadillac CTS coupe. The luxury sports car matched her Cadillac Escalade. She also had her light-purple '72 Chevy, with *beat*, on *Dicks* and *Lows*. And her forest-green BMW 750i, which mirrored the 328i convertible that she'd just bought for Lil Kim to whip. Of course, her favorite was the dark-blue Ford F-150 Kingcab, on 26's. She'd had it the longest and drove it the most.

After eating a quick breakfast at The Bedpost, Dee jumped on Route 81 and headed back to Americus. She knew that Lil Kim was going to pitch a bitch, however, when she reflected back on the wild-ass night she'd had with the freaky white stripper, she seriously felt that it had been worth it.

"So, umm," TrapGirl began, turning the volume down on the radio as she spoke. "What did your people say last night when you holla'd 'bout that?"

"Oh, shiiid, they gotta nigga on hold, for real... but, umm, I gotta nother plug in Albany," Dee said, lying her ass off. She hadn't holla'd at anybody last night about no work, because she still had ten kilos at Nelva's house from the last thirty that she'd copped from Smelvin. But if she made it seem like it was dry she could charge TrapGirl more for the work.

"What the peoples in Albany talkin' like?"

"I'll check for you, 'cause I need a few for myself... but it's gon' probably be 'bout 30,500."

"Damn?!" TrapGirl exclaimed and looked at Dee. "$30,500?"

"Yeah," Dee answered with an even tone and a straight face. "Shit been crazy."

TrapGirl sighed. "Aiight, fuck it, 'cause I gotta have it. But damn, $30,500?"

"That ain't shit for you, shiiid, you makin' $80,000 off a unit up there in Chat-Town. So what you bitchin' 'bout?"

"After payin' to get that shit shipped up there, plus payin' the workers... Dee, me and WattsDog got rent on three cribs and livin' expenses... Shiiid, $80,000 off a brick ain't really $80,000 off a fuckin' brick! It's probably more like $35,000."

"Well, at least you're eatin'. Some folks ain't doin' shit," Dee shot back.

"Yeah, true that. Which reminds me, what's up with Keisha and that strippin' shit?"

"What do you mean? It is what it is! The bitch lazy and she don't want shit *unless* a nigga *givin' it to her*. Shiiid, I tried, but I ain't my brutha and I ain't 'bout to be takin' care of no grown, leaching-ass bitches… She wanna lay up with broke-ass B-Easy, well, she better keep shakin' her ass. 'Cause I ain't *stuttin'* her."

TrapGirl didn't agree with Dee one hundred percent because Face Mob was supposed to always hold family down. Yet she decided to just leave it alone for the time being.

Chapter 21
The Right Thing?

"Here you go," the plump little dark-skin nurse said, handing Tracey a small bottle of pills. "There are fifteen pills in here. Take three a day; one in the morning, one at noon, and one at night; for five days, or until you begin to spot... You see, Ms. Carter, because you're twenty weeks pregnant there's no longer a clot inside of you, it's now a fetus," the nurse explained. "These pills will terminate the life inside of you before we go inside to –"

The nurse stopped short as Tracey broke down crying. She couldn't believe she was sitting in an Atlanta doctor's office about to kill her baby. It had been exactly twenty days since she'd written her *final letter* to Hitman, explaining that she was pregnant and simply unable to rear another child *alone*. In that four-page letter she'd bared her soul, stating that *if she didn't hear from him within the month she'd know that he didn't want the baby and she'd be forced to get an abortion*. The month had come and gone. There'd been no response. So here she was, crying for the life that was *not to be*.

The puggly little woman hugged Tracey. "Don't cry, baby... don't cry," she whispered. "Maybe, just maybe you should have it."

Tracey shook her head and withdrew from the nurse's embrace. She'd been at this point before with her first pregnancy. But Jai's father had somehow talked her out of having the abortion. And though it had been very hard raising her daughter alone, she thanked God everyday for allowing her to make the right decision – which was to keep her baby – because Jai was the absolute joy of her life and her sole motivation for carrying on.

Am I doin' the right thing? she asked herself.

"You have a choice, honey," the nurse said softly. "You don't have to do this."

"But, but he don't want the baby," Tracey cried, feeling as if she were dying with each word.

"Then he's a fool... there are programs you can apply for that'll help you financially – kids."

"It takes more than money and programs to raise a child. A child needs its father's love and support," Tracey stated, remembering the sad days when her daughter was left to shoot basketball alone. And the days when the school had programs and Jai had no father there to encourage her like the rest of the kids. She'd promised herself that she would not force another child of hers to go through such hardships. No, she couldn't have the baby.

Tracey wiped her sad eyes and took the bottle of pills from the nurse.

The lady felt bad for Tracey and fought back her own tears as she spoke, "Baby, when you see spotting, you'll have terminated the life. Come in the very next morning, but don't eat that night or drink anything before you come in. Your stomach must be empty. You'll also need someone to drive you home, because we can't discharge you without someone to take you home."

Just great! Tracey thought, because she was in Atlanta all alone. She'd left Baby Jai with her mother and the office with Sharon.

"Okay, that'll be fine," Tracey said weakly, knowing she'd have to figure something out before the time came.

She left the doctor's office hating Hitman for what he was making her do.

Tears began to fall anew as Tracey got into her teal-blue Infinity FX.

Why? Was once again the question.

Maxwell's LIFETIME played softly as she drove off to her hotel room at the Comfort Inn...

Chapter 22
Just Oughta

Just as Dee had figured, Lil Kim was super-pissed when she finally made it home from her night of partying and tricking in Atlanta with TrapGirl. So as soon as she went out to Nelva's, got the three kilos for her little partner and served her for the $91,500, Dee gladly took Lil Kim on a little shopping spree in Albany. Spending a few stacks on her woman always seemed to right the wrongs of her actions.

Now, parked at a red light in downtown Americus, in her fresh BMW 750i, Dee looked to her left and saw a cream 600 Benz roll up next to her. A frown instantly creased her face. *Fake-ass, bougie-ass, stuck up muthafuckas!* Dee said to herself, glad that the light changed before Sam and Black saw her.

Black had once been Face Mob. But ever since his DirTek investment began paying off, he'd distanced himself from the Mob. As far as Dee knew, Black had also bought a McDonalds and owned quite a few old buildings downtown — everything on Cotton Avenue, except for the bank, was now his.

Fuck him! Dee said to herself, feeling inside that if it wasn't for her and her twin brother, Hitman, Black wouldn't have shit. Yet the nigga didn't have the decency or common *good taste* to stop through and pay his respects to her. *I'm doin' big thangs, too! I'ma*

156

big-boy out here, too! Dee figured and felt that Black should treat her as such. She hated muthafuckas that forgot where they came from.

Making a left on Mayo, Dee heard her phone ringing. She looked at the caller ID and saw that it was her younger sister Sherry calling. She'd been calling all morning, but since Dee was already en route to the house she hit the *ignore button* on the phone. She knew exactly what Sherry wanted — what she always wanted — some money.

Dee pulled to the curb behind her father Clarence's Bronco. The new Honda Pilot EX-L SUV that she'd recently bought for Sherry and her two *badass* sons was parked in the driveway. No sooner than Dee'd opened the gate, Quan and Cameron came flying around the house. They both had pellet guns chasing the Rottweiler she'd bought for them, shooting at the poor dog as it ran.

"What the fuck?!" Dee yelled as the fleeing animal ran past her and a pellet meant for the dog missed its mark and hit her car door. "Y'all lil' muthafuckas, leave that damn dog alone!"

They both stopped in their tracks.

"Hey, Auntie!" they both yelled.

"I'ma fuck y'all two lil' bitches up... y'all done shot my fuckin' car!" she screamed, approaching them as she reeled off obscene threats.

"Shiiid," Cameron said. "Come on, Quan!"

And they were gone.

Before Dee could chase behind them the front door flew open.

"You ain't gotta be cussin' at my damn kids!" Sherry yelled.

"I'ma do more than cuss at them when I catch their asses," Dee answered her spoiled little sister. "What do you want? Why you keep callin' me, ain't you gotta man?"

Sherry sucked her teeth. "I need some money."

"Your ass need a job!"

"Child, I go to school. How I'ma go to college, study, work, and raise two kids, huh?" Sherry asked, rolling her neck and bouncing as she spoke.

Dee laughed. "You can take *raising kids* off of your lil' list, 'cause them two lil' bitches ain't got no home trainin' and no respect for nothin'!" Dee went into her pocket as she walked past Sherry, into the house. The place was a mess! Clarence sat watching EXCUSED on the 42" plasma.

"Hey there, girl," Clarence said in greeting.

"Hey there to you too, man," Dee replied mockingly.

The two had never shared a real father-daughter relationship.

Sherry took the money that Dee'd handed her and looked at it. A frown covered her pretty face. "Ut'un! Dee, I need more than this!"

"Girl, you crazy! That's $500. And I just gave your rotten-ass 'bout $600 a few days ago."

"I had to buy Cameron and Quan some new shoes and I had to buy my books with that money!" Sherry shot back angrily.

"Well, I don't need no books, them ain't my kids, and I ain't fuckin' you... so you best to call the nigga who is, 'cause I ain't givin' ya *nann* nother dime."

Sherry narrowed her already chinky-eyes and said, "I hate you! You make me so sick! I wish my damn brutha was here, then I wouldn't have to ask your ass for shit."

The comment hurt Dee a little, however, she was used to Sherry's shit.

She was about to turn and leave when Clarence spoke.

"You still runnin' 'round servin' evil, huh?"

Dee looked at him, not sure if he was talking about selling drugs or her lesbian lifestyle. "I don't know what you're talkin' 'bout," she said.

"Well, you just oughta," Clarence replied sharply.

"Just oughta what?"

"You just oughta let it go! Realize that your brutha made a tough decision that he thought was better for everybody... you oughta be thankful for the time y'all had together and know that the boy got his own life to live. He can't live for you, me, Sherry and everybody else," Clarence reprimanded his oldest child. "You just oughta be happy for him, wherever he's at, and get the larceny out your heart."

Dee wanted to say, *fuck you!* But instead she said, "You must be drunk, 'cause you don't know what you're talkin' 'bout... You trippin'." Dee told her father and exited the house before he or anybody else could see her cry...

Chapter 23
A Shared Love

Keisha was tired as hell. She'd been dancing all night at Magic City and did not have the strength or energy to make the long two and one-half hour trip back to Americus. She usually commuted back and forth on the days she danced — Wednesday, Thursday, Friday and Saturday — but tonight she just wasn't feeling the ride. *I'ma just grab me somethin' to eat, get me a box of Dutch's to roll this good 'dro in, and hit this Comfort Inn*, Keisha said to herself as she whipped her big white Navigator through the empty streets of Atlanta.

After getting the food and cigars, Keisha pulled into the Comfort Inn and got herself a single. She couldn't wait to hit that queen-size bed. *And I ain't gotta hear B-Easy's ass snorin' either*, she thought. *But I can't get me none of that good muthafuckin' head either*. Keisha absolutely loved getting her pussy ate and B-Easy had the *bestest* head she'd ever had.

As she juggled her food and overnight bag towards her room, she saw a familiar looking ride. *Damn, it look like I've seen that damn blue Infinity truck somewhere before*, she mused, trying to figure out just where she knew the SUV from. *Shit, probably some nigga that's spent his re-up money on me*, Keisha thought with a little laugh.

Once inside of her room, Keisha got naked and ate. She then rolled herself a nice fat blunt and smoked as she counted her take for the night. *Pretty damn good for a Thursday night*, Keisha reasoned, placing the $700 back in her bag. If she could hit them like that again Friday and Saturday she'd be straight. With that thought on her mind Keisha called it a night.

* * *

Front desk rang Keisha's room at exactly 10:48 a.m. Keisha was pissed. She'd just checked in at around 3:00 a.m. Tired and extremely irritated, Keisha smoked a half-blunt, showered and headed to the front desk. She noticed the Infinity SUV still parked in the same space it held when she'd arrived in the wee-hours.

Entering the hotel lobby, Keisha spotted a familiar face. *I knew I knew that damn truck from somewhere!* Keisha thought, placing the blue SUV with its owner.

"Tracey, what's up, girl?" Keisha greeted. "Long way from home... What you doin' up here?"

Tracey had seen Keisha enter the lobby and had hoped she would somehow overlook her, because she really was not in the mood for idle conversation. Besides, their relationship was not really friendly: She had been Hitman's woman and Keisha was his homegirl, so they just sort of knew each other and respected their lanes.

"I'm okay, Keisha... just tired. I'm up here taking care of some business," Tracey said weakly, offering a half-smile.

"Oh, okay," Keisha replied while handing the clerk her room card and getting her five dollars return. "Well, you take it easy, homegirl."

"Okay, you do the same." As Tracey spoke a yellow cab pulled up in front of the lobby. It was for Tracey. The cab was to be her ride to the doctor's office. She'd taken the pills that the nurse had given her and as promised, she'd began spotting yesterday evening — her unborn baby was now dead inside of her.

Keisha noticed Tracey walking slowly to the cab. The pretty dark-skin woman had a very strange expression on her face, which further added to Keisha's perplexing question, *why is she catchin' a cab and her car's right over yonder?*

"Tracey!" Keisha called out. "Girl, are you aiight?"

Tracey nodded instead of responding verbally. She was hurting so bad inside. So bad that it was impossible for her to mask it any longer. Standing there at the side of the cab, Tracey lost it. Great sobs overtook her as crocodile tears ran down her pretty face.

What the hell?! Keisha thought, hurrying over to Tracey. She immediately took the sobbing woman into her arms. Tracey melted in her embrace. She needed the affection. For five whole minutes Keisha held her in the parking lot as she cried.

"Excuse me, ma'am," the cab driver finally called out.

Keisha looked over her shoulder at him, still holding Tracey.

"Umm, I hate to disturb y'all, but I'm on —"

"My bad," Keisha said before walking Tracey over to her Navigator and sitting her in the passenger seat. She then took ten dollars from her overnight bag and gave it to the cab driver, along with the five dollars she'd gotten from the hotel clerk. "Sorry for holdin' you up, but she'll be ridin' with me."

The cab driver accepted the fifteen dollars with a smile and was off to his next fare.

"So what's up, Tracey?" Keisha asked softly as she drove away from the hotel. "I'm really not tryin' to be all in your business, but what's wrong, girl?"

Tracey sat on the passenger side of Keisha's Navigator, crying, lost to the pain that consumed her mind. A lot had been lost to her over the past decade: she'd lost her daughter's father to the Feds, she'd endured a couple of failed relationships and lost a few friends along the way, but nothing compared to the insufferable afflication that she was experiencing due to the lifeless embryo resting in her womb.

Keisha stopped at *Gloria's* restaurant. *Gloria's* had the *bombest* cheese-grits, fish and veggi-omelets in the world. Keisha made it her business to have breakfast there whenever she was in Atlanta.

"Tracey, come on, we can talk 'bout it over breakfast, my treat."

"Ut'un..." Tracey shook her head slowly. "I can't eat anything."

"Coffee or tea?" Keisha quizzed.

"Can't have anything on my stomach."

Keisha nodded and pulled off. She knew. Keisha had been down this road herself – a few times. She'd had three abortions. Of course, they hadn't bothered her the way this one was bothering Tracey, mainly because Keisha didn't have room in her life for children and definitely didn't care anything about the niggas she'd been pregnant from.

"You, umm, you holla'd at Hitman 'bout this?"

The mention of his name sent a shiver throught her body. Tracey shook the feeling off and looked at Keisha. "Talked to him 'bout what?"

"'Bout what you're doin'?"

Tracey sighed loudly. *God, why, why, why?* she thought and looked up towards the heavens before saying, "No... I haven't talked to him... But I know he doesn't want the baby," she whispered, sinking deeper into her sorrow with each spoken word.

"Don't say that, Tracey, 'specially since you ain't talked to him. I mean, like, how you figure he don't want the baby if y'all ain't talked?"

Tracey was a very private person, yet for some strange reason beyond her own understanding, she opened up to Keisha; a woman she knew so little about. Tracey explained the entire situation – the letter he'd left her, the many letters she'd written him and the terrible feeling that she felt inside. She'd never talked to anyone about her relationship and love for Hitman. No one knew that she was pregnant.

"I just don't know what else to do," Tracey finished.

"Well you don't have to do this," Keisha said, feeling sorry for her.

Tracey shook her head. "It's already done."

Keisha understood. "So where we goin'?"

Tracey gave her the address and they made the remainder of the trip in silence.

* * *

When Tracey woke up again her mouth was extremely dry and she was surrounded by darkenss. It took her a while, but she soon realized that she was back in her Comfort Inn hotel room. *How did I get back here?* she asked herself and tried to sit up.

"Awwww, shit," she moaned as pain exploded in her stomach and lower pelvic area.

Tracey reached between her legs and felt a fat sanitary napkin in her silk bikinis.

She then pulled back the comforter in a panic. Seeing that she only had on a bra and panties further confused the situation.

Forcing herself upright, Tracey turned on the bedside lamp. She saw Keisha laying asleep on the hotel room floor. That's when she remembered. The tears and the memories came back in a torrid flood... the smell of chemical disinfectant... the pushing in her lower-middle area... the loud vacuum-like sound... the pulling... the sucking and grinding... the vacuous feeling she'd been left with. As if the whole of her inside had been removed... the cold white sheets... the single bright light... the loneliness... the pain... the intense pain... and then the darkness.

My baby?!? Tracey thought, her face covered in tears.

She cut off the lamp in search of the dark.

She needed the darkness.

She needed it to cover the truth of what she had done.

The darkness was an escape.

Tracey hugged her pillow and drifted off to sleep.

* * *

The next morning when Tracey came out of her slumber, Keisha was sitting at the small table watching a muted TV screen. Tracey still felt the pain in her stomach and lower pelvic area, but managed to get up.

Keisha saw her struggling out of bed and immediately walked over to help her.

"I'm okay," Tracey moaned. She wasn't use to being semi-nude around another female.

"No you ain't... come on, I got you," Keisha said, helping Tracey out of the bed and into the bathroom. "Handle your business or whatever, and I'll help you back to the bed."

Tracey nodded and closed the door. Pulling her panties down she noticed all of the blood in her pad and almost passed out. She pee'd and wiped herself and noticed more of her life-fluid on the tissue and in the toilet. *Lord, please don't let me bleed to death... I know that 'Thou shall not kill' and all, but Lord, I just couldn't raise another child alone... I just couldn't bring an unwanted child here to be neglected by the daddy... and if somehow I was wrong in my action, then Lord, please forgive me*, Tracey prayed before flushing the toilet.

It was then that she noticed the box of pads. She picked it up and saw that one was missing from the box – she also realized that she hadn't been wearing those particular panties when she'd gone to the doctor's office. Keisha had at some point cleaned her up, changed her panties, and put a pad in them. She shivered at the thought, because she'd never been and never would be into women. *And I hope Keisha ain't either*, Tracey thought as she put on a fresh pad, washed her hands and exited the bathroom.

"Come on, Ms. Lady, I got you," Keisha said cheerfully.

"Thank you, Keisha. I really appreciate this," Tracey declared once she was back in the comfortable queen-size.

"Don't even sweat it. I got your meds, I got you some egg-drop soup and Ginger Ale soda, and I got your back, Tracey. Whatever you need, just holla."

Tracey almost started crying again as Keisha turned and put the egg-drop soup in the small microwave. Here was a street-hardened woman that she barely knew, doing more for her than she herself would've ever done for her – had the roles been reversed. Not that she was mean or selfish, because that wasn't the case. However, had she seen Keisha getting into a cab with a woeful expression on her face, she would've simply spoke, maybe said a quick prayer for her, but ultimately she would have gotten in her ride and rode off. *Damn,* she thought inwardly, *there are so many lessons in life. So many blessings. Lord, I thank you for this angel name Keisha.*

After eating her soup, Tracey took her meds and drunk two cups of Ginger Ale, which made her feel a lot better.

Keisha sat there with her and watched TV. She didn't even go to work at Magic City.

All of her time was spent catering to Tracey.

She helped her with her bath, gave her her meds four times a day, and ran out three times a day for Ginger Ale and egg-drop soup.

They talked often — whenever Tracey was not eating or crying.

Keisha learned a lot about the woman that she'd once erroneously deemed *bougie.* She now saw that Tracey was real *down-to-earth* and even funny at times. She saw now why Hitman loved her.

"Umm, Keisha, can I have some of that tea you've be makin'? I'm so tired of this Ginger Ale," Tracey stated.

"Some of this tea?" Keisha asked.

"Yeah, girl, some of *that* tea."

Keisha shrugged and said, "Aiight." *You're the one that asked for it now,* Keisha said to herself as she fixed Tracey a cup. She took two green tea bags and placed them in the little white coffee filter. She then dropped a few nice buds of 'dro in there and placed it in the hotel room's coffee maker. In no time the tea had drip-brewed, casting an exotic scent throughout the room. Keisha poured it up and flavored it with honey and a mint leaf. "Here you go," she said, passing it to Tracey.

"Thank you," Tracey responded and sipped. "*Mmmmm*, this is the bomb! It tastes better than it smells."

I bet it do, Keisha mused. "Umm, girl, you ain't on no probation or no shit are you?"

Tracey frowned at her. "Girl, no! Why you asked me that?"

Keisha shrugged and said, "Just askin'." She'd been brewing her weed and drinking it because she didn't want to smoke around Tracey — weed smoke often bothered non-smokers.

When Tracey finished her tea she was feeling too good. She laughed and talked until the sun came up. Keisha thanked God when Tracey finally fell asleep.

* * *

"Keisha, look, let me ask you something," Tracey said on their third and last day in the room together. She was feeling a lot better and was heading back to Americus that night.

"Go 'head, what's up?"

"What are you doin' up here in Atlanta?"

Keisha shrugged. "Strippin'," she answered with no shame in her game.

"Oh," Tracey mumbled, unable to picture herself employed as such. At one point she might've frowned on Keisha — or any woman for that matter — for stripping. However, Keisha's kind heart and golden personality had showed her another degree of God's mysterious blessings. "Keisha, why did you help me that day when I broke down cryin'?"

"'Cause I woulda wanted your help had the shoe been on the other foot... I had an abortion once, well, three times for real, and I had them alone. Like, my whole life I've been by myself. Everythang I know 'bout life I taught myself."

"What about your family?"

Keisha pointed to her ankle. Tracey saw the Face Mob tattoo.

"That's it. They're my family. Never met my sorry-ass daddy. My momma died so long ago I don't remember her. But, Hitman, I love that nigga. He ain't never told me no and he ain't never took advantage of me. He's 'bout what's right and he showed all us that. Folks talk 'bout we're a gang and he's a bad person, but that's only 'cause they ain't never been alone and they ain't never got to meet him... I guess, I helped you for him."

Tears were in both women's eyes. They both missed him so.

"Well," Tracey said through tears. "If you ever need anything, you better call me... because, I've been alone before and I don't ever wanna be that way again, girl... We're friends," Tracey finished, seeing exactly why Hitman loved Keisha so much.

Keisha wiped her tears and smiled. "I feel the same way, Tracey."

"Good! Now, can you make us some of that tea before we leave?"

Smiling, Keisha got up and did her thing, feeling good about having a new friend...

"Contrary to popular belief, there are no such things as *self-made* men and women. Everybody needs friendship, encouragement, and help. What people can accomplish by themselves is almost nothing compared to their potential when working with others."

— John C. Maxwell

Back In Business

Chapter 24
Slow Money

I started small time/ dope game/ cocaine/ I'm pushin' rocks on the block/ I'm never broke man... sportin' jewelry/ the 'caine/ the shit is rollin' hard/ you try to fuck me/ you'll get served/ wit' not regard...

Mr. Scarface pumped through the speakers of the custom utility van as Hitman navigated it through traffic. Flaco reached over from the passenger seat and unplugged the I-pod.

"Hell you doin', bruh?" Hitman questioned his main man.

"Why the fuck are you always listenin' to that *old-ass-shit*?"

"Boy, that's *gansta music!*"

"Fool, that's *old-ass* music!" Flaco shot back and plugged up his I-phone. "It's a new era, my niggie. Check out this *real gangsta music.*"

Last time I checked/ I was the man on these streets/ They call me residue/ I leave blow on these beats... Got diarrhea flow/ now I shit on niggas/ even when I'm constipated/ I still shit on niggas (Let's get it on!)... Got some Super Friends in the Legion of Doom/ They blowin' purple shit that keep me high like the moon... Yeeaaah/ I'm an affiliate/ I know Hitman... Yeeaaah/ I'm an affiliate/ I know Hitman... Yeeaah/ I'm an affiliate/ I know Hitman/ I'ma hater like you/ fuck my wristband...

Young Jeezy's TRAP OR DIE blasted, acknowledging the *Hitman*. And as things were, he and Flaco were the men on the streets of Dade County. Thanks to Flaco's dad, Santino, and $500,000 of his own hard earned drug money, Hitman was the proud owner of a two-floor eight-unit apartment building on 60th Street and 13th Avenue; a two-floor twelve-unit apartment building on 96th Terrace and 5th Avenue; and a duplex on 94th Street and 10th Avenue. So three times a week he and Flaco completed a circuit of the properties, cleaning, maintenance and/or collecting rent. It was a job for them, so they dressed the part — gray Dickie sets with *H&F Utility and Cleaning* on their shirt pockets and hats — and moved around discreetly in the brand-new custom utility van. The van was white, stocked with all sorts of tools and chemical cleaning supplies, a special stash spot; and big red, blue, and black graphics that read *H&F Utility and Cleaning*.

In-between maintenance stops and on days when no property upkeep was needed, they simply maintained the street — TRAPPED. Flaco had three *brick-buying* customers and a gang of *ounce* and *125 gram* consumers. The flow of *coke* was slow but sure — they'd only moved six kilos in the first two weeks of putting it out there. But Hitman wasn't tripping off of that, because he knew that the winner in his game was not the *fastest* but the *smartest*; and being patient in any situation was always *smart*.

...smoke purp by the pound/ Goose by the fifth/ re-up on the first/ then again on the fifteenth (Yyyeeaah!)... We trap or die nigga/ we trap or die nigga... You know these hoes love a nigga/ 'Cause they know we the truth/ Got the Chevy same color Tropicana orange juice (Yyyeeaah!)... We trap or die nigga/ we trap or die nigga...

Hitman bobbed his head to the *trap music*.

It was exactly 1:45 p.m. and they'd just finished cleaning and doing minor repairs at the 96th Terrace apartments and serving two *125's* to two of Flaco's people in Silver Blue Lakes. They were now officially off the clock.

Hitman pulled the van into the parking lot of *Respublica*, an old-fashion Spanish restaurant that sat in the middle of the plaza on 79th Street and Biscayne. It was not a very big or fancy eatery, however, the food and service was magnificent; so at any given day you could catch *big-money* chico's like Pit Bull, E4, Fat Joe, DJ Laz, Willie and Sal, or even the crooked *gangsta*, ex-mayor Martinez. Santino had turned his son and Hitman on to the highly regarded Spanish restaurant.

The Florida sun burned fiercely as they exited the van and entered the eatery. A Latin rendition of Chris Brown's SHE'S NOT YOU played crispy throughout the restaurant's sound system. A fair-skinned, plump, mild-age Spanish woman seated them and took their orders: *Ropa vieja platanito frito*, and malta mixed with canned milk to wash it all down.

The two friends devoured their meals as they discussed different measures of moving the 94 kilos they had stashed in the floor of one of Hitman's apartments. Had they been up in the Little A, Hitman would've *bammed* the units with no pressure. Nevertheless, he wasn't in Americus, where he'd done so much and gotten away with so much, that the police had tried to kill him; so he simply had to go with the flow.

"When this is done, bruh, I'm done. It's over, bruh. I've done too much," Hitman explained. "I'ma just send for Tracey and Jai, somehow, and get in the wind."

"I feel you, fool... Where you gon' go though, my niggie?"

"Somewhere where nobody knows me… where I can chill out and be the man that God made a nigga to be." Hitman laughed. "I might just father a son and name him Ismael."

Flaco smiled. "That'll be tight, my niggie, for real! I'll buy that lil' fool everything. He'll be my fuckin' nephew, dog."

They were both laughing, feeling the moment, when a tall Spanish man dressed in tan slacks and a white button-down shirt approached their table. His skin was tanned nicely and his dark hair was graying at the edges. A stern look coverd his face. Diamonds sparkled from the pinky-ring and expensive designer watch that rested on his left wrist and pinky finger.

"Ismael? Is *that-a-you*?" the man asked excitedly.

Flaco looked up and saw his father's oldest and dearest friend, Jose.

"Damn, hey, Jose, how you doin', man?" Flaco exclaimed, standing to embrace the man that had always been like family to him.

"Good, good," Jose replied, all too happy to see Flaco. "You *are-a* so big, you… what *have-a-you* been doing?"

"Workin' hard and tryin' to enjoy a little… sit down, Jose. This is my partner, Hitman. …Hitman, this is my dad's best friend, Jose."

Hitman and Jose shook hands and exchanged greetings.

Jose looked the youths over, noticing their work uniforms, he said to Flaco, "What *is-a* this clothes? I *know-a-you* don't workie." He'd known Flaco's father since the 1950's and they'd done plenty drug smuggling and hustling together. They'd also bought up a ton of houses and commercial real estate. Their investment guy, Elliot, was a beast with investment plans and he'd really set the two of them up comfortably. So he know that Flaco didn't need to work.

"I work a little. Me and my dog gotta property management and cleaning thing goin'. See here," Flaco said, passing Jose a card with their information on it. "We take care of about ten properties, not includin' my dad's stuff, because he doesn't pay us."

Everybody at the table laughed at Flaco's last comment.

Jose looked closely at the card and then back at Flaco and Hitman.

"I *have-a-something* for you two," Jose stated, standing to leave. "I *call-a-you* and we *do-a-some* business, okay?!"

Hitman and Flaco looked at each other and then at Jose.

"Okay," Flaco answered as he shrugged his shoulders.

Jose said his good-byes and quickly exited.

Chapter 25
A Real Job?

Boom! Boom! Boom! Boom! Loud banging sounded at Hitman's front door. He already knew who it was — Flaco — because no one else knew him or where he lived. His only associates were the tenants that rented from him.

Walking through the three bedroom, two bath, dwelling with the sunken den, Hitman grimaced as the loud banging ensued, *Boom! Boom! Boom!*

I'ma kill this crazy-ass-fool! Knockin' on my door like he crazy, Hitman thought. He'd just recently moved into the duplex on 94th Street and 10th Avenue for this very reason — living at Santino's house with Flaco was driving him crazy. Flaco was probably his *best friend* in the world, but living with him was like experiencing a never ending party. Flaco loved freaky women, sticky 'dro, alcohol, and loud music.

Hitman snatched the door open. "What? Crazy nigga, why you bangin' like the police after you?"

Flaco just pushed past him. "Niggie, I talked to Jose! We on, niggie!"

Hitman waved at the fine-ass older chick that rented the other side of the duplex from him. *Damn that's a bad old lady there*, he thought as she smiled and waved back at him.

"Niggie, you hear me, fool?! I talked to Jose!" Flaco exclaimed loudly, already seated on Hitman's leather sectional.

Closing and locking the door, Hitman sat across from his main man.

"Bruh, what the fuck are you talkin' 'bout?"

"Here," Flaco said, passing Hitman a piece of paper. "Look at this shit, niggie!"

It was a check for the sum of $50,000 made out to *H&F Utility and Cleaning.*

"Fuck is this for?"

"It's for use, fool!" Flaco jumped up, super-hyper as always.

"For what?"

"To clean and maintain Jose's hotel."

"Who is Jose?"

"My dad's friend, fool!" Flaco snapped. "You've been gettin' high on the low without me?"

"Mmaann, I ain't no fuckin' utility man, nigga!"

"Shiiiid, you are now, fool! You think I'm 'bout to give $50,000 back? I know you been gettin' high now, fool!"

Hitman shook his head slowly. He now had a damn headache. He didn't start *H&F Utility and Cleaning* with Flaco to actually *work.* He'd started it to maintain his property and Santino's, to put up the façade of a *hard working joe,* and to throw off the cops while he trafficked cocaine. *But this dumb-ass chico done really went out and gotta muthafucka a 'real job'!*

"Flaco, man, you trippin'."

"Nah, you trippin'!"

"You need to give dude his paper back."

"Shiiid, you need to get your ass up so we can go to work!" Flaco said and walked off to the kitchen. Removing a *Malta* from the fridge, he popped it open and drunk some before speaking. "Bruh, this is a good opportunity... We got $50,000 and a budget of $35,000 a month, niggie. That's $240,000 a year! You know how many bitches we can hire with that? You're always readin' that Malcolm X shit, well, niggie, you wanna help some fuckin' body, here's your fuckin' chance."

Hitman shook his head again. Flaco was a real piece of work.

"At least come with me and look at the shit... if you ain't feeling it, fool, I'll just give Jose the check back, niggie."

Sighing heavily, Hitman got ready and the two left.

Chapter 26
A Gold Mine

Yyyeeeaaah/ I'ma affiliate/ I know Hitman/ I'ma hater like you/ fuck my wristband... Nigga sneak this/ and that ain't how we play/ fuck wit' mine/ getcha drama like the DJ (That's right!)... Now tell me I ain't real/ this AR that I'm holdin' gotta gangsta grill...

Hitman's new theme music [Trap or Die] played loudly as Flaco exited I-95 and whipped up into the City Inn. Hitman could not believe his eyes.

What the fuck?! he thought, seeing the hotel that he'd spent so many nights at. The City Inn, which used to be the Days Inn, was once a nice clean hotel. Now, judging from its exterior, the place was a *hell-hole*.

Flaco parked and the two exited the van.

The parking lot was filled to capacity with cars and trucks of all kinds.

"Bitch! You think I'm somethin' to play wit'?" they heard someone yell.

"Ut'un, Daddy, I was just tryna," the girl tried explaining but was silenced with a hard slap to the face.

"No, Pre, you ain't gotta be hittin' her like that!" the other female yelled.

It was obvious that the chicks were prostitutes and the dude was their pimp.

Hitman wanted to intervene on the young girl's behalf, but he knew *that the heart and its mysteries could easily confuse the mind, blinding the foolish with what they perceived as love.* He remembered the situation with his sister Sherry and her abusive baby's father. A situation that no amount of intervention could rectify. Hitman wisely moved on past the trio.

Three running children, ages ranging from 6 to 10, blew past them, almost knocking Flaco over as they ran. They'd simply ran straight through the hotel's front door frame — the glass door had been broken out and only the metal door frame was there.

Hitman looked at Flaco with wide eyes. He thought about his two nephews — Cameron and Quan.

Flaco shrugged and stepped through the door frame. He was greeted by unfriendly stares and a miscellany of cheap perfumes and cologne.

Women in extra-skimpy short-shorts and skirts — most sporting wigs and too much makeup — lounged about the lobby. A few dudes in cheap suits stood around trying to look important.

It was as if Hitman and Flaco had somehow stepped onto the scene of one of those old *Blaxploitation* movies from the 60's or 70's.

"Umm, can I help you?" the black chick with the $100 weave, big lips, and huge tits asked. Her otherwise cute face was fixed in a frown and her smooth dark-skin was lightly covered in a sheen of sweat.

"Yeah, we're here to check out the hotel," Flaco said, staring hungrily at her juicy double-D's as he passed her their card. "Jose sent us."

"Oh," she replied simply and turned her back to them. She then bent down and began searching for something in a lower cabinet. Her tight white slacks were hugging her wide ass like a second skin. They were so tight and thin you could see the leopard print on her panties. When she turned back around to face them, both men were stuck with their mouths open. "Yeah, Jose told me 'bout y'all... Here, y'all gon' need these keys. They're for all the doors. And here," she said, going in a drawer below the register. "This here's a master card, it opens every room door."

"Okay, thanks, but... umm, what's your name?" Flaco asked after seeing no nametag on those big-ass titties of hers.

"Bambi," she replied with a smile. "My name's Bambi."

They thanked Bambi and walked over to the elevator. The doors opened and two children flew past them.

"What the fuck?!" Flaco stated involuntarily.

The mother of the two running children heard Flaco and rolled her eyes at him as she exited the elevator.

As soon as they stepped on the elevator, the stench of piss assaulted their noses.

"Gotdamn!" Hitman exclaimed.

"Fuckin' tell me about it," Flaco said, looking at the graffiti that covered the elevator's four walls and ceiling. "My niggie, what you think all these damn kids doin' here at this raggedy-ass hotel?"

Hitman shrugged and exited the pissy elevator at its tenth floor top.

The hallway didn't smell as bad as the elevator but it wasn't a place that they'd want to dwell in. Large areas of carpet was missing and the once white walls were covered in dirt and graffiti. Flaco pulled out a small pad and pen and began writing down a few obvious repairs. As they walked along the hallway, Flaco wondered what the inside of the rooms looked like. So he stopped and knocked on a door. After only a few seconds the door came open.

"Yeah, what's up?" the naked red-bone asked, staring at Flaco and Hitman as she stood in her door. Other than a few scars and some stretch marks, she was beautiful. "Did Pre send y'all up here?"

The two men looked at each other and back at the naked woman.

"Nah, but... umm, we work for the owner and we... well, umm, I think we need to check out the room so we can see what needs fixin'," Flaco managed to explain.

"Oh, aiight, y'all come in then, 'cause it's a few thangs that need fixin' up in here," the naked red-bone stated and stepped aside for them to enter.

The room was neat, but crowded with clothes and toys. There was a fridge, small stove and microwave. Hitman stood staring at the red-bone, a slight erection forming in the crotch of his Dickie pants. Flaco walked throughout the room noting repairs.

"Umm, 'cuse me, but how long have you been in this room and how much do you pay a day?" Flaco asked the broad.

"I been in here for 'bout like eight-nine months. And I don't pay shit, my section-eight cover it," the girl explained.

"Section-eight?" Hitman questioned.

"Yeah, I gotta son and a lil' girl, so I get section-eight."

"But this is a hotel," Hitman said.

"Shittin' me," the girl said. "This shit is like the projects! The tenth, nineth, and eighth floors are all section-eight... The lobby is mainly where we catch our dates... The fourth, fifth, and seventh floors is like New Jack City... For real, you can come up missin' in the City Inn. I came up in here nine months ago with my lil' peoples and ain't left since."

Flaco and Hitman stared at each other inquisitively.

Before either man could speak, a knock sounded at the door.

Red-bone turned to go and answer it. Her big red ass jiggled as she walked.

"Yeah?" they heard her say.

"Pre sent me up," a male voice replied.

"Come in, then," Red-bone said and she and the guy walked farther into the room. "It was cool rappin' with y'all, but as you see I gotta get this money, so –"

"It's cool. We'll be back later this week to fix your place," Hitman told the girl.

She nodded and walked them out.

When they were back in the dirty hallway and out of the woman's earshot, Hitman turned to Flaco, a big grin on his handsome brown face. "Bruh, you thinkin' what I'm thinkin'?"

"Niggie, if your mind's on money and money's on your mind, hell yeah! Fool, we've found a gold mine!"

This place was just like Eastview, Hitman thought.

Already counting their money, the duo headed for the elevator.

"Hey! Hey, y'all two!" they heard a female yell.

They turned to face her.

She was a cute, round white girl.

"Y'all here to fix shit?" she asked.

"Somethin' like that," Hitman answered.

"Well, I'm in room 1012 and I need some fixin'," she stated, hands on her hips.

Flaco wrote down the room number and they jumped on the elevator.

Chapter 27

Life & Death

...We trap or die nigga/ we trap or die nigga... You know these hoes love a nigga/ 'cause they know the truth/ gotta Chevy same color Tropicana orange juice (Yyyeeeaaah!)... We trap or die nigga/ we trap or die nigga...

Flaco reached over and turned the van's radio down as he pulled in front of Hitman's 94th Street duplex. The Delta Vert that he'd given Hitman was parked in the driveway behind Hitman's new Chrysler 300.

"My niggie, we gotta celebrate! What's up with tonight?"

"What you wanna do?" Hitman replied.

"Let's hit the Coco Cobana!"

"Fuck is that?"

"It's a Spanish club in Hialeah."

Hitman had never been there before. "Aiight, come get me 'bout eight." He exited the van.

"For sho'!" Flaco exclaimed and pulled off.

"Hard day?" Hitman heard a familiar female voice ask as he entered his fence.

It was his *fine-ass* tenant/neighbor. He hadn't noticed her sitting on her side of the porch when he'd gotten out of the van.

She always seemed to have something sexy on, Hitman thought as he took a seat on the steps — eye level with her *snatch*. She had her legs open and her shorts really weren't shorts at all — merely a layer of insubstantial fabric — because they did nothing to veil her *succulent opening* and shapely caramel thighs.

"It'll get better," Hitman answered her.

"Yeah," she said with a sigh. "That's what they say."

The two had shared a few meaningless conversations in the past.

If there was anything covetous in her intent it had gotten right past him. Other than her skimpy wear and warm smile, she didn't communicate anything sexual.

Hitman didn't have anyone in his life — relationship wise. And he hadn't had sex since that last night he'd spent with Tracey. Memories of that night were so vivid in his mind. Tracey's taste, smell, the feel of her wetness was etched in his brain. Most nights he masturbated in light of what they'd shared.

Feeling himself about to rise, Hitman rose and said, "You take it easy, Miss Donnie."

"I've told you about that *Miss* mess. Just Donnie," she straightened him, her eyes shifting to the tent growing in his pants.

"My bad, Mi-... Donnie," Hitman replied, apologizing for calling her *Miss* and for the embarrassing *woodie* he'd exposed to her.

She smiled that smile of hers and he turned, hurriedly he entered his house, wishing that he would've never stopped in the first place.

While showering, Hitman fought the urge to *jack-off* on the images of Miss Donnie's smooth legs and fat camel-toe print. It had been a while since he'd had any feminine affection.

He quickly toweled off, slipped on some Polo boxer briefs and poured himself a triple-shot of *Jack Daniels Black*. He downed the drink quickly and poured himself another triple. He had another six hours before Flaco was due to scoop him. The strong whiskey, muddled with his raging hormones, commanded him to go next door and beat that ole-ass pussy up, *'cause you know her fine-ass want it.* But common sense and respect for Miss Donnie demanded that he sit his ass down and watch the news.

Hitman sighed heavily. With drink in one hand and the remote in the other, he sat his ass down and watched the news. There was a special news bulletin concerning the fatal shooting in Sanford, Florida.

...Trayvon Martin, a 17-year-old student of Miami Carol City High School was shot to death while in Sanford, Florida visiting his father.

Reports indicate that Mr. Martin was walking home from the store in this gated community with only a cell phone and a pack of Skittles on his person, when he realized he was being followed.

At the time of this incident, Mr. Martin was on his cell phone with his girlfriend who heard the whole incident over the phone... the recorded conversation and the 911 tapes of Zimmerman's [the shooter] call clearly shows that young Trayvon was not the aggressor.

Public sympathy has poured in from the entire nation, with comments coming from the President himself, the nerdy looking white anchorman said and the scene panned to different individuals speaking on the tragic event.

The first woman said, "Trayvon was not a trouble maker, he kept to himself and made us laugh."

The second young woman, one of Trayvon's classmates and best friend said, "When I listened to the 911 tapes and heard Trayvon crying, I just couldn't believe it. That was my best friend...

I believe this is an eye opener. It took Trayvon's murder for some in America to wake up and see racism still exists..."

Another classmate said, "Trayvon was a very mature and nice person. I want Zimmerman to go to jail and be charged as a murderer!"

"Listen here, that cracka can talk that stand your ground sh— *beeep*— all he want to! But to shoot a young man who was unarmed and not be arrested can't happen! It's bullsh—*beeep*— and it ain't right. We ought to tear this bit—*beeeep*— up!" the angry middle-age man stated.

"I think it's fuc—*beeep*— up how fool gunned lil' one down. But it's even more fuc—*beeeep*—up how these fake as—*beeeep*— hypocrite muthafuc—*beeeep*— like Al Sharpton, Jessie Jackson, with his bitc—*beeeep*—as—*beeep*— all in front the cameras like some ho—*beeeep*— like they really care 'bout nig—*beeeep*— and shi—*beeeeep*— but had lil' Trayvon been convicted of some earlier shi—*beeeeep*— or had a lil' raw-half on him or somethin', wouldn't nobody be fightin' for him. He'd just be dead and the murder would've been swept under the rug. And for real, that's fuc— *beeeep*—up. 'Cause just 'cause a nig—*beeeep*— done been convicted or might get on a lil' *slight*, it don't mean he don't deserve justice," a young dude with long dreadlocks and a runny nose explained.

"I can only imagine what his parents are going through and when I think about this boy, I think about my kids, and I think every parent in America should be able to understand why it is absolutely imperative that we investigate every aspect of this and that everybody pulls together, federal, state and local, to figure out how this tragedy happened," President Barack Obama said before the cameras. "You know, if I had a son, he'd look like Trayvon. All of us have to do some soul-searching to figure out how does something like this happen..."

The camera then panned back to the anchorwoman.

As of now, Zimmerman is still uncharged... she said.

Hitman clicked off the TV wishing he'd never clicked it on. In that instance he thought about right and wrong. He looked at his own life and Trayvon's death. Hitman thought about God and wondered why God would allow him to continue to trap and let an innocent youth like Trayvon die, *murdered in cold blood?*

It was times like this that showed the world itself. The racism and injustice. The intense hate for a people, black people, trapped in this shit to die...

Chapter 28
Jazzy?!

…Why y'all trippin'/ I'm just fine/ 12:45/ It's 'bout that time/ Been netted all week/ Time to unwind/ Can't spell sober/ Lose my mine… This shit crazy/ Way to pack/ Rosé baby/ Waste two stacks/ Hardest thang in the lot/ That there mine/ Can't spell sober/ Lose my mind…

Young Jeezy's LOSE MY MIND blasted throughout the predominantly Spanish establishment. The *Coco Cobona* was the Spanish version of Jay-Z's 40/40 Club, only the *Coco Cobana* featured a full nude review with its expensive drinks, exotic cuisine, and bomb music selection. Tonight DJ Mil-Matik from Wilmington, Delaware's WJKS 101.7 FM was warming up the *one's and two's.*

Flaco and Hitman stepped up into the spot and found a table in the restaurant area of the club, which was located in the very back of the 64,000 square foot split-level club. The club was an old grocery store that sat off of 103rd Street — in Hialeah's warehouse district. The owners had gutted the building and completely refurbished it. Aside from having great food, a perfect blend of music and the largest dance floor in Florida, the *Coco Cabana's* biggest feature was the *32,000 square foot* glass floor that separated the bottom level of the club from the upstairs level. So as Hitman and the other seven-hundred-something club patrons partied, dined on exotic meals, or sipped expensive drinks, they could look up and view the scene upstairs — the best being the sexy women wearing short dresses and skirts. People came from everywhere to party at Hialeah's *Coco Cobana.*

Hitman ordered another bottle of *Jack Daniels Black* and watched as the G-string wearing, topless blonde sashayed off to one of the club's five bars to get his bottle. He'd never seen a night club as big as this one. Occasionally, he'd peek up at the shaking asses above him — surprised to see that some chicks were not wearing panties.

"Fool, you need to stop watchin' and VIP the damn thang one time, my niggie!" Flaco screamed over the loud music, taking a seat at the table. He'd just came back from the VIP for the third time. Each time he'd left with a different $750 chick.

"Nah, playboy, I'ma leave all the trickin' to you," Hitman responded, still looking at the asses above him.

"Fool, it's only trickin' when you ain't got it. I got it, my niggie, so I'ma ball."

When the waitress arrived with Hitman's bottle of *Jack Daniels Black*, Flaco promptly sent her back to the bar for two bottles of Ace of Spade.

* * *

A group of young strippers sat around their dressing room lockers counting their money, plotting out last minute dates and preparing to leave. It had been a long night of shaking ass, selling pussy — for those that choose to get that VIP money — and chasing tips. Now they were ready to go home and get some much needed rest — at least those that didn't have scheduled big money dates were going home. Jazzy was one. She counted out her $1,100 and placed the money in her overnight bag with the rest of her stuff. It hadn't been a great night, but it was a good one nonetheless. She'd stayed upstairs all night.

"*Mmmm, hmmm,* honey," one of the fine-ass Spanish strippers said to her partner. "We worked his ass, huh, girl?"

"We damn sho' did!" the girl's partner replied and the two high-fived each other.

A third stripper laughed as she counted out her $3,500. "These niggas are sweet as pussy-pie! They dumb asses out there robbin' banks and sellin' drugs just so they can come spend it with Sunshine... honey, I'm *servin'* these ducks."

"Shit, better we get it than the police." The Spanish stripper laughed her agreement and turned to Jazzy, who hadn't said anything the whole while. "Jazzy, girl, you better get off your little high horse and hit that VIP, where the real money's at... 'cause shit, I know you don't think you're better than us, like you're too good to sell some pussy. 'Cause, baby, we're all in here strippin' together."

Bitch I am too good! Jazzy wanted to say, but she held her tongue, because she'd already been through all of that tricking mess when she was younger. At age 15, Jazzy, named Jasmine by her father, who was serving 30 years in prison, had issues with her mother that forced her out into the streets; where she prostituted herself to survive. But thankfully, at age 16, Jasmine was blessed to have briefly come in contact with a very special man — one of God's finest and most caring. In less than an hour he'd been able to show her what she hadn't been able to see on her own — that she was worth much more than the life she was living. That night was her last night as a prostitute and she could not see herself going back to that. *I might be strippin', but I got my GED, my dreams and my pride*, she thought to herself. *And as soon as I save up this lil' money, I'ma get my own lil' place and enroll at Dade Community College. So, nah, fuck that turnin' tricks shit!* "I'm good, y'all do y'all and I'ma do me," Jazzy said to the three money hungry females.

"*Ppsstt!*" the Spanish stripper's partner said. "Well excuse the fuck outta us!"

"Yeah, for real, right?" the stripper named Sunshine commented before getting back to the money. "That one guy, the balling-ass Puerto Rican who fucked all three of us, what do you two think about him?"

"The dick was pretty good and he was fine," the Spanish chick's partner said.

The Spanish chick and Sunshine both looked at her like she was crazy.

"What?!" she asked, catching their cold gazes.

"I wasn't talkin' about his sex, stupid. What do you think about his pockets?"

"Oh, well, I think he has money. Shit, he paid $2,250 to fuck us."

"Yeah," the Spanish chick concurred. "Plus he's all jewelry'd up and just before I came back here the waitress took him two bottles of Ace of Spade. Shit, those bottles are $3,000 a piece!"

Sunshine nodded and whipped out her phone. "Y'all two go hold him down while I put this thang in motion," she said, dialing a number.

The two strippers grabbed their things and hurried off.

Jazzy shook her head in disgust. *Somebody gon' end up hurtin' one of them trifling-ass hoes*, she thought to herself...

Chapter 29

Hitman?!

Jazzy was so damn tired and sleepy she could barely carry her overnight bag. She could not wait to climb into her bed. This night life was truly getting the best of her.

Club patrons, employees, and other strippers all waved and called out to Jazzy as she promenaded through the sparsely crowded club. It was now 2:00 a.m. and the club had thinned out tremendously.

Passing the bar, Jazzy saw Spanish Lust and her stupid co-conspirator talking to a handsome, well built guy. He was Spanish and had a lot of jewelry on, so Jazzy figured that he was the Puerto Rican guy that they'd been discussing in the dressing room.

Probably gon' rob that damn boy, she thought, rolling her eyes at the two women when they looked her way. Jazzy was a real no-nonsense-type of chick. She was outspoken and often perceived as a *bitch* with a funky attitude by those outside of her circle — and being that she rolled alone no one really liked her. But that was cool by her. Life and the people in it had done enough to her and nothing at all for her. So her loyalties in life were to Jasmine, *fuck everybody else*. Being used was old news.

Jazzy hated going home to the confusion of her mother's household, but until she got her own there was no place else to go. She cursed herself for not parking up front. Not only because she was dead tired and hated walking, but also because of the fake-ass parking lot pimps with their lame-ass pick up lines and constant harassment. They pestered all of the strippers, but Jazzy they harassed the most — and it was very easy to see why. Jazzy was a total red-bone with long jet-black hair, sexy slated eyes, and pouty lips. Sylphlike to a degree, Jazzy was 5'8" tall, weighed exactly 121 pounds and posted measurements of 32C-24-36. Combine that with her naturally long lashed and *boss-bitch* attitude and it was quite easy to see why ballers came from everywhere to see her get naked. She was now 18-years-old and far more sophisticated — mentally and physically — than the 16-year-old tramp she'd once been. *God, I thank you for that day at the Days Inn*, she sort of prayed, inwardly remembering him. But he was probably dead or in jail, because that's what usually happened to the real street dudes.

Jazzy glanced to her right and saw a *clean-ass* 1967 Pontiac Firebird. The convertible top was down and the light from the light poles in the parking lot sparkled off of the Firebird's platinum-gray paint and 18" factory chrome and black rims. The car was tight work. And had it not been for the beautiful automobile, she would have missed him.

Jazzy thought for a minute that her eyes were playing tricks on her. Or perhaps her being so tired, maybe she was actually *dreaming on her feet*. She wiped at her sleepy eyes and looked a little closer. The realization of who she was looking at caused her to gasp loudly and drop her bag. *Oh my damn God!?* she thought, covering her open mouth in shock.

Hitman downed the last of his bottle and looked around the club. Everything seemed to be tinted in red and moving in slow motion. It had thinned out considerably, which to him was a good indication that it was time to go home.

"Bruh, you ready?"

"Shiiid, niggie, for another round of bottles?" Flaco answered.

"Hell nah! You know we gotta handle that business in the a.m."

"Yeah, fool, but we —" Flaco stopped mid-sentence. Two of his earlier conquests were eyeing him from the bar. "Hey, you wanna get those hoes and flex?"

Hitman looked. The two chicks were definitely bad, but he wasn't feeling it. "Nah, hell nah, I'm good."

"My niggie, I'm tellin' you, you don't know what you're missin'. That bitch Spanish Lust is crucial! My niggie, that bitch got that *zip tight!*"

"Count me out," Hitman told his main man. "Give me the car keys, I'ma be outside."

"For sho'!" Flaco said, tossing him the keys.

Hitman caught them and strutted towards the exit.

A warm Miami breeze greeted him on the outside.

It was sobering.

He looked around the parking lot and saw the many expensive cars, which made him question his being there. Why was he there? No answer came from within so he looked to God. The dark sky, God's heaven, hosted an array of bright stars. One in particular was blinking. He'd heard earlier in life that when a star burns out that it was indicative of life's final trial to man — death. *I wonder if that's the lil' dude Trayvon I seent on TV*, Hitman thought, his mind relenting to the pull of the *Jack Daniels Black*. Thinking of Trayvon made him think of Cameron and Quan. *That coulda easily been them on TV*, he mused, but was uncertain as to whether the world would have even cared.

A car started and its loud music broke his contemplation. Not sure as to exactly how long he'd been stuck there gazing into the heavens, Hitman shook it off and made his way through the parking lot.

Stopping in front of Flaco's new ride, Hitman admired it. It was a beautiful monster. From its color to the reworked lower valance and custom side-exit exhaust, the convertible Firebird separated itself from every car in the lot. Walking along the side of the car, Hitman rubbed where the door handle *would have been,* had they not been shaved. He hit the alarm, *chirp!* and the driver's door slowly popped open. *This is what $75,000 gets you, huh? Bad muthafucka*, he thought and slid inside. He then hit a switch and let the top down — for some reason he felt it brought him closer to God.

Slouched back against the soft black ostrich seats, Hitman found himself once again gazing up into the dark expanses of space that hovered infinitely over the earth. It had been over two years since he'd smoked a blunt, but right at that instance he wished he had one. Maybe even a guardian angel. *Yeah, a heavenly custodian to help a nigga through the wrong I'm doin'... 'cause it can't be right. Not when I've lost my dogs and been ostracized from the only place I ever knew as home... I finally found love, but even that's gone. Like the song said, 'Just let it die, with no goodbyes, details don't matter, we both paid the price'... But how long a nigga gotta pay?* he wondered. Knowing that when it was all said and done, life would be what life was, what it had always been, and he'd end up *Served Again.*

Hitman touched the 30" platinum Cuban-link that held a diamond crucifix and the four and a half karat white oval diamond ring, the ring he'd bought for a special someone, but had never given it to her. It was the only jewelry he wore. And he wore it as a reminder of the *dangers of love*. Lifting the ring and crucifix to his lips, Hitman kissed them and wished upon that blinking star.

That's when he heard a loud thud — as if something heavy had been dropped — and a woman's shriek.

Hitman sat completely up and saw *a fine-ass* red-bone standing there covering her mouth. She was wearing some purple satin short-shorts, heels and a satin floral print button-up shirt, which was almost completely unbuttoned, but tied above her navel, showcasing her smooth flat belly and juicy young breasts. Her smooth red legs seemed to curve for days and her long black hair hung perfectly below her shoulders. She was beautiful, yet familiar.

Where have I seen shawdy befo'? Hitman asked himself, thinking that maybe he'd seen her on one of those rap videos.

"Hitman!" the chick called out. "Oh my God, Hitman, is that you?"

He squinched his eyes, trying to focus and unlock the fog that the liquor had on his brain. The girl really did look familiar.

"God, I can't believe this!" Jazzy yelled with great excitement in her eyes and voice. She ran over to the driver's side of the car and hugged Hitman around the neck. "Where have you been? I've been callin' your phone like crazy! I even ride by that raggedy-ole hotel sometimes, thinkin' I might see you."

Then a light went off in his head. *Hotel? Jasmine?* he thought, breaking her embrace and looking at her again. *Damn!* he thought. It was her, but she'd damn sure changed a lot — in all of the right places. "Ja-Jasmine?" he finally stuttered.

She sucked her teeth and almost rolled her eyes at him. "Yes, Ja-Jasmine!" she replied mockingly. "And who you *thought* I was?"

Beyonce with more ass! he wanted to say, but simply said, "Damn, girl, you've growed all the way up." He shook his head slowly as he got out of the car, looking her over completely, he couldn't believe how fine she'd gotten. She looked nothing like the skinny little 16-year-old he'd met at the Days Inn.

"I have, *haven't* I?" Jasmine replied smartly and spun around for him to peep everything.

Smiling, Hitman said, "Yeah, you really have. But what's good with you? What're you doin' out here?"

Jasmine smiled back at him with a mixture of seduction and joyful innocence. "I'm out here lookin' for you," she retorted. "And I'm *sooo* glad I finally found you."

Her answer kind of threw him, but before he could respond they were interrupted.

"Todos esa curvas y yo sin frenos!" Flaco said drunkly, eyeing Jasmine.

Hitman and Jasmine both turned around to find Flaco standing there with Sunshine, Spanish Lust and their other stripper partner.

"What did you say?" Jasmine asked with an attitude.

Laughing, Spanish Lust translated what Flaco had said. "He said, 'All those curves and I ain't got no brakes'."

Jasmine sucked her teeth and rolled her eyes.

Flaco and the three strippers moved towards the car.

"What's up, fool? We 'bout to go party. Let's go."

Hitman wasn't going nowhere but home. He turned to tell Jasmine this, but she stopped him, speaking before he could.

"Umm, Hitman, check this out, let me holla at you over here." When they were out of earshot, she asked, "You with dude?"

"Yeah."

"Is he your peoples, *peoples*? Like, do you really vibe with him?"

"Hell yeah. We're like bruthas."

Jasmine sighed. "Well, umm, look, I don't want my name in this shit, and for real, I shouldn't be runnin' my mouth, but he don't need to be goin' nowhere with them."

Hitman raised an eyebrow. "Why?"

"Because those hoes are triflin'... and they're gonna rob him if he goes with them."

"How you know?"

"Look, it don't even matter. I've told you, now it's on you. But whatever happens, I don't want my damn name in it."

Hitman looked at her for a minute. "Aiight, let me holla at him."

"Hold up, boy!" Jasmine grabbed his arm. "You gon' ride with me, so we can finish talkin'?"

"I don't know, I got –"

"You gotta make me look good!" Jasmine said, cutting him off. "If you just go over there and say something to fuck up their plans and don't leave with me it's gonna look like I just pulled you over here to expose them."

Hitman nodded. "You're right, I'll be right back."

He walked over, pulled Flaco to the side and pulled his coat to the chicks' plot against him. Flaco's face turned red as fire.

"Just make up a lie 'bout something and back out, bruh. You feel me?"

Flaco nodded. "For sho'. I got you."

Hitman patted him on the back and walked off with Jasmine.

As soon as they were down the parking lot and getting into Jasmine's car, Flaco turned and got into his Firebird, mean-mugging the three strippers as he walked by.

"Poppi," Spanish Lust called out before approaching the driver's side. She caught the harsh stare. "What's wrong? We still party, right?"

Flaco looked at her and the veins in his neck popped out. "Bitch, you see this?" he asked, pointing to the three slashes in his eyebrow. "That means I'm fuckin' crazy, bitch! I'll fuckin' kill you bitches! 'Cause I'm fuckin' sick!" he screamed and fired up the Firebird's twin-turbo 427ci LSX engine. Without saying anything further he peeled out, smoking the parking lot as he sped off.

Chapter 30
We Both Know

... I know you've been hurt by/ someone else/ I can tell by the way you/ carry yourself... if you let me/ here's what I'll do/ I'll take care of you... I've loved and I've lost...

Rihanna's beautiful voice flowed smoothly from Hitman's home system.

Jasmine sat beside him on the love seat. Her pretty China-doll eyes danced as they talked. They'd arrived at his house only thirty minutes ago. And when Hitman had gotten out of the car, expecting her to pull off, to his surprise, Jasmine had also gotten out of the car and followed him inside of the house.

...What's a life with no fun/ please don't be so ashamed... I've had mine/ you've had yours/ we both know [we know]... They don't get you like I will/ my only wish is I die real/ 'Cause that truth hurts/ and those lies heal...

It had been a long time since they'd seen one another. And they had both changed a lot. Jasmine had thought about him so much over the past two years. Wishing that she could find him, wanting so bad to be with him. Because of him she'd improved herself, in hopes of showing him that she was worthy of his time.

Now here he was before her and she could not figure out what to say.

...I'll be there for you/ I will care for you/ I keep thinking you/ just don't know... Try to run from that/ say you're done with that/ on your face girl/ it just don't show...

Hitman couldn't keep his eyes from between her young thighs. She looked so tempting. Any man in his right mind would've been all over her. After all, she was beautiful. However, Hitman's heart was somewhere else — with someone else. And he'd never been one to mislead or take advantage of a woman's feelings for him.

...When you're ready/ just say you're ready/ when all the baggage/ just ain't as heavy... And the party's over/ just don't forget me/ We'll change the pace/ and we'll just go slow...

"So, umm, why didn't you ever call me?"

Hitman shrugged. "I left the number in the rental van."

"Well, why you ain't never answer the phone when I called you?"

"You're probably not gonna believe this, but I lost that phone," he answered half truthfully. The phone had been taken by the police. However, when it was returned they'd placed a bug in it. Once he found out he'd promptly used it to his advantage and gotten rid of the phone.

"Well, umm, did you ever think about me?" Jasmine asked, staring deeply into his eyes.

"Umm," he said, thinking of the best way to answer the question without hurting her feelings or leading her on. "Yeah, I've got a lil sister, so every time she does something good in school or whatever, I'd be like, I wonder if Jasmine's handlin' her business? You feel me?"

Yeah, I feel you. I feel you're fulla shit! 'Cause I ain't yo' lil' sister, she wanted to tell his ass, but instead she shared a more vulnerable side of her heart. "Well, I really thought about you, probably like everyday. That day I met you at the hotel really changed my life. I got outta that lifestyle I was livin' and got my GED. That's why I was blowin' your phone up. I wanted you to see what you'd done — when I walked that stage to get my GED... It was real hard a lotta times. And I ain't gon' lie, I did it for you."

"For me?" Hitman questioned, thrown by all that he was hearing.

"Yeah, for you!" Jasmine exclaimed, taking his hand in hers. "I've been through so much and nobody never cared 'bout me. Maybe my daddy, but he's locked up... So when you gave me them thousand dollars that day, it was like the closest anybody ever came to sayin' to me, *you're beautiful, you can be somebody and I love you*. At least that's how I took it... So, I said to myself, I'ma get my shit together, so when I see Hitman again he's gon' see a woman that's worthy of his time and affection."

"You got all of that outta me givin' you a rack?"

"Nah, plenty niggas have gave me money. I got all of that outta your actions! It was the things you said to me," Jasmine explained.

Her sentiments kind of choked him up a bit. He did care. He'd meant to leave a positive impression on her, however, he'd never meant for her to actually fall for him.

"Jasmine, you know you're a sweet lil' baby... but, umm, you met my girl didn't you? I mean, you remember I gotta lady, right?"

That bitch?! Boy, pulezzz! I'm finer than her, I'm prettier than her, and she can't be handlin' her business 'cause you ain't livin' here with her, Jasmine thought to herself. "Well, I'm not really trippin' off her. I'm my own woman and you're your own man. All of us are grown."

"Aiight, Jasmine, it's late."

"And?!" she said, rucking her brow. "I ain't got no where to go."

"But I gotta get up early, so –"

"So let's go to bed. I mean, we ain't gotta do nothing. And I'll cook breakfast for you in the morning," she said, smiling brightly.

Hitman laughed. "Girl, you're a trip!"

"So I can stay?" she asked excitedly.

"Yeah," he said laughing. "You can stay… but your ass is sleepin' in that guest room."

"What?"

"You heard me!"

"Are you serious?!"

Hitman didn't answer her, he just went in his bedroom and locked the door.

No this nigga didn't! Jasmine thought, laughing to herself. She was not use to men disregarding her advances. Normally it was the other way around. *Well, at least I ain't gotta go home… and thank God I finally found him!*

Jasmine went and climbed into the guest bed with the biggest smile on her face. Drake's lyrics were fresh on her mind:

You and all your girls in the club one time/ All so convinced that you're following your heart/ 'cause your mind don't control what it does sometimes…

In no time at all she was off to LaLa Land.

Chapter 31
When You're Ready

Hitman jumped up the next morning with a stir. He quickly looked around and saw that the sun was up and shining brightly through his window. *Damn!* he thought, jumping up out of his king-size bed. He'd overslept, something he never did. No matter how late he stayed up hustling or hanging out, he was always up before the sun rose. *This damn girl ain't been here ten-hot-hours and already fuckin' up my program*, Hitman mused as he entered the bathroom inside of his master bedroom.

Once he'd shitted, showered, and seen to his necessary hygiene, Hitman dressed in his blue *H&F Utility and Cleaning* work uniform and exited his bedroom. The smell of breakfast and Drake's lyrics met him as he neared the dining room.

"Damn, fool, what's up?" Flaco yelled with a mouthful of eggs, toast, and beef sausage. "You just gon' sleep all fuckin' day? You know we got work to do, fool!"

Jasmine was seated at the table with Flaco. She was drinking green tea. After laughing at the two friends' sense of playful comradery, she got up and went into the kitchen to fix Hitman a plate. She was wearing one of his T-shirts, which looked like a dress on her.

As soon as her back was turned Flaco began pumping his arms and hips as if he were having sex and mouthed the question, "Niggie, you splacked that pussy?"

Hitman waved him off and followed Jasmine into the kitchen. When they came back out they were both carrying plates and cups of orange juice. It was sweet of her to have fed Flaco but waited to eat her food with Hitman.

"My niggie," Flaco said loudly, always hyper and loud. "I'm so fuckin' proud of you!"

"For what?"

Flaco pointed at Jasmine. "I was startin' to think you was a fuckin' *gump* or somethin', fool! Always turnin' chicks down and shit. But now I see why. You had a fuckin' *dime-piece* in your pocket."

Jasmine just laughed her pretty little head off. She liked Flaco, he was cool and very funny. She was flattered that he thought she was Hitman's girl. After all, that's exactly what she wanted. That's also what Flaco wanted. He liked Jasmine and felt that she was good for his friend. They'd talked about a lot before Hitman had finally joined them. Flaco was very thankful that she'd opened his eyes to the robbery scheme that the strippers had plotted for him and assured Jasmine that she could always call on him in time of need. He'd even given her his cell number.

"I see you're a regular Kat Williams with the jokes this morning, huh?" Hitman said, laughing a bit himself.

"Nah, niggie, you need to loosen up... it's good to see you with her," Flaco answered seriously.

Hitman could see Jasmine staring at him out of the corner of his eye. She was eating up Flaco's every word. They both wanted a response to Flaco's statement, so he didn't give them one. If Flaco's thinking that he'd sleep with Jasmine, and her leading him to think that, made them both happy, then Hitman saw no need to kill their joy.

When he finished eating he called Jasmine to his bedroom.

"What're you gonna do, 'cause I gotta go to work," Hitman told her, indicating that it was time for her to go.

Jasmine caught his meaning but danced right around it. "Oh, okay, I'ma just clean up the kitchen and the bedrooms, and I guess I'll just have to chill out 'til you get back or whatever."

Hitman closed his eyes and rubbed his temple before speaking. This shit was going too far. He dug Jasmine as a friend and would help her with anything that she needed help with, but something inside of him was telling him to *send her away*.

"You don't have nothin' you need to be doin'? 'Cause I'll handle the dishes and shit when I get in. So –"

"Nah," Jasmine said, cutting him off smoothly. "It ain't no problem. I normally be sleep this time of day, so I ain't got nothing to do... you can just lock the lil' deadbolt and I'll clean up and sleep 'til you get back," Jasmine finished and walked off to clean up, like the issue had been mutually decided.

Chapter 32
Say You're Ready

The duo's very first stop was at Elliot's office to open up some new accounts for payroll. Based on what they'd seen of the City Inn they needed to hire twenty hardworking people, but knew that they'd have to make due with six, three males and three females — equal opportunity. Elliot also agreed to do the employee screening for five of the workers, Flaco already had the sixth man on deck.

With that done and out of the way, they headed over to the hotel. The scene was very much the same as it was the first day that they'd showed up to inspect their new million dollar trap. Hookers of all colors, shapes, and sizes were working the parking lot and lobby. Bambi greeted her two new supervisors with greetings that were cheerful, yet hinged on seduction. It was obvious that she was used to playing the game.

Their plan was to start in the lobby, hit the old lounge/restaurant area, and clear out the warehouse-dock area behind the restaurant — they were making that their office headquarters. Once that was complete they planned to refurbish the ballroom, which was also located on the first floor, just beyond the restaurant — the hotel rented the ballroom to One Love Baptist Church on Sundays and to the Nation of Islam Study Group on

Friday nights. Other than those nights the ballroom was empty. From there they would hit the tenth floor and work their way back down to the second floor — painting, repairing, and seeing who exactly was doing what. By the time they finished refurbishing the rundown hotel they planned to have the trap going HAMM!

When Flaco pulled the work van up to Hitman's place, they could hear Trey Songz's SEX AIN'T BETTER THAN LOVE blasting loudly from his side of the duplex. Flaco laughed, knowing that his partner had his hands full with the fast young beauty. Hitman sighed loudly and slowly got out of the van. He knew that Miss Donnie was probably having a damn fit over the loud music.

Hitman opened his front door and was met by the clean smell of pine oil and the aroma of curried chicken and rice. He looked in the kitchen for Jasmine and then on the coffee table for the remote to the sound system — he found neither. Frustrated, he checked the guest room and then the hallway bathroom. *Where the hell is this girl at?* he asked no one as he headed toward his bedroom. He pushed the room door open and there laying on her stomach with her legs wide open, in his bed in only a G-string, Jasmine lay talking on the phone. She did not see him enter because she was facing the headbord. Nor did she hear his approach because of the blaring music.

Hitman's anger slowly subsided as he stared into her meaty center. Her ass was so perfect. Not too red. Not too dark. Not too big. And surely not too small. Had she not had her shapely red legs open so that he could see the silky yellow material of her G-string hugging the fullness of her pussy, he would've thought she was completely naked, because her ass had totally swallowed the string holding her thong together.

Lord have mercy! Hitman said inwardly, feeling himself growing stiffer by the second. He also felt his anger returning, because he wasn't supposed to be aroused by her. And she wasn't supposed to be laying in his bed in only a G-string.

Picking up the remote that lay on his dresser, Hitman clicked off the sound system.

The sudden silence caused Jasmine to jump up and spin around to face him.

"Boy!" she screamed, her juicy titties bounced, but stood up firm. Her nipples were pinkish-red. "You scared the shit outta me."

"I'm the one that ought to be scared," he shot back, pointing at her nakedness. "You got the music all blastin', then I open my door and you're in my bed naked."

Jasmine sucked her teeth and rolled her eyes at him. "Aye," she said into her phone. "I'ma hit you back later, girl. I gotta go."

"Yeah, and you gotta put some clothes on."

Jasmine peeped his little attitude and started to *blink* on his ass. She'd cleaned up his whole house and cooked for his ass, but all he could think to do was catch a fucking attitude. *No! He got Jazzy Jasmine fucked straight up!* she thought as she pulled his big T-shirt back on. *Flaco might be right, this nigga actin' like a damn gump!*

"Okay, you straight now?!" she asked him.

I'm not 'bout to argue with this lil' girl, he told himself. "Yeah," he responded dryly and readjusted his stiff dick.

"Well, are you hungry?"

"I guess."

"Well go wash your hands and come eat," Jasmine commanded and headed off to the kitchen to fix their plates.

Hitman shook his head. Jasmine was just too much for him to handle. They weren't even a couple, yet here they were having their first lovers' spat. Hitman was a general and very much use to giving orders and controlling his troops; however, dealing with aggressive women was a real task for him. And everything inside of him was telling him to send shorty away.

I'ma send her ass away aiight... I'ma end up gettin' that slick-ass mouth, that's what's gon' happen... she ain't gon' keep gettin' out on me, he silently declared.

The two ate in relative silence. The food was damn good, he had to admit.

Jasmine got up when they were done eating and cleared the dishes.

Hitman stood to help her.

"I got it... I don't need no help," she sort of snapped at him.

Damn! Well excuse me, he thought as he moved toward the front door. He needed some fresh air — and time away from Jasmine's crazy-ass.

Seated on the cushioned bench that he'd bought from Home Depot, Hitman took a deep breath and slowly let it out. Again he wished that he had some 'dro to blow, but was very thankful that he didn't. Smoking weed was a habit that he didn't need. Especially with Jasmine already drivng him crazy.

He thought about Americus and wondered what Dee was doing. *Is she still mad at me?*

What is Keisha doing? *That's probably one girl I shoulda fucked.*

He wondered whether TrapGril was in town. *I hope Dee playin' fair with my lil' homegirl.*

Black? he thought. He knew that Black was doing good for himself. Black had really changed, but Hitman wasn't sure if it was for the better.

Then his mind shifted gears and switched to Tracey. *Damn I love and miss that girl!* He seriously wondered whether he should've asked her to leave with him. *Would she have come with a nigga? Was I wrong for leavin'?* Again he remembered their last night together. But just as fast as the images of him and Tracey entered his mine, flashbacks of Jasmine laying across his bed with her smooth, toned legs bussed-wide-open invaded his thoughts. *I don't 'posed to be thinkin' that!* he told himself.

"Get it together," he said out loud.

"Excuse me?"

Hitman jumped at the sound of the female voice.

It was *fine-ass* Miss Donnie standing there in some tight little coochie shorts.

"Talkin' to myself," Hitman said, a sly smile on his face.

"Loud music will do that," Miss Donnie replied, seating herself on the bench with him.

He snuck another peek at her fat lower-lips before saying, "I'm sorry 'bout that."

"No problem," she smoothly stated. "House guest?"

Hitman nodded. And before he could further explain, Jasmine came outside with her overnight bag slung over her shoulder and a triple-shot of *Jack Daniels Black* in her hand. She was wearing an orange cotton Dolphins sweatsuit.

"I'm 'bout to go to work," she said and passed him the drink she'd fixed for him.

"Aiight, thanks," Hitman managed to say. The situation felt awkward. Like maybe he'd just gotten caught cheating, even though that wasn't the case. "Jasmine, this is Miss Donnie, my tenant. And Miss –"

"Donnie," she cut him off. "Don't call me *Miss*, it makes me feel old," she finished with a smile.

Hmph! That's 'cause your ass is old! Jasmine thought but said nothing.

"My bad, Donnie, but this is Jasmine, my lil' partner."

"Hello, Jasmine," Miss Donnie greeted.

"Hello to you, too, *Miss* Donnie," Jasmine replied, purposely emphasizing the *Miss*. She then quickly turned her attention back to Hitman and said, "I'll see you later."

With that said, she sashayed off, putting a little extra in her switch because she knew that both Hitman and Miss Donnie were watching.

Chapter 33
Too Good To Be...

Boom! Boom! Boom! Boom! the loud knocking resonated from the front door. Hitman jumped up out of his sleep and snatched the Pocket Rocket from beneath the pillow. His walk to the living room was brisk — almost a jog. His heartbeat matched his steps. He hoped that nothing had happened with Flaco.

Boom! Boom! Boom! the loud banging came even harder.

"Yeah, who is it?" Hitman shouted from beside the door.

"Jasmine!"

"Who?" Hitman asked back, knowing damn well Jasmine wasn't banging on his door at 3:20 in the a.m.

"Don't play, Hitman! You know this me out here!" Jasmine yelled back, ending all debate as to whether it was her or not.

Hitman unlocked and snatched the door open. "Girl, are you crazy? You know what time it is?"

Jasmine came in with her overnight bag. She was still wearing the orange Dolphins sweatsuit. There were aqua contact lens in her eyes that he hadn't noticed earlier. They matched her orange, aqua, and white Air Max.

"Well, you know what time I get off, right?" she curtly replied.

"Yeah, but I didn't expect you to come over here."

Jasmine put her hand on her hip and rolled her neck as she spoke. "I don't see why not! I did tell your butt, clear as day, that *I'd see you later*. Didn't I?"

"*Later*, like tomorrow at regular hours. Or like next week for lunch. Like, I'll call you and we'll get together *later*," Hitman shot back, obviously pissed.

Sucking her pretty white teeth, Jasmine said, "Okay, I'm sorry if I didn't express myself to your satisfaction, but I'm here now, I'm tired, and I'm not gon' even argue with you. It's late and I'm goin' to sleep."

Jasmine walked off to the guest room and closed the door.

No this lil' bitch didn't just walk up in my crib at damn near 4:00 a.m. and beat me gettin' mad when I checked her 'bout the shit?! Hitman started to go right in that room and straighten her slick-ass, but he figured that she was probably naked by now and that would be another argument to be had. Deciding to hold off on the confrontation, Hitman went back to his master bedroom and went back to sleep.

* * *

It seemed that Hitman had just dozed off when light tapping on his bedroom door brought him out of his slumber. The sun wasn't beaming through the window so he hadn't overslept. Pulling the comforter up to his waist, Hitman told Jasmine to come in.

She opened the door and greeted him with a good morning and quickly left the doorway, leaving the bedroom door open. When she stepped back in she was carrying a food tray stacked with pancakes, fluffy yellow eggs and smoked beef links; fresh strawberries, orange slices and cream; and in two large flutes was chilled champagne. Destiny Child's CATER played softly.

The food looked and smelt great, but it was a far second when compared to the way Jasmine looked and smelt. Her hair was swept up into a bun. The black silk teddy hugged her every womanly curve — stopping just below the spot where he knew her succulent *pleasure mound* was waiting to peek out. *Diamonds* was her fragrance. Looking at her was like watching the sun rise over the Atlantic in the mountainsides of Nassau — something you would have to experience to understand its true beauty. Jasmine was what romantics spent a lifetime trying to create.

Hitman felt an instant erection.

As Jasmine sat the tray down and began arranging things on the large king-size bed, Hitman got up and did everything that men did in the bathroom every morning before facing the cruel world. Jasmine was laying with her back to the headboard, eating a ripe strawberry with cream covering it, when he exited the bathroom. The food tray sat beside her, leaving his side of the bed open for him to lounge.

Hitman really didn't know what to think. He knew exactly what she was thinking, but it was not that type of party whereas he was concerned.

"You hungry?" Jasmine asked before swallowing the last of her whip-cream covered strawberry and sucking the cream residue from her delicate fingers.

He knew that he was supposed to be mad at her, but something inside of him wouldn't allow him to stand his ground and decline her invitation.

"Yeah, I could eat," he said reluctantly.

Jasmine smiled brighter than the sun.

He loved her smile.

"Well sit down then," she sang seductively. "And let me cater to you, 'cause you deserve it."

Hitman positioned himself on his side of the bed and Jasmine started out by finger-feeding him a strawberry with cream covering it... then an orange slice. After eating an orange slice herself, Jasmine fed the both of them eggs, pancakes, and sausage from the same fork. Occassionally, they sipped from their champagne flutes. Jasmine never stopped looking into his eyes. She was loving her moment. Hitman couldn't wait for the last morsel of food to be consumed so that he could end this little game that she was playing.

"You want desert?" Jasmine asked seductively.

"Nah, lil' momma, but thanks. The food was good."

"How 'bout the service? Did you enjoy my caterin'?"

"If I was into the romance thing, it would've been perfect. But shawdy, I'm thuggin' it, you feel me," Hitman lied through his explanation. *It would've been perfect if you had been Tracey,* was actually the truth.

"Well excuse me, thug, my bad." Jasmine gave him attitude and exposed a little more thigh and buttock than he was ready to see under the circumstances.

She took the tray back into the kitchen and started cleaning up.

Hitman quickly dressed for work, knowing that Flaco would soon be there to pick him up.

"So, look, Jasmine, I'm 'bout to head off to work in a few," he said, entering the kitchen where she stood washing dishes.

"Okay." She continued doing what she was doing, not even turning to face him.

"Okay, what are you gon' do? 'Cause I gotta go."

"What do you mean, *what I'm gon' do?* You know I ain't got nowhere to go," Jasmine said, meaning it both figuratively and literally. "I was just gon' clean up and then go to sleep, that's it."

Hitman shook his head slowly. This shit with Jasmine was going too far. "Jasmine, look, this is my space, lil' momma, and I'm used to livin' a certain way, and —"

Jasmine stopped him mid-sentence. "Oh, so I'm in your way?!"

"I didn't say that!"

"You might as well!" Jasmine snapped back. "You act like I'm just layin' 'round. Like I don't get your food together three times a day! Like I don't clean up behind me and you! Like I don't get up and go my ass to work. I've been bussin' my ass tryna show you I'm cool peoples and that I'll go above and beyond my duties to see my peoples happy."

"But I'm not your peoples, Jasmine. I gotta lady."

Tears welled up in her pretty eyes. "You know what? Nigga, fuck you!" Jasmine said. "You want me outta your way, cool, I'm gone... you're too good for somebody like me, but it's all good."

Jasmine stormed off and locked herself in the hallway bathroom.

"Damn!" Hitman said out loud. This is exactly what he didn't want to happen. Because there was no doubt as to whether he had love for Jasmine. It just wasn't the kind of love she wanted. "Jasmine," he said, tapping lightly on the bathroom door. He could hear her crying as he stood there. "Jasmine," he repeated.

"I'ma get out of your house... just leave me alone," she replied through tears.

A horn blew out front. He knew that it was Flaco.

"Jasmine, I gotta go... we'll talk when I get back, okay."

He stood there waiting, but there was no response. Only more crying and sniffling.

Hitman sighed heavily and left the house.

Chapter 34
Take Care

Hitman basically stumbled through his day. They managed to complete the work on the lobby and their new office area. The work on the restaurant/lounge was left incomplete because they had yet to convince Jose to buy the new cooking range, oven, and other necessities. Still, he was pleased with what they accomplished.

When Flaco pulled up to his crib, Hitman just jumped out. He wasn't in the mood for jokes or small talk. All he wanted to do was clear the air with Jasmine and hopefully salvage their friendship.

Opening the door, he was greeted by the soulful wails of the heroine of all scarred women... *I'm not gon' cry/ I'm not gon' cry/ I'm not gon' shed no tears... No I'm not gon' cry/ 'cause this is not the time/ you're not worth my tears... I know there are no guarantees/ love second chances/ sometimes it seems unfair to me... Look at the circumstance...* Mary J. Blige sang.

He could smell the aroma of steak and potatoes. That surprised him. He had not expected Jasmine to cook under the current circumstances.

Slowly he walked towards the guest room, where he found Jasmine writing in a tablet.

She saw him standing in the doorway and looked up in his direction.

"Hey," he said, staring at her.

"What's up?" she replied, setting her tablet aside.

"You okay?"

"Yeah, I'm good," Jasmine said, standing. "You hungry?"

"Yeah, I could eat somethin'."

"I got you," Jasmine told him and walked off to the kitchen.

Hitman washed up and then followed her to the dining area.

There was only one plate on the table. It was full of steak, potatoes, and wild rice.

"You not eatin'?" Hitman sat down.

"Nah, I ain't got no appetite." There was sorrow in her voice.

"Well, after I eat, you wanna talk?"

"I'm good... It really ain't nothin' to talk about. I'ma just leave — give you your space."

"So you fucked up with me?" he asked, feeling bad about the way things were going down.

"Nah." She shook her head. "I can't be mad at nothin' that happened."

"Then why are you lookin' and actin' like that?"

"Because... I guess, because I finally met my hero and he wasn't who I thought he was," Jasmine stated and left the room.

Hitman didn't know what to say or do. He sat there playing over his food, trying to come up with the right words. Nothing came to him.

Jasmine reappeared, dressed in tight jeans, a tight baby-T, and four-inch heels. Her overnight bag was slung over her shoulder.

"I'm gone."

"Okay, you be easy, lil' momma."

Jasmine waved and walked out.

Hitman ate a few more bites of food and placed the plate in the microwave.

He hoped that Jasmine would be okay...

When he walked into his room he smelt her perfume. *Diamonds.*

There was a note on his bed. Picking it up he read:

Well, I guess this is my official good-bye. I'ma miss you. And maybe one day when your nights get a little bit colder, you'll realize just how much love and warmth you had in me. I'll never forget you! And again, I wanna thank you for what you did for me back then.

On your bed you'll find an envelope. It's $1,200 inside. The $1,000 you gave me two years ago and $100 for each night that I stayed in your house. Now it can never be said that Jasmine doesn't pay her way. Maybe that was the problem. You thought I was a free-loader out to live off of you when in reality I ONLY WANTED TO LOVE YOU!

Take care,
Jasmine

Hitman picked up the envelope. Sure enough $1,200 was inside. He felt like a complete jerk. He didn't want her money. He only wanted to be her friend and see her doing good for herself.

He dropped the money and the note onto his bed and fell down beside them.

"...[it] ain't a nigger living who doesn't know fear; we live in it all our lives, like a fish in water. We just have to learn how to use it... Damn near the deadliest people in the world... but killing each other all these years instead of the people who put all that fear and anger inside them..."

— Sam Greenlee [The Spook Who Sat By The Door]

The Re-Up

Chapter 35
Gucci & Luey

"So you're ready to re-up right now?" TrapGirl asked Lip as she drove out to the rendezvous spot. They had to meet secretly because Lip was a Crip and wasn't supposed to buy dope from her.

"Yeah, I'm ready right now!"

"You got everything?"

"Yeah! Damn, TrapGirl, you know I'm good."

"Nah, nigga, I don't know shit! And I've told your country-ass 'bout sayin' my name over your phone!"

"My bad," Lip apologized. "I got the whole eight-five."

"Eight-five? Nigga, you owe *twelve-seven-fifty*!"

"Hell nah! I already talked to WattsDog 'bout that *dirtbike* money."

"How the fuck you gon' holla at WattsDog 'bout my muthafuckin' money?"

"Aye, look shawdy, I ain't –"

"Nah, nah," TrapGirl cut him off. "I gotchu, just come on. You by yourself, right?"

"Yeah."

"Aiight, see you in a few," TrapGirl said and ended the call.

This pussy-nigga! TrapGirl fumed. *I guess he think I'm pussy 'cause I gotta pussy. Well, I'ma show this bitch*, she said to herself, thinking over different scenarios. *I'ma make him check that tire… nah, I'll have to ride 'round with him. Somebody might peep us together… I got his ass, though.* She continued thinking as she parked the stolen 2008 Nova. She adjusted the hotel towel over the bussed steering column. Just as she got out of the car she saw headlights approaching. It was exactly eight o'clock and darkness was shadowing the old closed down gas station, which sat on a dirt road on the outskirt of town.

TrapGirl peered closely into the car when it stopped and saw an extra head. It was his bitch, Val. *This nigga done brought his bitch?! I just asked this lying-ass nigga was he 'olo and he said yeah*, TrapGirl thought, shaking her head.

"What's up?" Lip said, towering over TrapGirl's little frame.

"Who's that in the car?" she asked, but already knew.

"Oh, umm, nobody… just Val."

TrapGirl sucked her teeth. "Come on, let's count this money."

TrapGirl was just what her name stated — a *trapstar*. She was short in statue and even shorter on patience. Truthfully, she was a very pretty chick — brown skin, doe-eyes, naturally long lashes and big juicy lips; long black ponytail, perky little B-cups, and a 34" bubble-ass that she kept covered in baggy jeans, shorts or sweatpants — so she always had something to prove, because she felt that her being small and sexy made big ugly niggas think she was sweet.

Lip noticed the thin leather gloves on her hands as he passed her the money. "Why you got them gloves on?" he asked.

"I'm anemic. My hands get cold easy," she lied with ease.

"Oh," Lip replied, taking a Mr. Good Bar from his pocket and ripping into it. Lip looked around their dark surroundings and then over at TrapGril. He liked her. Not like normal people liked others, Lip liked the fact that she was small and wanted to dominate her sexually. While staring at her sexy mouth and eathing his candy bar, Lip noticed the towel on the sterring collar. "Aye, why you got that towel over the steerin' thang?"

"Nigga, why your ass askin' so many questions? You 5-0?" TrapGirl snapped.

"Don't play with me!"

TrapGirl was about to finish counting the money when a loud tap on the passenger window startled them both. They looked and saw Val standing there with her mouth poked out and her hands on her wide hips.

Lip rolled his window down. "What, Val?"

"Ut'un! Ain't no *what*. You said five minutes! That was fifteen minutes ago, Lip. I got shit to do, boy. And you know the mall gon' be closed if you don't hurry up," she complained.

"Aiight, Val."

Val turned to walk off.

"Nah, hold up, lil' momma!" TrapGirl yelled, putting the money under the seat. There was really no reason to count it anyway.

"Excuse you?" Val said, staring at TrapGirl like she'd lost her mind.

"I got somethin' for you." TrapGirl got out of the car and began walking toward the trunk. Lip and Val followed. "You like that Luey and Gucci shit, ma?"

"Umm, yeah, why?" Val answered slowly.

"'Cause my connect up in New York, he's one of them pretty, fly-ass *panchos*. Always gotta be fly. So he always givin' me my work in big Gucci and Luey bags. I got 'bout ten of them and don't use them. You want them?"

"Yeah, how much?"

"Free, I ain't gon' charge you... I fuck with Lip and you're Lip's ole-lady. Feel me?"

"Thanks!" Val cheered.

"Yeah, that's a bet," Lip gave his two cents.

"No problem, yo." TrapGirl popped the trunk. "They right in there."

"Where?"

"Up there, fool... reach up in there by that Mal-Mart box back there," TrapGirl instructed him.

Lip leaned over into the trunk and *BOOM! BOOM! BOOM!* TrapGirl hit him twice in the back and once in the head, spraying the whole trunk with his blood and what little brains he had.

"*Aaaaaaaaaaaaaah!*" Val yelled in horror.

BOOM! TrapGirl pulled the trigger on the snubnose .45, sending a slug into Val's stomach. The woman fell, staring up at TrapGirl with scared, pleading eyes. *BOOM!* TrapGirl put the last bullet right between her eyes.

Tossing the empty gun next to Val's lifeless body, TrapGirl flipped her phone open and called WattsDog. As she waited for him to pick up she got the money out of the car and began walking up the dirt road.

"Hello?" WattsDog finally answered.

"Come get me!"

"Where you at?"

"Walkin' up the dirt road, leavin' the old Phillips 66."

WattsDog said bet and they both hung up.

Chapter 36
After The Money

"You did what?!" WattsDog screamed after hearing what TrapGirl had just told him.

"Maaann, fuck that nigga," TrapGirl said nonchalantly, sparking a blunt from the ashtray.

"Bit-" WattsDog started to say, but caught himself. TrapGirl gave him an evil gaze through the haze of weed smoke. WattsDog knew better than to call her a bitch. "My bad, TrapGirl, but are you crazy? You know Lip's a Crip!"

"Fuck the Crips!" she shot back. "They need to know I'm Face Mob."

"You shouldn't have done that, man... I told you that shit was dead!"

TrapGril chuckled. "It's dead for real now. Him, the situation, and his bitch."

"You killed Val?" WattsDog yelled.

"Yep."

"Fuck did you do that for?!"

"'Cause he brought her with him... And I'm glad he did, 'cause I know the bitch helped spend my muthafuckin' money."

"You trippin'."

"Nah, you trippin'! Everytime a nigga get in the red they come cryin' to you, runnin' game, and you fall for that weak-ass-shit! A nigga owe, his ass gon' pay. I don't give a fuck if he's a Crip, Blood, GD, Vice Lord, or *ann* other click. I gotta have mine."

"TrapGirl, those were peanuts. So what we letta nigga get a 125 here or an ounce there. We beatin' 45 grams outta an ounce. That's a 500 and a big-eighth over. Then we hittin' most of that shit in dubs. Man, fuck them lil' crumbs. You gotta give to get."

"*You* gotta give to get. I ain't gotta give a nigga shit unless he's Face Mob... And I damn sho' ain't gon' let no nigga take nothin' from me... 'cause that's what it is. They feel like they takin'. Pretty soon we won't be able to serve up here 'cause niggas won't respect us... Nah, fuck all that. If you ain't want Lip dead you should've served him yourself... and anybody gotta problem with Lip bein' dead, they can get it too. 'Cause when it comes to my money, I don't give a fuck. 'Cause after the money, besides Face Mob, I ain't got nothin' else."

WattsDog shook his head. He knew it was going to be some bullshit behind Lip getting killed, the only question was how soon? TrapGirl had done some dumb-ass, *nut-ball* shit that was probably going to get them both killed.

"You know you're crazy, right?"

TrapGirl nodded her agreement. "Just hope they know I'm crazy and fall back. 'Cause I'm too stupid to be scared and I ain't got enough sense to fall back."

WattsDog sighed and said a quick prayer for their safety as he entered Chat-Town city limits.

Lip had been playing some vicious games. And like that old saying about the chickens coming home to roost, he'd just gotten what his hand called for. TrapGirl wouldn't lose one bit of sleep over his death, however, she would put as many to sleep as came her way concerning Lip's timely demise. *Fuck every last one of them bitches!* she thought to herself.

When they pulled up to TrapGirl's crib, she hopped out, expecting WattsDog to pull on off. But that wasn't the case. WattsDog jumped out as well.

"What're you doin'?" she asked.

"Shiiid, hangin' out," he replied.

This nigga scared! TrapGirl laughed to herself. "Come on, homie, I ain't gon' let the Crips get you."

"Maaan, fuck you!"

They both laughed and went inside.

Chapter 37
The Wire

The three men sat around the sparsely decorated office going over profiles and reviewing recordings from wire taps. They'd been at this particular campaign for two years. They saw most of what was seen and heard most of what was said. Therefore, operation TRAP OR DIE was steadily building momentum. These were not typical field agents and operation TRAP OR DIE was not a conventional campaign. Tyrannical would be the one word to describe these operatives and their operation, because they answered to no one. They were not the law — they functioned above it. Their job was to get positive results. They attained results by manipulating factors until their desired outcome was achieved.

"Should we investigate the murder scene?"

"No. We'll let the locals do the foot work and simply hack into their files."

"But what if they miss something?"

"We'll compensate… The less we're seen the stronger our position… they'll get us what we need and we'll get exactly what we want."

"I hope you're right… His death was a set back… and we have no way of linking her to it."

"She did it. His last conversation was with her."

"So why wait?"

"Why not wait?"

"She's as slippery and resourceful as he is. Anything could happen."

"He's right," a third agent said.

"No, but he has the right idea. As of right now we have nothing to tie him into this."

"If she's killed we'll never get that link, sir."

"If she's killed, well, she's not the one we need."

One agent nodded his agreement.

"So what shall we do?"

"What we do best, sir... We stir things up and see if she's our girl. And hopefully, when the bodies stop falling we'll have our guy."

The other two agents nodded their approval and made preparation to resume operations.

Chapter 38
Oh Yeah?!

...the shit was rollin' hard/ you try to fuck me/ you'll get served/ wit' no regard... So don't test me 'cause/ I'm tired of teachin' lessons/ and muthafuck you and that bullshit you stressin'...

Scarface's bloody drug anthem banged loudly from the trunk of TrapGirl's money-green and gold hard-top '63 Impala. Her silver and gold 100-spoke Daytons stopped rolling when she hit her switches — dropping that bitch in the dirt — and killed the high-performance Big Block 400.

Dressed in a dark-brown Dickie short set, all black Jordans, and dark Gucci shades, TrapGirl tucked her snubnose .357 and hopped out of her vehicle. WattsDog, wearing Polo jeans and shirt, and matching Polo sneakers, hopped out behind her. In his pocket rested a small nine-shot 9mm.

This was TrapGirl's daily routine. Every morning she came to the Mess Hall —a small eatery that served the best steak, gravy and home style potatoes on the planet — to have breakfast. She entered the place and found her regular table near the back. She and WattsDog both sat facing the door. A group of Crips were also in the Mess Hall having breakfast. TrapGirl acknowledged them like she always did and ordered her food.

WattsDog ordered coffee and toast. His appetite was shot. Every two minutes his eyes went from the door, to the group of Crips, to TrapGirl and back to the door. His nerves were seriously on edge. WattsDog, 5'10" and 190 pounds, was high-yellow and cool as a breeze — normally. He wore his hair cut low and brushed into deep 360 degree waves. The women loved him. And any Mob would be proud to have him on their team, because he was smart, responsible and he could follow orders. He just was not about that trigger-play. Not to insinuate that he was soft, because he'd fight in a heartbeat and maybe even shoot if he was forced to. WattsDog was a thinker and a certified *trapstar*, and that's what he chose to focus on. That's what made him and TrapGirl's partnership so successful. They were opposites that greatly complemented each other's talents. However, at that moment, as he sat nervously sipping his coffee, WattsDog was thinking that TrapGirl's talents may have gotten them into a deadly situation in which no amount of diplomacy could get them out of. He was scared. His mind was telling him to leave, go home, leave the whole situation alone. After all, they had made plenty money in Chat-Town. Their re-up had been steady over the eighteen month period they'd been serving the locals and the return on their investments had been great. *Yeah*, he thought, *we need to leave this shit alone and head back to Americus.* Of course, he knew in his heart that TrapGirl wouldn't leave. Not like this. She'd consider it backing down or running. No, she wasn't leaving and he couldn't leave her. *Maaann, I wish I could holla at Hitman! I know he'd know what to do. And he's the only nigga TrapGirl will listen to,* WattsDog thought, wishing he'd never came to Chat-Town.

They finished their breakfast without incidence. TrapGirl smoked her morning blunt as they headed to the trap house. The raggedy two-bedroom shotgun house made more money a day than it was actually worth when it was brand-new. WattsDog and TrapGirl pulled at least $11,000 a day out of the house; and that did not include the weight that they served.

When they pulled up there were a few crack-fiends getting served on the front porch. TrapGirl pulled her Impala around back and dropped that bitch in the dirt. She loved her Chevy. It was her toy. Something she'd never had coming up as a child. TrapGirl had come up broke, dirty, and hungry. She'd always been the dirty little girl with the big lips. Up until she met Hitman she'd never had a friend. Until she clicked up with Face Mob she'd never had a family. That's why she loved Hitman so much. She'd die for him without a second thought, because he'd seen more than a dirty little girl with big lips when he'd looked at her. He had seen someone that only needed a little love and some help. He gave her both. Now, at 17, she had more than most niggas twice her age — money, cars, and cribs. Dudes that she'd once been fond of were now jocking her fresh. But she just gave them the deuces. Thinking that just maybe Hitman would be hers... or she'd be his. That had always been her fantasy. Her little secret. Of course she'd eventually realized that it would never be. Pain. That was the reality of it. But just like all of the torment that life had dealt her, time healed it, and the experience improved her character — made her stronger.

"Hey there, baby!" Auntie said with great excitement. "Here you go, nice and cold, just like you like it."

"Thanks, Auntie," TrapGirl replied, taking the Peach soda from the thirty-something-year-old crackhead. TrapGirl really had love for the lady, despite her drug addiction. Auntie had done nothing but look out for her and WattsDog since they'd arrived in Chattanooga almost two years ago, bringing all of her smoker buddies to cop from them, and pointing out the people to deal with and the people to stay away from. Her help had been key to their success and TrapGirl made sure that she was straight.

"TrapGirl," one of their four workers said. "This from last night."

"Aiight, bet," TrapGirl replied, taking the stack of dirty money.

"You heard 'bout ole-boy?" the duded asked.

"Who?"

"Lip."

"Nah, what's up with his bad paying-ass?" TrapGirl asked in return, playing the nut-role.

"Shiiid, somebody fucked that boy over!"

"Get the fuck outta here."

"No bullshit."

"When?"

"Last night. They found him shot to death in the trunk of a stolen car... him and his ole-lady."

TrapGirl stood up, mock shock covering her pretty brown face. "Val's dead?"

The dude nodded yes.

"Damn, Lip's busta-ass might have had that comin', but they ain't had to *splash* Val," TrapGirl stated, playing her role to the fullest.

WattsDog came in, catching the end of her performance. He shook his head sadly, because TrapGirl was full of shit.

"Aye, that shit from yesterday is gone. We gotta rock some more down and hit the table," WattsDog said.

TrapGirl downed her soda and they left for the stash house.

Chapter 39
Super-Crip

Nike sat on his all blue couch, sandwiched between two blue-black females. They were Cripettes, the female counterparts of the Crips. They came in all shapes, shades, and sizes; however, Nike was a Super-Crip, so he wouldn't deal with a red Cripette because anything red was Blood in his eyes. All of his females were so black that they looked blue. While he himself was light-brown skin, 6'2" and weighed 215 pounds. He wore his hair in seven long braids that hung down his back. Chat-Town was his. And he ruled it as such.

Before him and his two fine black Cripettes sat his three lieutenants. Nike had received a phone call from his Aunt Fay in the wee-hours, crying over his cousin Lip's brutal murder. Now he needed answers. He needed to know who was big and bad enough to kill a Crip in Chat-Town. And not just any Crip, but the cousin of Nike — *the Super-Crip Anybody Killer.*

"So what happened, cuz?" Nike asked.

One of the men shrugged. "It's like this, cuz. I rapped with cuz-o maybe 'bout ten o'clock, cuz. He had his *ball-and-chain* with him, you dig. Far as I know, they was 'bout to hit the mall, cuz."

"Yeah, cuz, I holla'd at him over by the car wash. Him and Val was eatin' chicken and shit, cuz... straight up."

"Did he say anything 'bout makin' a move? 'Cause he came and got five-bands from me, 'cause I ain't have no dope and he needed a lil' somethin' to hold him over," Nike said, thinking that his cousin's murder was probably a robbery gone bad.

"Aye, you know what?! That nigga did ask me 'bout some dope, cuz. But all I had was a *dirtbike* and I wasn't 'bout to sell that… But, damn, who else might've had some dope?"

"That lil' bitch TrapGirl and that nigga WattsDog got work. I know that for sho'."

"You talkin' 'bout the cute lil' bitch with the big lips? Her and that pie-ass red nigga?" Nike asked.

"Yeah. They serve on the other side, outta that ole-ass wood house," one of the lieutenants answered.

"Hell nah! Ain't no way those two killed Lip!" Nike said with assurance.

One of his men started to tell him that TrapGirl really wasn't no punk and that he'd seen Lip talking to her and the dude WattsDog on more than one occasion, but instead he held his tongue. He didn't feel like arguing with Nike. When Nike decided an issue that was a wrap. So if he said TrapGirl and WattsDog couldn't have done it, well, *they couldn't have done it.*

"Look, my lil' cousin is dead and my Auntie Fay is sad… I love my Auntie Fay! She raised me and fed me when my momma died. Lip was like my brutha, cuz!" Nike stated, his eyes flashing blue rage. "I gotta reward for whoever get me the muthafucka that killed Lip. Cuz, I want them dead! *Ten-stacks* for whoever body them."

"For sho', cuz!"

"Hell yeah!"

The three men said, rubbing their hands together as they stood and left.

Chapter 40
She's A Thug

...niggas throw ya sets up/ bitches throw ya blocks up/ niggas hold them K's up/ bitches get them Glocks up... Yeah/ it's murder in the air/ niggas ridin' tonight/ let them slugs fly thugs if ya 'bout that life... Grave filla/ I'm 'bout killin' you know this/ Head splitta/ catch a nigga and leave his chest wide open... 'Bout that bread/ got bond money nigga/ contract killa/ got long money, nigga...

Raw-Nitty's blood soaked lyrics filled *Club Menagerie* — formerly known as Dough-Dough's. The club had a wild crowd. It was always packed to capacity on Saturday nights. Lip had once been a regular at this rowdy hot spot. So the Crips had all decided to do-it-big for their fallen comrade — his funeral had been held the day before.

With no knowledge of the special Crip gathering, TrapGirl and WattsDog entered the club. Everywhere they looked they saw blue bandanas and/or blue T-shirts with RIP LIP LOC written on them. There were also regular club goers in attendance, however, blue dominated the scene.

Dressed in her usual Dickie set and Jordans, TrapGirl spotted Youngin — her *worker/play thing* — posted up in a booth. A bad yellow-bone was posted up with him, seemingly helping him enjoy the night. TrapGirl tapped WattsDog, who was Ed Hardy down from hat to shoes, and they walked over to Youngin's booth. TrapGirl walked up and sat right between the two of them.

"Youngin, tell your lil' buddy to go play," TrapGirl ordered and began rolling a blunt.

"Aye, umm, I'ma holla at you a lil' later," Youngin told the girl.

She sucked her teeth and rolled her eyes at TrapGirl. "It's like that, Youngin? You just gon' try me?"

"Don't trip, lil' momma," WattsDogg said, sliding in beside the angry yellow-bone. He put his arm around her shoulder, allowing her to peep the big diamond bracelet and big diamond pinky-ring. "We just gon' trade partners. Youngin gon' get her and I'ma get you. How does that sound?"

The girl looked from his bejeweled wrist and finger, and saw the handsome face with the gold Cartier frames accentuating it and knew exactly who he was. *Damn, you right, I ain't gon' trip, 'cause WattsDog's money-getting-ass is a definite upgrade!* she thought before saying, "Ut'un, hold up, I don't know you like that, dude. I mean, I ain't no *jump off* for no niggas to just be *tradin'* me like I'm cheap stock. Nah –" she popped, playing her hand.

What-the-fuck-ever! TrapGirl thought, not giving a fuck whether the bitch stayed or left, because she'd already taken what she wanted — Youngin. TrapGirl had been dealing with him on a sexual level for about a year now, but their relationship was not serious, at least not on her end. Fucking around with Youngin was more so a thrill for her. She loved the fact that he worked for her, meaning she controlled his livelihood, so no matter who he was with or what he was doing, she could have him if she pleased. Not to mention the fact that Youngin had a pretty good *pipe-game* and a *fire-cracker* head. All sorts of bitches were always jocking Youngin, bitches way prettier and far finer than TrapGirl, which only added to the satisfaction she got from controlling him.

"Dig, shawdy, maybe I said that wrong," WattsDog capped, preventing the girl from leaving. "Youngin got peoples, you dig? He with my lil' sister right there, been with her for 'bout a year... Me, I'm tryna get me some peoples, you dig? My back's strong, I'm kindhearted, and I got plenty money. Now what's good?"

Yellow-bone nodded and licked her thin lips. "Well, okay, since you put it that way... I guess we can vibe and maybe do whatever."

WattsDog nodded and waved a waitress over.

TrapGirl shook her head sadly. *Duuummmb, bitch! All that beauty and body with nothin' to think with*, she said to herself.

* * *

As the night wore on, Nike sat in his section of the club drinking, smoking, and watching the scene closely. He didn't do too much mingling, because he wasn't exactly sure of who he could trust — outside of his two sexy black Cripettes and his three lieutenants. Somebody had violated his status. They'd killed his cousin. And something inside of him told him that the killers were inside the club with him — possibly one of his own.

Through this fog of muddled thoughts, Nike watched TrapGirl go back and forth to the dance floor. She seemed to favor *aggressive music*. Something about her gestures, her choice of clothes, and choice of music arrested his interest. It intrigued him greatly to see so many hustlers and popular street dudes stopping by her table to *holla* at her. A few of his little homies — Crip Soldiers — even paid respects to her. *Is this lil' bitch really gettin' it like that?* he asked himself. Since his rise to Super-Crip he hadn't been playing the blocks like he used to when he was just an up-and-coming hustler. Back then he made it his business to know exactly who was who and what they were doing. This whole situation with Lip getting killed had opened his eyes to an important fact — *I'm out here slippin'... I'm losin' touch with the streets.* What further augmented the epiphany was the realization that he was the leader of the Crip Gang but he barely knew any of the Crips present. *I really gotta tighten up!* he told himself. *I also gotta see what's really good with this lil' hoe, TrapGirl.* He really felt some type of way about her, but wasn't quite sure if the intrique was sexual, maybe relationship wise, or if he wanted to rob and kill her. Either way, he really wanted to get to know her.

* * *

If it wasn't for the Hennessey/ and thug livin' from my enemies/ my brutha still be alive and a part of me... So I say a prayer for that playa/ and I tote fi' everywhere I go/ ...[see] it's kinda hard when you missin' ya dog/ another name on the wall...

Trick Daddy came beating through the club's speakers.

"Oooooh, shit," TrapGirl got up, grabbing Youngin's hand as she stood. "That's my shit right there! Come on." She finished off her E&J and coke and pulled Youngin to the dance floor.

The yellow-bone rolled her eyes. *Bitch!* she said under her breath and faced WattsDog. "Watts, why come you always be with her? Ain't she a dyke or somethin'? 'Cause she sho' dress like one."

WattsDog smiled and pulled her super-close to him. They'd been drinking all night and smoking *seven-gram* blunts of 'dro. He was feeling too good. And judging from her low-eyes and open speech, she was feeling just as good.

"Dig, shawdy," WattsDog whispered in her ear, kissing her neck and rubbing her pussy as he talked to her. "You... you think... lil' momma... a dyke?"

"She... umm... she look like... one."

"Tell the truth... you like... the way... she thug it, huh?"

"If... she... was a ... nigga."

WattsDog had three fingers in her pussy and his tongue in her ear. Twice she'd tried to kiss him, but WattsDog had turned his head, because this wasn't *loving*, it was *thugging*. And she loved it, because her pussy was wet like rain.

"Damn, Watts, you... you got me... so hot," she whined.

"You real hot?"

"Yeah."

"You think my lil' homegirl is pretty?" WattsDog asked, trying to stick a fourth finger in her wet pussy.

"Ye-ye-yeah... I guess, you know... if she did her hair... and like... you know... dressed like a girl."

"Like a girl, huh?... Keep it real with a nigga... you like... girls?"

"Like, maybe... maybe how... they, they look." Yellow-bone was about to cum.

"If I asked you... to let my... girl... suck that pussy... would you?"

"I don't know, Watts... I ain't never —" she whined and spasmed. "Damn, boy!"

"Want me to stop?"

"Nooo!"

"What do you want?"

"Some dick."

WattsDog whipped it out.

She grabbed it and rubbed it. She squeezed it and held it. She wanted it inside of her.

"Watts, baby, you got me... tooo hot!"

WattsDog stuck his pussy-coated fingers in her mouth.

She sucked them greedily.

"Taste good?" he asked.

"*Mmmmm, hmmmmm!*"

"Will you suck my lil' homegirl's pussy like that?"

"If... you... really... want me... to," she moaned, sucking his fingers and jacking his hard dick.

WattsDog knew that the animal-ass bitch was *bicurious*. Most bitches were. They just needed the right motivation. And even though he knew for certain that TrapGirl had never had a sexual experience with another woman, he knew that she'd thought about it and would probably one day succumb to the curious urges. At times like this he really missed Dee. Because the two of them had freaked so many hoes together. And even though Dee didn't play that *dick shit* — he'd never had sex with Dee — he'd had *hella* fun flipping hoes with her.

At that moment WattsDog was about to blow.

"Damn... baby... don't fuck up... my jeans," he managed to say.

Yellow-bone felt his dick throbbing and knew exactly what was up. She lowered her head and covered his dick. She didn't bob her head, she just held his dick in her mouth and applied pressure with her lips and tongue.

WattsDog shook and cursed.

His sperm slipped over her tongue and down her throat.

"Damn!" he said aloud.

Yellow-bone drained the last of him and stood.

"I'll be right back. Let me go clean up, baby."

"Aiight," WattsDog said with his eyes closed.

She laughed and walked off.

"Damn, bruh, what's up?" TrapGirl asked when she and Youngin walked back up.

"You wouldn't believe me if I told you," WattsDog said, still trying to compose himself.

TrapGirl laughed. She felt him, because she was feeling a little horny herself. "Well, me and Youngin' 'bout to slide. How you and yellow-girl gon' do it?"

"Shiid, we slidin'!"

When the fine-ass yellow-bitch came back, WattsDog ran his spiel, she told her friends she was leaving, and they bounced for a night of fun.

Chapter 41
Nobody's Fool

The next morning they dropped the fine yellow coquette off at her momma's house in the projects and headed over to the Mess Hall for breakfast. The trio were all hungry and couldn't wait to feast on the house 24 ounce steak, home style potatoes and thick onion gravy.

After dropping the growling '63 on its belly, TrapGirl, Youngin, and WattsDog slid out and entered the small black-owned restaurant. The aroma of the southern home cooking greeted them as soon as they walked through the door. As far as they could see, the usual motley group of patrons were inside and everything seemed to be in normal order.

"Hey there, y'all... Just get y'alls' regular table and I'll be right over," the aging black owner of the eatery said as she got fresh milk, coffee, and sugar for them. She usually left the table waiting to her waitresses, but TrapGirl had been spending good money in her restaurant for almost two years now, so she was special and the owner wanted her to know that she was special and very much appreciated. "Here you go," she said, smiling as she poured the three of them coffee. "Baby, you havin' your regular?"

TrapGirl nodded and gave the pretty black woman her best *little girl* smile.

The lady smiled in return, but she wasn't fooled. She hadn't lived the long years she'd survived in Chat-Town by being no fool. No, she knew that TrapGril was not an innocent little girl. She knew exactly what the pretty young girl was into, because she saw the big money, the jewelry and the fancy car that she drove. It pained her to see young blacks, so beautiful and ambitious, losing their lives to the cruel streets.

"Okay, baby, comin' right up... and you two, what're y'all handsome men havin'?" she asked with a wide smile.

They gave the woman their orders and drank coffee as they waited for their food to arrive.

"You know we only got one brick left, right?" WattsDog said to TrapGirl.

She shrugged and drunk her coffee before saying, "So that means we should have plenty money in the safe."

"Yeah, it do. But it also mean we need to re-up."

"I feel you... I need a break from this shit anyway. I just hope Dee don't be with that bullshit."

"What bullshit?" WattsDog questioned her.

"You know, havin' me waitin' and shit," TrapGirl half-lied.

She really didn't like the wait, however, she'd been feeling *some type of way* about their business with Dee as of lately. The last two times she'd gone to Americus and shopped with Dee, she'd been held down there for four-to-five days when normally her trips were only two-to-three days. The excuse [or reason] being *that her people weren't straight*. Which also resulted in TrapGirl paying $30,500 a brick instead of her regular $28,500. All of this made her reflect on the conversation she'd had with Keisha concerning Dee's *supposed disloyalty to the Mob*. TrapGirl once again pushed it out of her mind. *Nah, Dee got me... If anybody 'bout that Mob Life it's Dee... she wouldn't try me like that*, TrapGirl thought as their food arrived.

Chapter 42
Product of My ....

True to his word, Nike rose early with the sun the following morning. He, his two Cripettes, and his head lieutenant all climbed into his big blue Suburban. He needed to see the streets. To feel the tension and reconnect himself to the neighborhood haps.

Early in his *coming of age*, he'd seen that anybody who was somebody in the streets always started their day with breakfast at the Mess Hall. It just always seemed to be the thing to do. So Nike instructed his lieutenant to go there.

When they arrived the place was packed as always. Nike scanned the room and didn't recognize one person at first. Then on second glance he peeped the focus of his night's contemplation — TrapGirl. The thuggish little baby hadn't left his thoughts since he'd seen her in the club. A sly smile crept onto his smooth brown face as he saw the owner of the establishment serving TrapGirl and her party personally. It had been a long while since he'd come into the happening little eatery, but he knew that the owner didn't wait tables — not even in her younger days. *Yeah, the lil' bitch is definitely somebody and she's really doin' somethin' big*, he thought.

A cute little waitress came over with menus.

Nike spoke up before she could say a word. "We don't need no menus. Just get us whatever she eatin'," he ordered with boss-certainty and pointed at TrapGirl. "And add their bill to mine... the change is yours."

"Thank you," the waitress said with a smile and took the three crispy $100 bills from his hand. "Your orders will be right up."

The boss Super-Crip watched the young waitress walk off, his thoughts consumed with approaching TrapGirl. It was as if he'd just stepped off of the porch for the very first time. As if he had never spat or been exposed to game — which was totally not the case. At one point in his life, when game was all he had, he'd been *Boss-Game Nike*. However, the large amounts of money and status he'd gained over the years had nullified his dependency on game to get what he desired in life. Somehow he'd lost his tact for the streets.

He tore into his steak when their food arrived. The well done steak was prepared just the way he loved it — minus any blood, because he had no love for Bloods. He kept an eye on TrapGirl as he ate. A few people had stopped by her table in passing, acknowledging her status. No one had so much as looked in the direction of his table. As if they didn't recognize the overlord of their town. Nike had had enough.

"Hey, go tell that lil' bitch that I paid her bill, breakfast is on me. All I ask in return is a few minutes of her time," Nike told one of his Cripettes.

The shiny-black female put down her fork and sashayed over to TrapGirl's table.

Nike saw the exchange of words and then saw TrapGirl look in his direction.

He gave her a slight head nod.

She nodded back and said something to the Cripette, who simply turned and came back to the table.

"I told her."

"And what did she say?"

"Good lookin' on the breakfast, she appreciated it... but if you wanna holla at her and your legs ain't broke, then what's stoppin' you."

Nike smiled. Anything else from her would've been a disappointment. "So that's what the bitch said, huh?" he asked rhetorically.

"Yep! That's what the bitch said," the pretty black Cripette echo'd and began eating her food.

* * *

WattsDog, Youngin, and TrapGirl all watched as the thick black female sauntered away from their table with her tight blue spandex pants pulled all up in her big juicy ass.

"Damn!" WattsDog exclaimed. "Youngin, boy, you seen the camel-toe on that hoe?"

Youngin was about to answer, but caught TrapGirl looking at him and thought better. "Nah, I ain't look at shawdy like that," he lied, knowing that the girl was the finest chick he'd ever seen in his young life.

TrapGirl wasn't tripping off of the chick at all. After all, she didn't do fish at all — she was a strictly beef sausage type of chick. A lot of people got that fucked up about her because of the clothes she chose to rock and also because of her strong demeanor. But that didn't bother her one bit. As long as they respected her fucking mind, they could think what they wanted to think. At present she was thinking about the dude Nike. Damn, I wonder what this busta-ass nigga want? If it's 'bout that nigga Lip, I'ma spazz! she told herself and felt for the .357 she had tucked in her waistband, beneath her shirt.

WattsDog didn't show it, but he was scared as hell. He also felt for the .9mm in his pocket and prayed to God that he wouldn't have to use it. God, please, I hope these fools don't trip up in here, he thought.

Youngin had no idea what was going on, because nobody except for WattsDog and TrapGirl knew that she'd killed Lip... At least that's what they thought.

TrapGirl watched as Nike approached their table.

She had to admit, he was tall, golden-brown, and fine as hell.

His long braids complemented his handsome face — giving him just enough pretty boy to go with his rough thug appeal.

"What's good?" he greeted the table, but kept his gaze fixed on her.

Youngin and WattsDog mumbled something that he didn't hear, because his eyes and mind were both focused on TrapGirl's eyes and juicy lips.

"Ain't really nothin'," Nike watched her sexy-ass lips articulate. *Damn she gotta sweet lil' voice*, he mused. "Can I holla at you right quick?"

TrapGirl shrugged. "Can you?"

He smiled. "You got that... but can we speak without your goons?"

Goons?! These two scared-ass niggas? She wanted to laugh, but instead said, "We could, but I'ma tell them what we rap 'bout anyway."

"And I won't be mad at you, lil' momma, 'cause that's all on you," Nike shot back, feeling his swag slowly coming back.

TrapGirl smiled at him. *You might've been aiight if you wasn't a Crip... and, umm, if I ain't knock your cousin's fuckin' head off!* she thought, sizing him up with her pretty doe-eyes.

"It won't be but a minute. And I promise, I won't hurt you," Nike said teasingly.

TrapGirl nodded. "Aiight," she told him and turned to WattsDog and Youngin. "I'll be out in a minute, y'all."

They both got up and Nike sat down.

When they were out of earshot Nike started talking.

"So what's your name?" he asked her.

"What's yours?" she countered, but continued before he spoke. "But befo' you answer that, I'ma let you know that I already know it, just like I know that you already know mine... so, what's really up, Nike?"

He laughed openly. "Damn, TrapGirl, you sure are hard."

"I'ma product of my rough environment... My surroundings, niggas like you, and hard times made me like this."

Well, this damn sure ain't gon' be easy, he thought. "You said, *niggas like me*. I take it that you must *think* you know me."

"You can take it that way, and you can also *think* whatever you like, it's all on you... but know this, bruh, I ain't make it to where I'm at *not knowin'*."

This bitch gotta real jazzy mouth. I wonder if it's that slick with a dick in it? Nike eyed her seriously. Her rough exterior wasn't a façade. She was the real deal. "Shawdy, are we beefin' or somethin'?" he finally asked.

TrapGirl raised a brow. "Are we?"

Nike laughed again and raised his hands in mock surrender. "Lil' momma, dig, I ain't lookin' for no problems. I just peeped you at the lil' get together for my dead cousin and you kinda caught my eye, that's all... then I just seen you over here and figured I'd thank you for *payin' respects to cuz*."

TrapGirl wasn't sure where he was going with that *payin' respects to cuz shit*, so she checked the trap. "Your dead cousin? Who you're talkin' 'bout?"

"Lip, my cousin Lip got killed last week and you was at the club when we threw the party for him."

"Nah... I mean, I was at the club, but I don't know no Lip."

That kind of threw him, because everybody in Chat-Town knew Lip's crazy-ass.

"Well, I ain't gon' take up too much more of your time. You stop bein' so mean, lil' momma, and hopefully I'll see you around."

TrapGirl nodded and stood.

Nike stood also and the two went their separate ways.

Chapter 43
Artful Thoughts

...is this world 'bout to end/ and if not/ then explain to me how come I'm losin' my friends... and why I'm livin' wit' my kin/ and why I'm fifty-grand short from gettin' me a brand-new Benz... It's kinda hard for the Black man/ I watched the million man march for the Black man...

Trick Daddy played though the boom box in Nike's stash house as he, two of his lieutenants, and his two ever present Cripettes counted duffle bag after duffle bag of wrinkled, smelly bills of small denomination. His plug had called an hour ago telling him that the work was in order, so he had to hurry and get his money together for the cop. It was the best news he'd had in a while, because they'd been out of dope for almost three weeks.

Nike's lieutenants and the two super-bad, super-black Cripettes were all surprised to see Nike actually helping out, since his only job seemed to be giving orders.

Money was piled everywhere.

Someone walking in or glancing the room in passing would've thought it was a billion dollars in there. But in actuality it was less than a million, the small bills just made it seem like so much. Nike was only copping fifteen birds. However, he allowed his lieutenants to spend their money with him, thereby increasing his buying power and bringing the price-per-bird down some. With his men's money, he was buying twenty-four kilos for $660,000 — that's $27,500 a unit, fifteen for him and three each for his three lieutenants. They usually copped twice a month.

The whole time they were counting and re-stacking the money, Nike's mind was filled with thoughts of TrapGirl. He thought about the way she danced at the club. He replayed the conversation that they'd had at the Mess Hall two days ago. Her voice played like lyrics to a slow jam in his mind... so saucy. *Tempestuous*. He could gape at her big sexy lips and never get tired of looking at them... Her eyes. *Inquisitive*. One might even say *salacious* or *ingenuous*. Those doe-like orbs of hers told many stories that were very much the same — bitingly maniacal. If it was true that the eyes were the window to one's soul, then it was clear that TrapGirl didn't have one... *All of this*, Nike thought, yet he found himself wanting her... *All of this he felt*, yet he still wanted to duct-tape and rob her...

Chapter 44
Keeping it Mobbing

East of Chat-Town, on the border of Dalton, Georgia, TrapGirl and WattsDog were in her Cleveland, Tenneessee home. The large split-level house had four bedrooms, three bathrooms, and a four-car garge. She'd only had the place for about six months and no one besides her and WattsDog knew where the house was. Cleveland was only a forty-five minute drive from Chat, so TrapGirl had no problem driving back and forth everyday. And whenever she didn't feel like driving home she simply crashed at the stash house in Chat, got a hotel room, or slept in the raggedy old trap house.

TrapGirl and WattsDog sat in her spacious living room counting up the *buy money*. She'd already gotten in touch with her mules — an old white couple she'd met a year ago — and gotten her rental car. The mules would be driving the Dodge minivan that she'd had fitted with a large stash spot.

"So you sho' you wanna snatch five?" WattsDog asked, rubber-banding the last G-stack and tossing it on the table with the other $151,500.

"Shiiid, we got to! If Dee tax us $30,500 a piece, which I know she is, we gotta get more work to cut back on the trips and whip a lil' extra out the shit, 'cause for real, we ain't seein' no real bread runnin' back and forth with three, 'specially not at $30,500 a lick," TrapGirl explained.

WattsDog agreed with her, but added, "You don't *think* that maybe we should shop 'round some? You know, she fam and all, but she ain't the only person with dope."

"Nah," TrapGirl said. "We ain't doin' no shit like that. We're Face Mob, nigga! And Dee makin' it happen. The price just high right now, it'll drop. And when it do, everything will be back to everything... Shiid, niggas ain't wanna shop 'round when prices was sweet, so we ain't shoppin' 'round now."

"Look, TrapGirl, I ain't mean it like on no dis-"

TrapGirl cut him off. "It don't even matter how you meant it. It's over with. We gon' get this money and keep it mobbin'. Feel me?"

WattsDog nodded his agreement and left the shit at that, because he knew that the bitch was crazy. Her eyes said it all. She was pixilated and dangerous when it came to people outside of her circle — and even more so when she sensed disloyalty amongst people in her click. You were either a friend or a foe to TrapGirl, there was no in between.

"So, ummm, what's up with ole-boy?" WattsDog asked, referring to Nike.

"He *think* shit sweet."

"What you mean?" WattsDog quizzed, a bit of worry in his voice and facial expression.

"Nah, he ain't hip to me *splashin'* Lip," TrapGirl clarified. "The nigga want some pussy."

"Huh?" WattsDog yelled like he just knew she had to be either bullshitting or gone crazy.

"My nigga, you better act like you know!" she said. His reaction had offended her a little, like she wasn't pretty or bad enough for a raw nigga with money.

"I ain't mean it like that, now."

"You couldn't have... shiid, just 'cause I ain't walkin' 'round with my ass and pussy hangin' out don't mean niggas ain't checkin' for it."

"You know I ain't mean no bullshit, TrapGril," WattsDog reiterated.

"It really don't matter, playboy... 'cause one thing 'bout me, I know my worth. And when you know your worth, you get everything you got comin' outta life. The petty shit, it rolls off like water down a hillside," TrapGirl retorted and went to pack for her trip, because the *re-up* was at hand.

Chapter 45
The Message

Nike's head lieutenant had just come back from putting the *re-up* money in the Suburban when his cell phone began ringing. The ID read OUT OF AREA. The wise young street soldier did not do OUT OF AREA calls, because they were normally from muthafuckas he didn't care to talk to. Ignoring the call, he sat down across from Nike.

"So when are they gon' be ready?" he asked his big homie.

"Any minute now. You know Graig and them Mexicans don't trust no niggas, so they always hittin' at the very last minute with a location. And if we ain't there in fifteen minutes with the money, we're hit," Nike explained.

The dude's phone had stopped ringing, but quickly started back.

He looked at it again, it still read OUT OF AREA.

"Fuck is this callin' me?" he mumbled.

"Answer the muthafucka and see!" Nike snapped, tired of hearing the shit ringing.

Nike didn't own a cell phone. He either got one of his Cripettes to make calls from their phones or he used a pay phone, because too much shit happened over phones.

"Yeah?!" Nike's lieutenant answered.

"I know who killed your homeboy," the caller said. His voice was clear and free of emotion.

"What?!"

"I know Lip's killer."

"Who the fuck is this?!"

"I'm sending you a recorded phone message. I'm also sending you a print out of Lip's call log. The last number on the log is the last person Lip talked to; that's the number of his killer."

"Man, who the fuck is this?!"

The line went dead.

"What happened, cuz?" Nike asked his man after seeing the fucked up expression of his face. "Who was that?"

"I, I don't know, cuz," the man answered.

"Well what did he say?"

"Ma-ma-man, he talkin' 'bout he know who killed Lip."

"What?!" Nike asked, standing up.

The phone rung back.

The dude looked at it and saw that it was a message.

He accepted it and saw it begin to load. He hit the button again. A conversation played out:

So you ready to re-up right now? A female voice asked.

Yeah, I'm ready right now. They both caught Lip's voice.

You got everything? Nike knew the female's voice but couldn't place it.

Yeah! Damn, TrapGirl, you know I'm good. Nike couldn't believe his ears.

Nah, nigga, I'on know shit! And I've told your country-ass 'bout sayin' my name over your phone!

My bad... I got the whole eight-five.

Eight-five? Nigga, you owe twelve-seven-fifty!

Hell nah! I already talked to WattsDog 'bout that dirtbike money.

How the fuck you gon' holla at WattsDog 'bout my muthafuckin' money?

Aye, look shawdy, I ain't –

Nah, nah... I gotchu, just come on. You by yourself, right?

Yeah.

Aiight, see you in a few.

The message ended.

Nike's blood began to boil instantly. *That lil' evil, no-good-ass bitch! She told me that she didn't even know Lip! But here she is on the phone settin' up a drug deal,* Nike thought. He turned to his lieutenant and asked, "Who was that who gave you this? Who called you, cuz?"

The dude shrugged. "I don't know, cuz! But it sounded like a cracka!"

"A cracka? Cuz, get rid of that phone!" Nike commanded. "Then we gon' kill that bitch! But first we gotta handle this *re-up*."

The story continues in the third installment:

STILL S3RVING: The Reckoning

Get it now!!! Available on badlandpub.com and amazon. com.

PLEX PRESENTS:
NO TURNING...
Nathan "Big Nation" Welch

PLEX PRESENTS

LOVE & THUGGIN

BY BO BROWN

CRUMBS TO BRICKS

BY CAPO CAT

Part One

PLEX PRESENTS:

GET IT HOW YOU LIVE

Volume 3hree

PLEX

sOmEThInG 2 DiE 4

A Classic Novel
By PLEX

BADLAND PUBLICATIONS
PO Box 11623
Riviera Beach, FL 33419-1623
www.badlandpub.com

Name:

_____

Address:

_____

City: _____ State: _____ Zip: _____

Title	Author	Price
STREET RAISED: The Begin...	Mike Harper	15.95
BOO BABY: The Secret Of...	PLEX	15.95
STREET RAISED: The Raw Deal	PLEX	15.95
BUCKIN' DA' DICE Vol. 1	BOOK GANG	15.95
NO TURNING...	Big Nation	13.95
ONE LOVE	PLEX	13.95
SERVED: With No Regard!	PLEX	15.95
SUGAR	Mike Harper	15.95
LOVE & THUGGIN	Bo Brown	15.95
CRUMBS TO BRICKS	Capo Cat	15.95
EROTIC DESIRES	BOOK GANG	13.95
PROMISCUOUS	PLEX & C. Williams	10.95
GET IT HOW YOU LIVE	Big Gemo	13.95
GET IT HOW YOU LIVE II	Big Gemo & PLEX	13.95
GET IT HOW YOU LIVE III	PLEX	14.95
sOmEtHiNg 2 DiE 4	PLEX	14.95
Young-N-Thuggin	Troy Jones & PLEX	14.95
LIL ONE: Blood Investment	K–1 & Bino	15.00

$3.75 (S&H) for 1-5 Books _____

For quantities over 5 add $ .75 per book _____

www.ingramcontent.com/pod-product-compliance
Lightning Source LLC
Chambersburg PA
CBHW060535260626
47161CB00003B/910